INDIAN RIVER CO. MAIN L

W9-AIQ-636

3 2901 00587 4434

Indian River County Main Library
1600 21st Street
Vero Beach, FL 32960

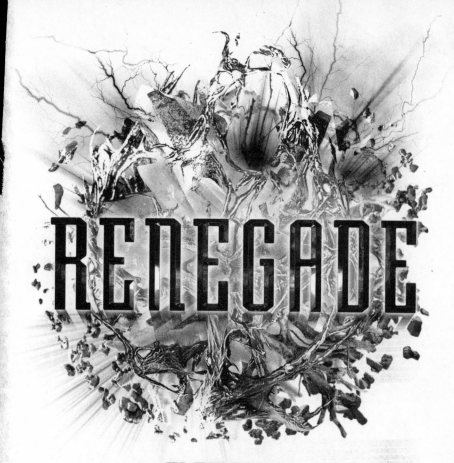

RENEGADE

AN *ELEMENTAL* NOVEL

BY ANTONY JOHN

DIAL BOOKS
an imprint of Penguin Group (USA) LLC

DIAL BOOKS
Published by the Penguin Group
Penguin Group (USA) LLC
375 Hudson Street
New York, New York 10014

USA/Canada/UK/Ireland/Australia/New Zealand/India/South Africa/China
penguin.com
A Penguin Random House Company

Text copyright © 2014 by Antony John
Map illustration © 2014 by Steve Stankiewicz

Penguin supports copyright. Copyright fuels creativity, encourages diverse voices, promotes free speech,
and creates a vibrant culture. Thank you for buying an authorized edition of this book and for
complying with copyright laws by not reproducing, scanning, or distributing any part of it in any
form without permission. You are supporting writers and allowing Penguin to continue to
publish books for every reader.

Library of Congress Cataloging-in-Publication Data
John, Antony.
Renegade : an Elemental novel / by Antony John.
pages   cm
Sequel to: Firebrand.
Summary: Thomas and his friends use their elemental powers as they fight the ultimate battle
for their home on Roanoke Island in a dystopian future United States.
ISBN 978-0-8037-3685-6 (hardcover : alk. paper) [1. Fantasy. 2. United States—Fiction.] I. Title.
PZ7.J6216Ren 2014
[Fic]—dc23
2013043847

Printed in the United States of America

1 3 5 7 9 10 8 6 4 2

Book design by Jasmin Rubero
Text set in Electra LT Std

The publisher does not have any control over and does not assume
any responsibility for author or third-party websites or their content.

3 2901 00587 4434

To Edie

Atlantic Ocean

The Colony

Shallowbag Bay

Pond Island
Bridge

Store

Bridge

Clinic

To the mainland

Lookout

The shelter

Grove

Watertower

The Sound

Broad Creek

HATTERAS ISLAND

ROANOKE ISLAND

To Bodie Lighthouse

N

0   2 miles

CHAPTER 1

A mile behind our ship a sleeker, nimbler vessel carved through the ocean. The crew of five stood against the prow rail, faces turned toward us. They couldn't see us from so far away, but that wasn't the point. Dare, my uncle, the pirate captain, just wanted us to see him.

"They're gaining," said my friend Alice under her breath. She leaned against a crate for support. "They're going to catch us. Soon."

I wanted to remind her that her element—the ability to heighten her senses—didn't work as well hundreds of miles from our home on Roanoke Island. None of our elements did. But anyone could see that the other ship was lighter and faster.

I raised my binoculars. Lowered them again. I didn't need to see Dare's colorful arms to remember the man. I only had to think of Griffin, my younger brother. He was resting below deck on a pile of blood-soaked blankets, his lacerated skin and open wounds a shocking reminder of the lengths to which

Dare was prepared to go to get his hands on the *solution*—a mythical cure for the Plague.

Plague. For sixteen years we'd lived in isolation on Hatteras Island, protected from the rats that had consumed the mainland and the disease that had decimated the population. Waterways, too wide for the rats to cross, had kept us safe. But water was no deterrent for Dare and his men. They'd burned our Hatteras Island colony to the ground, and driven us to neighboring Roanoke Island. When they'd seized that island by force as well, we'd taken to the ocean in search of a new home.

We'd found it too: a self-sufficient colony operating in the remains of Fort Sumter, near Charleston. I'd dared to dream that the worst was behind us. But it had only taken a few days to realize that this new colony harbored secrets too. Once again we'd escaped, but not before Griffin had been bitten by rats; his friend Nyla, as well. We wouldn't know for another day if they'd contracted Plague, but if they had, they'd be dead before the end of the week.

"Thomas." My older brother, Ananias, tapped my shoulder. "If we want to go faster, we need to get more out of the sails."

I looked at the massive pieces of dirty white canvas already pulled taut by the wind. "How?"

He swept his right arm through the air, indicating the other elementals on deck. They were staring at the approaching ship too, and on their faces they wore the same expressions of defeat I felt on mine.

"We need more," he said.

"More what?"

"Wind. Helpful currents—"

"Our elements don't work well out here," I reminded him.

"Neither does my shoulder." He pointed to the sling over his left arm, and the patch of dried blood where he'd been shot the previous evening. He'd always appeared strong to me—trusted by our Guardians, and confident in his ability to conjure fire—but now his voice carried a hint of desperation. "Our elements are all we have."

Before I could reply, Dennis approached us. At nine, he was the youngest member of the colony. Physically, he was doing better than the rest of us, but the events of the past couple weeks had taken a heavy toll. Gone was the sheepish smile, the trust in our Guardians, and the unshakable optimism, replaced by a cold, neutral expression that I couldn't read at all.

"Let's combine," he told me. "We can do more if we join our elements."

Until recently, I hadn't even known that I possessed an element. Everyone else my age hadn't realized it either. The Guardians had kept us in the dark, afraid that if I tried to use it, I'd hurt someone—maybe even a Guardian. Now I took Dennis's hand and allowed my energy to flow, giving him extra power, boosting his element. He began to shape the air around us. A gentle breeze circled our legs and rose up, gathering force, until he unleashed it on the sails.

The sailcloth strained but didn't tear. The masts creaked

but didn't break. The ship lifted slightly in the water, and as the sound of waves crashing against the hull grew louder, I knew we were moving faster.

Around us, everyone was still. No one spoke. They didn't want to distract us. But with each passing moment it was harder to stay focused. Staring at the endless expanse of ocean before us, I wondered where we were going. Would Griffin still be alive when we next made landfall? How would any of us survive when we already knew there was no food and water on board?

"Keep going." Dennis's voice was small, imploring. "Please."

I refocused, and the wind picked up again. But my energy was waning. During our escape from Sumter, I'd leaped from the fort into shallow water and sliced open my chest. Now, as my heart beat faster, pain flared through me. I tried not to let it show, but holding it inside just made me angry.

"This is useless!" I shouted. I pulled away from Dennis and broke the connection. "We can't keep this up forever. We're just delaying things, that's all."

"What other choice do we have?" demanded Ananias.

I had no answer for that. As our ship returned to a slower pace, I think that we were all wondering the same thing: What hideous things would Dare do when he captured us?

I turned to Nyla's brother, Jerren. Jerren was injured too—a bullet wound on his right forearm—but he was a Sumter native, which meant he knew about the vessel that was pursuing us. "Tell us about that ship," I said.

He exchanged a glance with Alice. They'd become almost inseparable during our short time on Sumter, and I got the feeling he was anxious not to step out of line now that he was among relative strangers. Alice responded with a brief nod.

"It's a reconnaissance ship, mostly," he said. "Short-range missions. Good for intercepting slower vessels too."

"Intercepting?"

"Capturing," he clarified. He was sweating, and his dark skin had an almost reflective sheen. "Without your elements, we won't outrun it."

"Maybe we don't have to. As long as we keep moving, we don't have to outrun Dare. He can't board a moving ship. What if we conserve our elements until they get closer?"

"Then what?" asked Dennis. He kept his hand outstretched, urging me to combine again.

"Then we make sure that every time they try to pull alongside us, their ride gets a little more bumpy—extra wind, turbulent water."

Ananias was first to nod in agreement. Then Alice. Dennis too. My father, eyes still fixed on the trailing ship, gave a murmur of consent. Under different circumstances, I'd have been amazed to see us unified. But there was one omission: Jerren. And his opinion was the most vital of all.

"What is it?" I asked him.

Jerren hesitated, as if he were weighing up how much to tell us.

"Give me the binoculars, Thomas," my father said.

I eased the cord over my head and handed them to him.

Alice was already following his eyes, honing in on whatever it was he thought he was seeing. I kept my attention on Jerren, though. "Is there something we should—"

Alice inhaled sharply. I spun around as a puff of smoke rose from the fast-advancing ship, followed by a noise like a clap of thunder. There was a moment of stunned silence, and Father yelled, "Get down!"

I shouldn't have hesitated. Shouldn't have watched that plume of smoke, and wondered what it meant.

As I dove for the deck, the explosion threw me several yards.

CHAPTER 2

I slammed into the deck, shoulder first. Ears ringing, head pounding, I fought to catch my breath. Beneath me, the ship slowly righted, though waves continued to crash against the hull.

"What was that?" yelled Ananias.

Jerren pulled himself off the deck. "That's Dare's way of telling us to stop and surrender."

"He could've hit us," added Alice.

"Could've, but didn't. It was a warning shot, that's all."

"That's *all*?" repeated Ananias.

Jerren touched his wounded arm gingerly. "I used to hear them saying they had weapons that could sink another ship instantly. I don't think it's an accident the explosion happened thirty yards away. A full-on hit would've blown us apart."

Dennis shook his head like he was woozy. Alice lumbered toward the stern rail to see what Dare was planning next. My father helped me to stand.

"Dare won't destroy us," said Ananias. "He wants the solution, right?"

"He can sink this ship without hitting it," Father explained.

Jerren nodded. "A close-range explosion might crack the hull so we take on water. When everyone abandons ship, Dare will stick around to rescue the solution from the wreckage . . . but *only* the solution. The rest of us will drown."

"You seem to know a lot about Dare's plans," shouted Ananias, grimacing from the pain in his shoulder.

"Do you think I'm wrong? I've seen what evil people are willing to do to get what they want. My parents were killed by the man they trusted most of all. So you'd better believe it: If Dare wants Griffin, he'll do whatever it takes to get him."

Ananias didn't reply, but the way he bowed his head looked a lot like surrender. "Then let's reef the sails," he said. "We have to show Dare we're—"

"Down!" Alice shouted.

The word was barely out of her mouth when another explosion turned the surface of the ocean inside out. I was tossed to the deck. Water poured over us in a deluge, while a wall-like wave tipped the boat sharply to one side. I slid across the wet deck and came to an abrupt stop against the deck railing.

"The sails," Alice yelled. "Dare has to see we're giving in."

Dennis began working the mainsheet winches with Jerren. They reined in the massive ropes that raised the sails. I crawled to the next winch, where Alice was already turning the handle.

"If we let Dare board this ship, we're as good as dead," I muttered.

The muscles in her upper arms strained as she turned the winch. "Who said anything about letting him on board?"

"What about the sails, Alice? We're surrendering."

"No, we're not." As the sails tucked away, she locked off the winch. "We're saying don't blow us up. We're saying come over here and let's have a fair fight."

"Fair fight? They have weapons that can sink us."

"And we have elements."

"Not here we don't. We're too far from Roanoke Island for them to work properly. Even when they do work, they're only good for a moment, and then we lose control."

I waited for Alice to fight back, to tell me I was wrong or unreasonable. It wasn't in her nature to back down. But this time, she swallowed whatever she was going to say. "So what do you want us to do, Thom?"

"I don't know. I just know I can't let them take Griffin. Dare's pirates died trying to capture him on Roanoke Island. The Sumter chief was so sure Griffin's blood could cure Plague, he almost killed him. The next time Dare comes face-to-face with my brother, Griffin's dead, I'm sure of it. And I won't let that happen."

"Nor will I," she said gently.

Alice cast an eye around the ship and took in the flurry of activity. Her mother, Tarn, tall and lithe like Alice, staggered on deck. She'd been below when the explosions occurred and must have fallen. A cut above her right eye was bleeding

9

freely. She wiped at it with the back of her hand, smearing blood across her face. It didn't hold her back, though. She began helping my father with the sails.

Everyone was working as a team, but what good was that now?

Alice puffed out her cheeks. "What if we hide in the secret passageway below deck? The one that goes from the captain's cabin. Dare hid out there for days after we left Roanoke. He was a stowaway, and we never even knew it."

"Because we didn't know the passage existed. But Dare sure knows about it. And even if we're not found straightaway, we'll have nothing to eat and drink. There are no supplies left on this ship, remember?"

"What do *you* want to do, then?" she snapped. "All I hear is, there's no food and the ship's too slow and—" She broke off suddenly, eyes wide open. "Wait. You're right!"

"About what?"

She didn't answer, but spun around and shouted to Jerren: "How much food is there on the Sumter ship?"

He shrugged. "They normally keep about a week's worth. Why?"

Alice turned back to me. "We need to switch ships."

I figured I'd misheard her. "What?"

"Think about it. If we switch ships, we can go faster than them. We'll have supplies, and weapons. They'll have to give up the chase. We just need the right bait to lure them on board."

"And what would that be?"

"Griffin."

"No way! They'll capture him."

"Not if he's not here," replied Alice cryptically. She pointed to the ship closing in on us. "That's a smaller vessel than this one, and the deck is lower. They'll be able to see us from a distance, but when they get close, they won't have a clear view of our deck. So here's what we do: As they approach, we make sure they can see us . . . *all* of us. Then we disembark on the blind side as they get ready to climb aboard. When they don't find us on deck they'll figure we're hiding below. While they're searching for us, we swim around the bow and claim the other ship."

I watched the Sumter ship. Dare could attack at any moment. He wasn't stupid and he wasn't careless. He was a cold-blooded killer; anyone who stood in his way was brushed aside. Alice knew that as well as anyone.

"There's no way it'll happen like that," I told her. "It'd take a miracle."

"At this point, miracles might be all that's left."

"In case you've forgotten, Griffin's not the only injured person on this ship. How are Ananias and Jerren going to swim with gunshot wounds?"

"I can make it," said Jerren, joining us.

"Taking Alice's side, huh?" I huffed. "No surprise there."

Jerren flicked sweat from his forehead. "This isn't about sides. Dare wants Griffin, and the other men want revenge. We ruined their colony. Released Plague-ridden rats. They're not interested in taking prisoners. They want the solution,

11

and they'll take Griffin straight back to Sumter. The rest of us will die here."

"Forget it," my father said, joining us. He must have been listening. "We'll surrender. Appeal to their conscience. It's the only way."

Alice snorted. "Dare kidnapped you and left you in a ship's hold to die. The Sumter colonists locked you in a cell. How did appealing to everyone's conscience work for you then?"

A few weeks before, Father would have had the final say. He and the other Guardians would have gathered in private, talked it out, and told us their decision. But now he and Tarn were the only Guardians above deck, and it was clear that neither of them had an alternative plan to offer.

"Inviting them to board our ship is crazy," Tarn said.

"And trying to outrun their ship is impossible," replied Alice. "So I say we give my plan a try. Worst-case scenario, they catch us in the act and do what they planned to do to us all along."

In the silence that followed, I looked at the worn-out faces around me and realized that they'd already resigned themselves to exactly that fate.

CHAPTER 3

Father and Ananias returned to their posts. Jerren too. "I still don't see why those men will go below deck just because we're not here," I told Alice.

"Actually, you and I *will* be here."

"What?"

Alice looked around to make sure we weren't being overheard. "They *know* us, Thom. You were Chief's favorite back on Sumter, and the way these men see it, you betrayed his trust. The moment they see you, they'll be focused on revenge, which means they won't be focused on anyone else. We're just trying to give everyone a chance to get away, right?"

She was right. The chief of the Sumter colony had singled me out and spent a lot of time with me. It was obvious now that he'd been probing for information, but to the rest of the Sumter colonists, it must have appeared as an act of kindness. And how had I rewarded that kindness? By pushing Chief to his death.

I pursed my lips. "I thought you said that Griffin's the bait."

"He is. You're just the distraction." She gave an anxious smile. "We'll be waiting for the men as they board. They're going to force us to tell them where everyone's hiding. We'll hold out just long enough that they don't get suspicious. Then we'll take them below deck . . . and strike."

"Strike?"

"Oh, come on." She rolled her eyes. "You know what we can do when we combine elements. Your power plus my fire . . ."

"And if it doesn't work?"

"Then we'll have given Griffin and everyone else a chance to escape. We'll have drawn the men away from all the other weapons on that ship too."

With the sails reefed, we were gliding to a stop. The warm southwesterly breeze fluttered the edges of the canvas like a hummingbird's wings thrumming to hold it precisely in one place. In contrast, the Sumter ship continued to slice through the swell. The men on board were fanned out against the prow railing, each one straining for a better view of their prize.

I admired Alice's decisiveness, but I didn't share her optimism. What if the Sumter men fought back? What if they weren't interested in taking prisoners at all? They could shoot us on sight.

And what about Dare? He was a seer. What if he'd already foreseen her plan?

She waited for me to say that I was in. Finally, with no alternative to offer, I did exactly that. "All right," I said. "I'll go tell everyone downstairs what's happening. They'll need time to prepare."

"And I'll join you in a moment."

I ran below deck, my wounded chest throbbing with every stride. I stopped in front of the door to Griffin and Nyla's cabin, and gathered myself. If Alice's bravado was just an act, it was one I needed to copy.

My brother and Nyla lay side by side in the cramped cabin, nothing but a few dirty blankets between them and the dusty floor. Nyla gave a weak smile as she saw me. Griffin couldn't even manage that.

Neither of them showed signs of Plague yet, but it was hardly a consolation. On Sumter, Griffin had been imprisoned inside a glass cube with a pack of rats—a brutally efficient way to determine if he was the mythical solution. With his hands and feet bound, he hadn't been able to move away or fend them off, and I'd been too slow to stop the attack. Now his entire body bore the evidence of that encounter. Being deaf, he wouldn't have heard the sound of his own cries, but they must have reverberated through his skull just as powerfully as they'd seared through me.

We. Leave. Ship, I signed to him.

To my surprise, it was Nyla who signed back: *What. Is. Explosion?*

For someone who'd only begun learning Griffin's sign language a few days ago, Nyla had uncanny understanding. She was already more fluent than some of the Guardians who'd known Griffin his entire life. It was a clear sign that she cared about communicating with him more than they ever had.

Sumter. Ship. Following. Us, I signed. There wasn't time to explain any better than that.

Where. Go. Now?

Other. Ship.

Nyla looked at me like I was crazy, which was probably justified under the circumstances. She obviously had other questions, but struggled to find the signs. As long as she was with Griffin, she preferred to sign, rather than exclude him.

Griffin rolled onto his side and met my eyes at last. He looked tired and worn, much like the tunic he wore: stretched and beaten and bloodied until it was barely recognizable as the thing it used to be. I felt tears forming, but held them back. My brother needed strength, not weakness—we all owed him that.

Where. Journals? he signed, his gestures fluid but painfully slow, as if he were signing through water.

I wasn't sure I understood. *Journals?*

Journals, he repeated stubbornly. *Logbooks.*

Who cares? I wanted to sign. I couldn't believe that with everything else going on, Griffin was still thinking about the logbooks we'd found in Dare's cabin on our journey to Sumter, and the journals we'd found buried in the sand near our Hatteras Island colony. We were fighting for our future; the past had never seemed less important to me.

Where? he repeated stubbornly.

How could I tell him that the journals and logbooks were back at Fort Sumter? In our haste to escape, no one would

16

have thought to retrieve them. Who would have been able to, in any case?

Then I remembered something. The previous evening, Alice and I had discovered our colony's third and final journal—the one that promised to unlock our final secrets.

We. Find. Missing. Journal, I explained.

Griffin's face brightened. He didn't seem as tired anymore. *Where. Journal. Now?*

Cabin, I answered, pointing along the corridor.

Griffin shuffled as if he was about to stand, but I raised a hand to stop him. *Prepare,* I said. *We. Leave. Soon.*

I ran along the corridor to the cabin where I'd spent the night. My closest friend, Rose, was still in there, stretched across the floor. Her cropped blond hair was matted, clothes soiled with blood from cuts on her neck and a gaping wound on her side. She'd suffered a brutal knife attack on Sumter. Seeing her now, stoic and immobile, it wasn't difficult to imagine that she could have died.

"Dare's catching up to us," I said. "We have to leave the ship."

Rose inhaled, and released the breath in a long sigh. "I can't."

"Didn't you feel the explosions?"

"I just . . . can't."

She'd suffered so much over the past day, but there was no way I was leaving Rose on the ship.

I knelt down and slid my arms under her. It was a risky thing to do. Unless I was combining, my element seemed to

17

work itself into people, hurting them. It was the side effect of my element—the *echo*, we called it—and it was what had kept everyone at arm's length my whole life. Even now, as I lifted her up, I could feel my element pulsing lightly. The only reason Rose didn't pull away was probably because the discomfort was negligible compared to the rest of her pain.

She ran her fingertips gently across my chest. "You look rough," she said.

I raised an eyebrow. "We've both looked better."

Smiling bravely, she coiled her arm around my neck, and rested her head against my shoulder.

I kicked the door open and stepped into the corridor. Only then did I remember the journal I'd promised to retrieve for Griffin. I turned awkwardly and peered inside. The floor was bare, except for a blanket.

There was no time to waste, but I had to find that journal. So I slipped back in and flicked the blanket away. There was nothing underneath.

"What are you doing?" Rose whispered.

"Where's the journal? I have to find it."

"Last time I saw it, it was right next to me."

I wanted to leave. There wasn't time for this. But how difficult could it be to find a journal in a cabin as small as this?

I looked again, but someone had taken it. And from experience, I knew better than to think it was an accident.

CHAPTER 4

Footsteps pounded on the stairs. Alice appeared in the doorway, but seeing Rose in my arms, she hesitated. Her expression turned unusually sympathetic. "We really need to hurry," she said.

Rose was groaning now. Not from the pain of her injuries, I suspected, but from my element, which grew stronger as my pulse accelerated. On Sumter we'd practiced combining, so that my element channeled *through* her instead of *into* her. But there was no way that she could engage her element now, not when she was so weak. When she stopped grimacing, it was only because she saw my expression and didn't want me to feel bad.

"Here," said Alice. She stood with her back to me and tapped her shoulders. "I'll carry Rose. You make sure the others get on deck."

I wasn't sure that Alice would be able to support Rose's weight, but I helped Rose onto Alice's back anyway. Alice took off up the stairs as easily as if she were carrying a sandbag across the beach.

I returned to Nyla and Griffin's cabin as they emerged. They staggered along the corridor and paused before the stairs. I offered to help them, but Griffin waved me off.

Up on deck, I counted heads. We were all present, looking bedraggled and forlorn. Even Rose and Dennis's mother, Marin, was there, short and stocky, her features wrenched into an all-too-familiar scowl. I hadn't seen her caring for her daughter below deck or helping the other Guardians above; but then, it was no secret that we'd brought her on board against her will. She'd clung to the dream of a new home on Sumter, and hadn't appreciated being rescued. Even now I wasn't sure that she realized how vulnerable she'd been. If we'd left her there, she wouldn't have lasted the night.

Ananias tilted his head toward the approaching ship, which was about a quarter mile behind us. "They're watching us, so keep low. They mustn't see what we're doing."

Across the deck, my father lowered a rope ladder over the port side, readying for the escape.

I scooted over to Alice. She fixed her eyes on the ship, searching for any clue that might give us an advantage. "Same five men," she murmured.

"There might be more below deck," I reminded her. "Maybe some injured crewmen too."

"I don't think so. Anyone who was injured wouldn't have been able to make it on board—not with everything that was going down at Sumter. No, they're operating with a small crew. And it's our job to get those men onto this ship and trapped below deck. If we do that, there's nothing to stop us from getting away."

"And if we can't?"

She peered at me from the corner of her eye. "Just think of Griffin, and Rose. You know what's at stake."

My father was already helping Tarn and Marin onto the rope ladder, so I crawled across the deck and joined them. When she saw me, Tarn furrowed her brows. "I don't like this," she said.

"We don't have much choice," I replied. "Dare will be here any moment."

She exchanged a glance with my father. "How did you all escape from Sumter, Thomas?" she asked. "From what I've heard, you were trapped in a room. Chief and his men were armed. Dare was there too. So what happened?"

I couldn't be sure, but her tone sounded suspicious. It annoyed me, that. With Dare closing fast, and others waiting to descend the ladder, I didn't have time to answer, or even to consider why she'd ask me that question now. I turned my back on her and beckoned Nyla and Griffin over.

One by one, the elementals slid first one foot and then the other onto the ladder. The rope was strong, but the ladder shifted from side to side as the ship rocked in the swell. The healthiest of our crew—Tarn, Marin, Dennis—treaded water, waiting to assist the injured.

When it was my father's turn to go down, he paused. "I'm staying with you," he said.

21

Alice, who was on the other side of the deck, spun around. "No. Only Thomas and me. Dare has a history with you, Ordyn," she reminded my father. "We need him to believe he'll get no resistance from us."

Still my father hesitated. Then, as the Sumter ship sailed toward our starboard side, he followed the others into the water.

I raised the rope ladder and untied it, hiding all evidence of what we'd done.

"May as well throw it in the water," said Alice, joining me. "We won't be needing it anymore."

"How are we going to get onto the other ship?"

"The deck's lower than this one. We'll jump."

I tossed the ladder over the side. It floated for a moment, and then sank. When I turned around, Alice was crouched beside the hatch door that led below deck. "Once the men are trapped down there, you get out, hear me? Even if I don't make it, you bolt that door and board the other ship."

"I won't leave without you, Alice."

"Yes, you will. And if I have to, I'll leave without you too. Because this is bigger than either one of us, you hear? This is *everything*."

The Sumter ship pulled alongside us. The sails had been reefed, allowing the vessel to glide to a halt. As Alice had said, it was lower in the water, so I couldn't see anything except the masts, but I could just make out the men's faces peeking at us over our ship's railing. Each of them held a gun.

An object flew onto our deck and landed with a clatter.

Before I could get a good look at it, it was dragged backward, scraping angry lines in the wooden planks. With a clang, it anchored against the railing—a hook, tethering the ships together.

Instinctively I edged closer to Alice. "You ready?" she asked.

I didn't even know for sure what was about to happen. "Yes," I lied.

A hand appeared on the railing. Then an arm. For a moment, I considered attacking him before he had a chance to get on board, but Alice gripped my sleeve and held me back, forcing me to stick to the plan.

We edged toward the Sumter ship, close enough to see a sliver of the deck. Close enough that when, with a twitch of her head, Alice directed my attention to the water, I made out the heads of the elementals as they slid to the far side of the ship. None of the men was paying any attention to the ocean, though.

My father was watching me. Ananias was as well. They were waiting for a nod, the signal that they were clear to board the Sumter ship. Neither Alice nor I could give it yet, though.

The first Sumter colonist slid over the rail and landed on the deck. Someone tossed a rifle up to him. He pointed it at us, hands shaking, and yelled, "Ship's secure."

Alice had the appearance of a cat poised to pounce.

Another man labored to climb aboard. He was older, bald. As he took up position beside the first man, he rubbed his leg and frowned.

A third man joined them. Even older. Even slower. When he caught his rifle, he took several moments to aim it.

I wanted to ask Alice if she'd noticed the men's condition when she'd spied the ship. Was *this* why she wanted them to board—because they were possibly even weaker than us?

As the fourth man joined the others I afforded myself another glance at the deck of the Sumter ship. I feared Dare more than all the rest of the men combined, but he wasn't climbing the rope. I couldn't see him at all.

"Where's Dare?" Alice demanded.

"Preparing," replied the first of the men.

"For what?"

"You know why we're here. Now where's the solution?"

Alice took a small step forward. Immediately, the men jammed the rifles against their shoulders, arms rigid, eyes wide. From their body language it was obvious that they were wary of us. Maybe even afraid. Alice shuffled back again at the sight of four restless trigger fingers. Whether or not they intended to harm us, it seemed all too possible that one of them might accidentally fire his weapon.

"The others are below deck," said Alice.

"Then bring them up."

"So you can take the solution and kill the rest of us, you mean?"

The man glanced over his shoulder. "We have other weapons than rifles. Less lethal, but possibly even more painful. Would you prefer it if we used those?"

"Actually, I'd prefer it if Dare came on board to bully us himself. He's one of us, you know."

The man laughed. "An elemental, yes. And we can see how much he likes you. Enough to lure you to Sumter. Enough to watch you die—"

He broke off at the sound of footsteps from the Sumter ship. Dare emerged from the stairwell, and regarded the men coolly. "What's going on?" he demanded, voice smooth yet menacing.

"The solution's hiding out below," answered the man, sounding less confident than before.

"So what's stopping you? *You* have guns. *They* are children. Get him now."

"What about our ship?"

"I'll guard this ship. Just make sure you take those two below deck to guide you. And if they resist or refuse," Dare added, like it was an afterthought, "just burn the ship. Fire has a tendency to make even the smallest creatures scatter."

CHAPTER 5

You heard Dare," the man told us. "Lead on."

When Alice held her ground, he stepped forward and jabbed his rifle into her stomach. She stumbled and fell. Instinctively I reached for the barrel, but before I could pour my element along the metal shaft, shocking the man, Alice grabbed my ankle. "Don't do it, Thom," she muttered. "Think of the others."

The men stared at the deck planks, as if they were visualizing people hiding out below. But I was looking at the ocean instead, and the figures floating beside the hull of the Sumter ship. Rose lay on her back in the water, eyes closed; it was probably only her element—water—that prevented her from drowning. Ananias and my father continued to watch me, waiting for the sign to board. But with Dare still on the Sumter ship, that would be suicide.

"Let's go," the first man said. "Now!"

Head down, shoulders slumped, Alice led us to the hatch. If the men were suspicious, they didn't show it. But they weren't taking any chances, either. Two of them pointed their rifles at her, while the others nudged me along behind her.

I stole a final look at the Sumter ship, and our families bobbing up and down in the water. There was nothing I could do to help them, or to warn them that Dare was still on board. It seemed obvious now that someone would stay to secure the Sumter ship. But why did it have to be Dare?

A rifle barrel snapped against the backs of my legs, urging me onward. Alice and I pulled open the large hatch door and let it swing onto the deck with a crash. I figured that Father would know that sound and realize we were heading below deck. Since I hadn't signaled to him, he'd also know there was a problem.

I was first through the hatch. I walked down the stairs slowly, keeping the others close behind. Although I couldn't see them, I was sure that if we were bunched up, it would be harder for the men to move their weapons about.

The worn wooden stairs creaked under the weight of six people. The men were breathing heavily—was it from exhaustion, or fear? True, they had guns, but they must have realized that they were heading into the bowels of the ship, where they'd be outnumbered by elementals.

Sure enough, the footsteps stopped. "I'll wait here," said the last man in the procession. "We need to cover ourselves." There was a murmur of agreement. "I don't think the girl should go on, either. Doesn't take both of them to show us where everyone's hiding."

I craned my neck to check out the men's positions on

the stairs: two immediately behind me, rifles raised; another two behind Alice, also poised to fire if provoked. Each man grasped his weapon with both hands, which meant that they didn't have hold of the rail that ran along the wall.

Alice gave a slight nod and flexed her fingers in readiness. "Go ahead, Thom," she said calmly. "I'll be right here."

I spun around and grabbed the two rifle barrels immediately behind me. My pulse was racing and my element surged through them, shocking the men. Alice whipped her hands back and jerked the other men's rifles forward. Off-balance and without a free hand, all three of them tumbled down the stairs and careened into my two guards. I jumped out of the way as the five bodies crashed to the base of the stairs.

Alice seemed to take the brunt of the fall, but she was also the first to emerge from the pile. One guard separated himself from the others and tried to extricate his rifle, but he was still fumbling with it as I kicked it into his chest. Another man ripped it from him and swung it toward me.

I grabbed Alice's outstretched hand. Even before we combined—before the fire leaped out—I imagined it. Felt it, even—the shape of the flame and the intensity of the heat. And as the fire burst through the air, it was exactly as I knew it would be.

The men shrank back. Not one of them held on to his weapon.

It was tiring to combine, though, and Alice seemed surprised by it, maybe even unsettled. Barely a moment passed before the flame weakened. Sensing it, the men shielded their faces with raised arms and edged toward us. Alice and I backtracked halfway up the staircase, anxious to escape while we still had control.

One of the men retrieved his rifle, but the wooden stairs were smoldering. Smoke obscured his view. He aimed the barrel in our direction, but there was only a harmless click as he pulled the trigger. *It must be the heat,* I thought, but neither Alice nor I waited to find out. As he roared in anger, we scrambled up the remaining steps and rolled onto the deck.

I slammed the hatch door and Alice slid the large steel bolt across, imprisoning the men below.

"Let's go," she said.

We were halfway across the deck when there was a new sound: blunt objects pounding against the hatch door. It bulged slightly with each strike, straining the hinges.

"They're going to break through," said Alice. "We need to get everyone on board the other ship, and quick."

"Are you crazy? Dare's still on it."

She ran a few steps and peered at the ship. "He's not on deck."

"So?"

"So this is our chance. Give me a moment and signal to the others to get on board. And whatever happens, keep that hatch door closed."

Right on cue, the men struck it even harder than before. One of the hinges came up with it, freeing the metal screws from the splintered wooden deck.

Alice took off running. She stretched one foot onto the

deck railing and launched herself across the gap between the ships. I held my breath as she landed on the other deck with a thud and rolled to a stop.

I couldn't tear my eyes away until she stood. Favoring her left leg, she hobbled over to the stairwell and out of sight.

Beside me, four rifle butts drummed in alternation, rocking the hatch door. The men were like trapped hornets, growing fiercer with every passing moment. They would break through soon, it was obvious.

I scanned the deck for something to use against them. There were no weapons here. No other elementals with whom I could combine. But there was a large wooden crate, so I pressed my back against it and drove with my legs, sliding it toward the hatch.

Another hinge broke free from the deck, but with some of the crate resting against the hatch, the door didn't budge at all as the men pressed against it. I took a deep breath and pushed again so that the crate was centered over the hatch. Enough to hold them back for a little while longer.

I sprinted across the deck and leaned against the rail. Father was signaling frantically from the water. Tarn cradled Griffin in her arms. With only one good arm each, Ananias and Jerren struggled to stay afloat.

Where was Alice? Where was Dare?

I was scared for her, but she was right: We couldn't wait any longer. No shots had rung out from below deck, so maybe Alice hadn't found Dare. Or he hadn't found her. Either way, getting everyone on board would increase our chances of overpowering him.

I climbed over the rail and jumped onto the deck of the Sumter ship—not as dramatic as Alice's leap, but the landing hurt plenty. There was a lightweight metal ladder hooked over the deck rail, so I unclipped it and carried it to the bow, secured it to the rail, and extended it into the water.

Father drew the others closer to him. I would have stayed to help them climb, but a loud crack from the other ship confirmed what I'd feared: The crate wasn't heavy enough to keep the men trapped.

It was hard work to climb back up the other ship. The rope tethering them together was thick, with razor-sharp wisps that pierced my skin. No wonder the Sumter men had labored to cross from one vessel to the other.

As I reached the deck, the chest moved slightly. A hard thump from below and it dipped as though it were sinking.

"You need to go," I yelled to the elementals on the next ship. For a moment I wasn't sure that anyone except Ananias had made it on board, but then Jerren climbed over the rail as well and the two of them sprinted to the mainmast, following my instructions. I released the metal grappling hook that held the ships together and tossed it onto the deck of the Sumter ship.

Still no sign of Alice or Dare. Something was terribly wrong.

I grabbed a wooden pole from the deck and stood guard

beside the crate, which was perched precariously above the hatch. I just needed to give the others time to get the Sumter ship moving, but with each strike from below, the crate shifted. As a narrow gap opened up to one side, I drove the pole through and stabbed blindly. One man cried out. Another grabbed the end of the pole and wrenched it, dragging me forward. I landed on the crate. Hard.

The hatch door finally gave out.

Sprawled across the crate, I dropped onto the top stair, which promptly collapsed under the weight. I reached up and grabbed the edges of the deck as the staircase crashed to the ground.

My legs dangled uselessly below me. I knew that if I let go, I was as good as dead. It wasn't a question of *if* the men would kill me, but *how*. One of them broke free from the carnage and found a rifle.

Ananias was shouting my name. Father too. Even with all the other sounds—the men's groans and the creaking ship—I clearly heard the fear in their voices.

Summoning all my energy, I swung one leg onto the deck, and then the other. I kept waiting for the man to fire. He wouldn't miss from such close range.

The bullet never came.

I pulled to a stand. The Sumter ship loomed large before me, but not as close as before. Too late, it dawned on me that the reason they'd been shouting to me is because they were leaving. Everyone stood against the railing, arms stretched out as though they might catch me as I jumped.

As I ran across the deck, the last thing I heard was the men screaming Dare's name. Maybe they were imploring him to stop us, or maybe they were angry for listening to him. I didn't care anymore. I was too focused on getting away.

Just as Alice had done, I drove one foot onto the top railing and launched myself at the Sumter ship as it eased away. The air rushed past me, the ship seemed to draw closer, and I honestly believed that I was going to make it across.

Instead I came crashing down in the water. I was close enough to feel the hull as it brushed past my fingertips.

I sank under and resurfaced as the stern glided by.

I was stranded.

CHAPTER 6

floundered in the ship's wake. Whitecaps lifted and dropped me. Water swirled around me. And the Sumter ship, crewed by elementals, pulled away.

From behind me came the sound of breaking glass. When I peered over my shoulder, the men we'd trapped inside Dare's ship were smashing the portholes.

"Thomas!" someone shouted.

I turned back in time to see my father launch himself off the back of the Sumter ship. Clasping a rope in his right hand, he sailed over me and landed a couple yards past me. For a moment, he was still, the rope slack in the water. Then it pulled taut, wrenching his arm.

I grabbed his free arm as he skimmed past me. Dragged along behind the ship, we slipped under and resurfaced again, over and over, stealing a breath every chance we got. Father's face was a mask of pain as he fought to keep hold of both the rope and me.

I lunged for a piece of the rope and caught it in my free

hand. Ahead of us, Alice, Tarn, Ananias, and Jerren pulled the other end toward them.

I blocked out everything except my hand on that rope and the desperate need to breathe.

"Take it, Thomas," Father said.

There was another rope in the water just ahead of us. I slapped at it and wrapped my fingers around the end. Straight-away, Ananias tied off the rope securing our father and turned his attention to me. With everyone else helping, he dragged me toward the ship's stern. I was so close that I could literally touch the hull, but there was nothing for me to hold on to.

"Don't you let go!" Ananias screamed. "You hear me?"

I didn't answer. Just clasped the rope in both hands as they pulled me from the water. Inch by inch I broke free of the undertow, first my shoulders, then chest, and waist, and legs. Progress was quicker now, but I was forced to take my full weight or risk losing my hold on the rope. I hugged it tight against me, and shut out the pain from the wounds on my chest.

"I can grab his arm." This from Tarn as she leaned over the metal rail. "I've got you, Thomas."

She pressed her claw-like fingertips deep into my arms, securing me. I focused on keeping my element inside me, limiting the echo. Even so, it seemed like an eternity passed before I was able to get a hand onto the railing, and Tarn grimaced the whole time.

The others grabbed my tunic and legs. They pulled me over the railing and deposited me roughly on the deck. There

35

they left me so that they could attend to my father, who was still floundering in the swell.

I tried to keep my eyes open but the sun was bright and the salt stung. I gave up fighting and filled my lungs with the fresh breeze instead. In the background, voices grew louder and more excited as my father's rescue progressed.

Someone touched my arm. Fingers ran across the back of my right hand. "I was scared we'd lost you," said Rose.

It was a relief to feel her there beside me. "Uh-uh. Seems like everyone wants to keep me around."

Her breath tickled my ear. "You and Alice did it. I don't know how, but you pulled it off."

"So they're not following us?"

There was a moment's pause as she adjusted her position to regard the ship. "They're opening the sails right now. They're going to follow, all right."

I punched the deck. "I trapped them. How did they get out so soon?"

"Dare probably helped them."

"What?" For a precious few moments, I'd forgotten about Dare. Now the name set my pulse racing so fast that Rose pulled away from me immediately. "When did he cross to the other ship? *How* did he cross?"

Before she could answer, there was a loud groan as my father collapsed onto the deck a couple yards away. I should've been overjoyed that he was safe, but I couldn't get Dare out of my head.

"Hey," coaxed Rose. "This ship is faster, remember? We're free now."

Free. I could tell that she meant it, but I couldn't shake the feeling that she was wrong. I opened my eyes and looked around me, still searching for Dare even when he was gone.

Father was wheezing. "Thomas?"

"Here," I answered.

Just hearing me speak seemed to calm him. He lay still as the giant sails above us flapped in the wind, and the ocean slid by, putting precious distance between us and our pursuers.

While Ananias and Tarn tended to my father, Alice approached me. I shielded my eyes as I looked up at her, silhouetted by the bright midday sun.

"Your chest is bleeding nicely again," she said.

I touched my tunic, and felt the telltale sticky wetness. It would hurt even more once the rest of me stopped aching. "How about you?" I asked. "I saw that crazy jump you did between the ships. You didn't have to be so dramatic, you know."

She stared at her left foot. "I didn't want to give Dare extra time to react. Anyway, I thought I'd nail the landing. Serves me right."

"Where is Dare now?"

"What?" Alice tilted her head. "You didn't see him?"

I was sure my heart skipped a beat. "No. Why?"

"I heard him below deck," she explained, "so I went down. Couldn't find him anywhere, though. Then I heard footsteps on deck. Figured it was you. By the time I got back up, you'd gone. And Dare was following you onto the other ship."

I couldn't bear to look at the others. "Did anyone else see him?"

"No," said Ananias. "He was out of sight by the time we got on deck. . . . You really didn't see him?"

"I was kind of busy, you know? The hatch door gave out, and I fell. I only just got away before one of the men fired at me."

"I'd say you had a lucky escape," said Alice.

"Lucky? Don't you get it? Dare's a *seer*. What if this is all part of his plan?"

Ananias smiled. "Then I like his plan. Sure beats blowing us out of the water."

The others seemed satisfied by this. More than that, they seemed relieved. But I wasn't.

How had I missed Dare? Why had he allowed me to escape? For that matter, why did he let me live at all?

And how long before everyone else started to ask the very same things?

Alice saved me from the silence. "Come on," she told Jerren. "There's work to do."

"Where are you going?" demanded Marin.

"To find the galley. The Sumter colonists kept this ship stocked: food, water, maybe even medicine. No one's eaten since yesterday. Rose's and Griffin's wounds are going to get infected if we don't clean them soon."

"What about the other ship?" asked Ananias.

"We're faster," said Alice.

"But we don't know where we're going."

Alice didn't miss a beat. "Yes, we do. We're going back to Roanoke Island."

Marin snorted. "In case you've forgotten, we risked everything to *leave* that place."

"Then where else should we go?"

"There must be other colonies."

"Sure. Just like Sumter. And look how that turned out."

"Pirates control Roanoke now," said Tarn. "It's why we left."

"No. We left because *you* were too weak and injured to fight back," spat Alice, waving a finger accusingly at her mother and Marin. "And now my sister is dead, and my father too."

"But Roanoke Island is in ruins."

"So we'll rebuild."

Tarn placed a hand on her daughter's arm. "We don't have the technology."

Alice shook her off. "We don't need technology to survive. To eat."

"There's nothing there for us anymore!" shouted Marin.

"You sure about that?" Alice took a step toward Marin. It was a signal that she wouldn't back down anymore; a reminder that she was taller and more powerful too. But as Alice turned her gaze to me again, I knew exactly what she was about to say, whether or not the time was right. "The pirates have a prisoner on Roanoke," she announced. "A Guardian, no less."

My father pulled to a seated position. He shook his thick

wavy hair, spreading droplets across the deck. "There are no Guardians left but us, Alice," he said, indicating himself and Marin and Tarn. "I can promise you that."

Alice gave a single nod, as if she were giving his statement proper consideration. "I know that's what you think, Ordyn. But you're wrong."

"Then who is it?"

She raised an eyebrow. "Go ahead, Thom. Tell them."

Everyone was silent now. They must have sensed that the information, whatever it was, would change everything. Only, I didn't want to be the person to share it. How could I possibly explain that my mother was still alive, thirteen years after the Guardians had supposedly watched her die?

"Who is it, Thomas?" Father asked.

I felt caught. And played too—Alice had diverted attention away from herself and onto me. Even Jerren seemed surprised and uncomfortable at the turn of events.

I cleared my throat. "It's Mother," I said to Ananias, because I couldn't bear to face Father. "Our mother is alive."

CHAPTER 7

Father glared at me, as if I were playing a cruel joke on him. "Why are you saying this?" he growled. "Are you and Alice so determined to return to Roanoke that you'd make up this . . . this hideous lie?"

I wished I had proof enough to convince him, but according to legend, my mother had died on the morning after Griffin was born. That's what we'd always believed, anyway.

"It's no lie," said Jerren softly. "I saw her. When Dare visited Sumter a month before you arrived, she was with him. She even told me you'd be coming."

"You saw a woman, that's all," snapped Ananias. "She could've been anyone."

Jerren raised his hands, palms out like he was preparing to deflect punches. "She arrived with Dare—the only woman on board his ship. The pirates treated her differently too. Respectfully."

"Then she was his wife."

"No. They're related. If you saw her, you'd understand."

Ananias seemed ready to argue another point, but when he looked at our father, he stopped.

"Skya . . . died," said Father to Marin and Tarn. He licked his chapped lips. "You saw her drown."

Marin nodded. "We saw her facedown in the ocean, yes. She was badly wounded, Ordyn."

"You saw her *drown!*" he roared.

Tarn cleared her throat. "I watched Dare pull her from the water. Watched him cry as he dragged her on board his ship. She was dead. It was obvious. All the Guardians saw it."

"Really? Or were you just too cowardly to help her? Why risk getting hurt when she was taking the punishment for you, right?" Father was shaking, and it had nothing to do with his saturated clothes. The turmoil of the past thirteen years played out on his face. "You told me that Skya was dead!"

"She *was!*" Tarn frowned as she realized how ridiculous that sounded. "You know better than anyone how she was during those last few weeks—how she was always talking about the solution; saying she'd do anything in the world to save Griffin. When she drowned it seemed like she'd known all along what would happen. You know what I'm talking about, don't you? She was a seer."

Ananias looked at our father, then at me. The events of the past couple weeks had left him a shell of his former self. What was he thinking now that he'd discovered our mother had been alive all these years?

Just as importantly, what would Griffin make of the news?

I rolled onto my side and stood. My chest constricted. With every heartbeat, a searing pain spread across me.

"Where are you going?" Alice asked.

"I think Griffin deserves to know the truth as well, don't you? Just a shame that he'll be the last to know."

Alice must have detected the anger in my voice, because she brushed by me.

"You going to beat me to it, then?"

She flicked her head dismissively. "No. I'm going to look for food and medicine, like I said I would. It'd be nice if your wounds could heal before your mother has to see them."

Now I was really angry. I felt caught in the middle of a fight I hadn't even started. We should have been celebrating an improbable escape. Instead, Alice had risked fracturing our group to make sure that we'd set a course for Roanoke.

"Why did you make me tell them about my mother, Alice?"

"Don't you think they ought to know?"

"I think it should've been my decision."

She raised an eyebrow. "Want to know what I think? I think I just distracted everyone from the most awkward question of all."

"Which is?"

"How you didn't notice Dare joining you on the other ship. And why he chose to let you live."

Determined to have the last word, she turned her back to me and headed downstairs. I didn't follow, but lumbered across the deck to the prow. Griffin hadn't moved from the ladder they'd used to board the ship. Nor had Nyla. But where Griffin was lying down, Nyla was sitting bolt upright, facing forward, as if she'd already consigned everything behind us to the past.

Griffin watched me with narrowed eyes, like he knew I had something important to say. I sat beside him and stretched out my legs.

The signs came slowly at first. I wasn't sure how to tell Jerren's story so that it would make sense. Griffin didn't stop me, though. He didn't ask any questions either. Just let me tell it all in my own words.

When I was done, he glanced at Nyla. *We. Know*, he signed.

I looked at Nyla too. "What's he talking about?"

"We already know everything," she explained. "I've known for weeks. Ever since Jerren told me about the conversation he had with your mother. When we all escaped from Sumter yesterday, I had to tell Griffin the truth. He deserved to know."

Though Griffin couldn't hear a word, he nodded in agreement. I searched his face for signs of anger or concern, but unlike Father and Ananias, he seemed completely at peace. *All. Right?* I asked.

Griffin's lips twitched upward in a smile. *Always. Think. Mother. Die. For. Me.* He let out a long sigh. *Mother. Alive*, he continued, emphasizing the last word. *Not. My. Fault. Anymore.*

I thought back to the day before. When Jerren had found his parents' bodies hidden on an island near Fort Sumter, he'd said he felt *relief*. Four years of wondering if he could have

44

saved them were dispelled in an instant. Looking at Griffin, I saw that same relief now. From now on, he wouldn't have to carry the guilt of believing that our mother had given her life to save him. Not as long as she was still alive.

We. Find. Her, I promised him.

He returned a nod, but it wasn't convincing. Griffin didn't place much weight in promises or blind optimism. At thirteen, he was younger than everyone but Dennis, but he appeared as wizened as the Guardians as he raised his hands and signed: *You. Have. Journal?*

I hadn't thought about the journal at all. Didn't want to think about it now, either. We'd just escaped yet again, but we weren't in the clear yet. Dare was giving chase, and our crew was in mutiny. What would yet another journal prove?

Where. Journal? Griffin pressed.

Not. Here, I returned. *Gone.*

I didn't bother to point out that the journal would have been ruined if any of us had attempted to swim with it. I didn't tell him that it was already gone when I visited Rose, either. Whatever those journals might have exposed—more secrets and lies, no doubt—was in the past now. The sooner Griffin moved on, the better.

Only, he wouldn't move on, of course. Over the past couple weeks, as we'd battled pirates and storms and rats and death, Griffin had never let up in his desire to learn about our past. Now that he'd been exposed to rats, and almost certainly contracted Plague, it seemed less likely than ever that he'd give up his search for the truth.

What kind of brother was I for thinking that he should?

I couldn't go back and find the journal for Griffin. But maybe I didn't need to. It could only have been taken by someone who had visited Rose's cabin on the other ship. Someone who had known what secrets the journals contained, and who wanted them kept that way.

All signs pointed to a Guardian. But which one?

Griffin's and Nyla's eyes drifted past me. Someone was crossing the deck toward us.

It was Jerren. "You'd better come below deck," he told me.

"Is there a problem?"

"Not if you're hungry, or need medicine. But if you were hoping to find a stash of weapons, you're out of luck."

"Where are the guns, then?"

"I don't know. But like I say, you should come with me. Alice found this room, and . . . well, it's not like anything you've ever seen."

CHAPTER 8

Jerren led me down the stairs and along to the stern. The corridor wasn't as gloomy as the one on Dare's ship. Instead of wood paneling, the walls were white, though flaking and crumbling in places. Open doors revealed cabins filled with makeshift beds built on wooden crates, and roughly folded blankets. If the accommodations weren't as comfortable as our cabins on Hatteras Island had been, they weren't far off.

The ship wasn't large, and in less than twenty paces we stood before the farthest door. Jerren opened it wide.

This was no cabin. Desks ran along either side, built to follow the contours of the curved walls. Above each one were three sturdy metal shelves. They were lined with books and machines. No space had been wasted.

"What is this?" I asked.

"I figured you could tell me. They never let me see it. To be honest, they never let me on board at all."

"I thought you said—"

"That it was a reconnaissance ship, yes. And that it was well stocked. Doesn't mean Chief let me anywhere near it. He always said I was too young, but now I think it was because he didn't trust me."

"Can't imagine why," I deadpanned.

Jerren gave a low chuckle. "After everything he did to us, it feels good to have gotten the better of that guy."

"Yes, it does." I felt embarrassed for having trusted Chief. "We owe you our lives, you know that? Without you, we never would've escaped from Sumter."

Jerren shrugged. "Yeah, well . . . Nyla and me owe you *our* lives too, right? We had no future there. Maybe we'll have better luck on Roanoke."

I took a box from the lowest shelf and opened it. There were maps inside. I opened each of them and laid them side by side. "Look at this stuff. There's nautical maps of Charleston Harbor. Maps of the whole east coast of the mainland."

Jerren picked up a small book and flicked through the pages. "The other ship didn't have this much stuff, did it?"

"No. But something tells me, Dare doesn't need it either."

"You really think he can sail without maps?"

"Yes, I do. That's why I won't feel safe no matter how much distance we put between us and the other ship. He knows these waters differently than everyone else, I think."

I moved on to a desk lined with machines and ran my fingers across them lightly to see which of them still worked. Three flashlights gave off a dull glow, while a radio emitted static. The next machine was a piece of flat, circular glass surrounded by metal. The glass was dark and blank, but as I ran my fingers along the metal edge, a green dot appeared in the center. A thin shaky line ran above it and down to the left.

Just like everything else I touched for the first time, the machine startled me. It wasn't so much the dull ache that hovered in the background every time I used my element, but the surprise of what I was able to do. During our escape from Sumter, Jerren had shaped and redirected sound, but that had been the extent of his element. For me, every new machine was a mystery I was unearthing. My element felt limitless.

"What's that?" asked Jerren. He pointed at the green dot.

"It's a satellite navigation system," came a voice from the doorway.

I hadn't heard Tarn enter. She leaned against the doorframe, tired eyes lingering on the glass screen before me. When she opened her mouth to speak, a sigh came out first. "I never thought I'd see one of those things again."

"What does it do?" I asked.

"Tells you where you are."

"We know where we are. We're on the ocean."

Tarn smiled. She moved closer to the machine. "That dot there is us. And this jagged line to the northwest is the Carolina coast. This machine isn't just telling us we're on the ocean. It's telling us exactly where we are on the ocean."

"How exact?" Jerren asked.

"Hard to say, without knowing the machine. But I'd guess it's accurate to within a couple boat lengths."

Jerren let out a long breath.

"How does it work?" I asked.

Tarn shifted her weight from one foot to another. "It's called triangulation. This is going to be impossible for you to understand, but there are machines in the sky called satellites. They run on solar power, which is why they're still going, I guess. They send signals, which are received by this machine. The signals arrive at different times depending on how far away they are. This machine then calculates our location based on those three points in space."

"How did the machines get up there?"

"We sent them," answered Tarn. "Many years ago. Before the Exodus and the Plague. It's kind of crazy to think about it . . . how the only machinery that hasn't suffered over eighteen years is the stuff we put in space."

"Not the *only* machinery," I reminded her. "This thing works too." I removed my finger and watched the dot blink out. Then I touched the machine again and savored the control as it sparked to life. Here at last was a reminder of what my element might contribute—there was power in controlling a machine like this, and I was only just beginning to realize the potential. "Does it work on land?"

Tarn watched me from the corner of her eye. "It should, yes."

"Then we'll always know where we are." I tapped the glass. "What about other ships? Can we see them?"

"I don't know exactly what this system can do. But I have a feeling you'll work it out." She turned to leave.

"You know a lot about this stuff, Tarn."

She paused. "There was a time all of us depended on the

ocean. And knowing how to stay alive on it." She sounded wistful.

"So you know how to operate some of these other machines, then?"

"No." She closed the door soundlessly. "Look, Thomas," she said, quieter now, "I know we've kept things from you — all of you — but we need to stick together."

"What do you want me to do?"

"Talk to Ananias. Alice too." She flashed a look at Jerren, as if this affected both of us. "She's shutting me out. I don't know why, but I do know that if we can't work together, we're all going to die before we reach Roanoke."

I wasn't sure what to say to that. In the event, I didn't get to say anything, because a cry came from down the corridor — a girl's voice, short and sharp. It came to an abrupt and unnatural stop, as if someone was covering her mouth.

Jerren flashed me a look. "That's Nyla."

We piled out of the room together. Griffin was inside the first cabin on the left, awake, resting on a nest of blankets. I joined him, certain that Nyla, his constant companion, would be in there too.

She was gone.

CHAPTER 9

G riffin craned his neck to see me. Then he caught my expression, and frowned. *All. Right?* he asked.

Yes. If Nyla was in trouble, I didn't want him to know about it. Yet.

Jerren had continued along the corridor without me, bouncing off the walls in his haste, unable to protect his good arm. Nyla had only screamed once, but he seemed to have a very good idea of where the sound had come from.

"Jerren!" I shouted.

He didn't stop. Just blundered all the way to the last door, which he opened swiftly. Alice was standing right there, a tray in her hands. "Nyla dropped a water canister," she explained.

Sure enough, Nyla was on her knees, mopping up a pool of water with a handful of rags. "Is she all right?" I asked.

"She's fine," said Alice.

But Nyla had her back to us, and she still hadn't said a word. "Are you all right, Nyla?"

She nodded, but didn't turn around. "It was a shock, that's all."

Jerren knelt beside his sister and eased the rags from her hands. "It's okay," he told her. "Everything's okay."

Alice pressed the tray into my hands. "While you're here, you may as well take that up."

Tarn joined us then. She tried to peer around Alice. "Nyla sounded petrified," she whispered.

Alice's expression shifted—no longer patient and concili-atory, but fiery. "Yesterday she found her parents' bodies. She got bitten by rats. Now she might have Plague, and she's scared to death."

"We know what happened," I said.

"So why was no one tending to her? Griffin too," she added, glaring at me.

"Something came up."

"Did it now?" She tapped the tray. "Well, I've prepared the food. Is it asking too much for you to serve it?"

The tray was covered with fresh green leaves and cured fish. Jerren wasn't wrong when he said that the ship was kept stocked and ready. But as I headed upstairs I didn't feel partic-ularly hungry, just confused and chastened.

The afternoon was late, the sun already low in the sky as I emerged on deck. Tarn was close behind me, hands full with water canisters. We set everything on the deck, shooing away the gulls that swooped down to steal our food.

Father was at the wheel, while Ananias stood at the stern,

watching the pursuing ship through my binoculars. I joined him. Dare's ship was trailing us by over a mile now, but I didn't comment on it. It would have seemed like tempting fate to say out loud that we were steadily pulling away.

Ananias lowered the binoculars. "When we switched ships earlier, Alice saw Dare join you on the other ship."

"I didn't see him. I promise."

"I believe you. But why did he let you escape? I mean, he could've killed you, or trapped you on that ship. Kept you hostage until the rest of us surrendered. Instead, it's almost like he hid from you. You have to admit, it's weird."

"Yes, it is. Unless he *wanted* to be back on his ship."

Ananias handed me the binoculars. "Then what's he doing *now*?"

I aimed the binoculars at the distant ship. Four men stood near the prow, facing us. But Dare wasn't among them.

"Alice says Dare looked unarmed as he boarded that ship," continued Ananias in a low voice. "Maybe the Sumter men decided to get rid of him."

I waited for Dare to reappear, to raise his colorful arms and wave, tormenting us even as he was losing the battle once and for all. "Dare's a seer. He won't disappear as easily as that."

"Maybe they know he let you escape . . . like he let you escape from the gunroom on Fort Sumter."

I lowered the binoculars. I had the feeling these questions weren't really about Dare at all. "What are you getting at?"

He met my eyes. "Why does Dare need you alive?"

"I don't know what you're talking about."

"Don't you? You really haven't wondered how all this is happening to *you*?"

"All *what*?"

"Oh, come on, Thomas. A few weeks ago you were an afterthought in this colony. Didn't even realize you had an element at all. Now you and Dare have this game of cat and mouse going, and he seems to know every move we make before it even happens. Kind of a coincidence, isn't it?"

"It's not a coincidence. He's a *seer*."

"I'm just saying—"

"*What?* What are you saying, Ananias?" I reminded myself that this wasn't the old Ananias talking. He was still grieving for Eleanor, the girl he'd loved, and in shock from discovering that our mother was alive. But I couldn't hide my anger. "In case you haven't noticed, Dare's *your* uncle too. And it was *our* mother he didn't kill, not just mine. And you know what else? He's not the only one with a history of violence. Seems the Guardians have blood on *their* hands too."

"Sounds like you're quite sympathetic to him."

"Not sympathetic. Just sick of everyone's lies." I lowered my voice as Alice and Jerren joined us on deck. "Believe me, if Dare isn't dead already, I'll stand with you and finish him off. That, I can promise you."

I figured that Ananias would have more to say. Until recently, he never would've let me have the final word. But maybe that was what was really at stake here. This wasn't about Dare, or the Guardians. It was about *us*—how our roles had been reversed. For years he'd looked out for Griffin and me, while the Guardians groomed him to take charge of the colony. Now there was no colony, and Griffin and I were at the heart of everything that was happening. Where did that leave him? What was his role now?

Ananias walked away. He took a plate of food from Alice and ate, keeping his distance from both Father and me.

He wasn't the only one eating in silence. Everyone seemed to be splitting their attention between mouthfuls of cured fish and the chasing ship. The quiet didn't feel peaceful either, but uncomfortable, as if we didn't know what to say to each other anymore.

It was almost a relief when Dennis piped up. "I saw how you helped us escape from Sumter," he told Jerren. "Your element's kind of weird."

Jerren chuckled. "I think it's weird that any of us can do what we do."

"I guess so. How many elementals are there?" Dennis asked no one in particular.

Tarn and my father exchanged glances, but Marin didn't look up at all. "It's not important," she answered.

"It's important to me."

Father cleared his throat. "Years ago, there were thousands of us, but most lived too far from Roanoke for their elements to work. Some probably spent their whole lives not even knowing what they could do. Elements fade throughout adulthood, especially if they're not used."

"Someone should've told them about it," said Dennis indignantly.

Tarn took over as Father gave a resigned sigh. "Most parents who left Roanoke did it so their children could grow up free from the burden of an element."

"You mean, there could be hundreds of children out there who have elements, and they don't even know it?"

"In the past, yes. But not now. Not anymore."

Dennis picked up a spinach leaf and dropped it again. "What about a solution?"

"What about it?"

"I mean, what if Griffin's not the only one?"

"Solutions are elements that fix an existing problem. So only a child born since the Exodus could be a solution. And to be honest, I don't think there are many children left," Tarn said. She swallowed the last words, no doubt thinking of her daughter Eleanor, who had died only a few days earlier.

Another awkward silence. This time, Marin broke it. "I hear you grew up on Fort Dauphin, Jerren. That's a very long way from Roanoke Island. I'm surprised your element worked at all down there."

"It was really weak," he admitted. "Hardly an element at all. But the one time I used it on people, it surprised them. Just me being able to twist sound at all . . . they didn't know what to make of it, you know?"

"And what about your sister? What's Nyla's element?"

He shrugged. "She doesn't have one. At least, not that I know of."

"A child without an element. Or maybe a child who doesn't understand her element." Marin raised her eyebrow provocatively. "Just like Thomas, really. And we all know what's happened since Thomas found out what he can do. Kyte and Joven and Eleanor are dead, and I don't believe for a moment they'll be the last to die."

I was about to fight back when Dennis beat me to it.

"Stop it!" he yelled. He faced his mother, small hands clamped into fists at his sides. "Why are you always like this?"

If Marin had expected resistance, it certainly hadn't been from Dennis. Now she stared at him with narrowed eyes, as if he were a stranger who looked vaguely familiar. "If you've finished eating," she said coolly, "I suggest you choose a cabin. You must be tired—"

"I'm not tired!" Dennis looked fit to explode. "The only reason we're alive is because of Thomas. Jerren and Alice too. On Sumter, Chief had plans for *me*, not you. It was *me* he wanted to keep around in the colony. Don't you see? They would've gotten rid of you just as soon as they could. You would've died, or been killed, and I would've been all alone in that place."

"You don't know that," Marin replied, but for once her words lacked conviction.

Dennis regarded his mother with a pitying expression, as if he were the adult and she, the child. "Father's gone, Mother," he said. "The things he said . . . they don't matter anymore. Thomas isn't what you think. We have to stop looking at everything through Father's eyes."

I didn't know what to say. The conversation didn't include me, but I was at the heart of it. And if there was one thing I'd thought I knew, it was that Dennis would never question his mother.

Now that it was clear Dennis had no intention of leaving, let alone going to bed, Marin stood instead. But as she left, she looked at me with an expression I'd never seen before, wondering and uncertain. And though she didn't say a word, that look communicated plenty. It was the first time I felt that she wasn't looking straight through me.

Finally, her eyes shifted, back past the stern to the ship pursuing us. Straightaway her mouth fell open and her expression changed. But she didn't find a word to express her shock.

CHAPTER 10

We jumped up as one. I braced myself for discovering that Dare's ship was closer than before. Instead it took me a moment to see the vessel at all. It had changed course, and was heading due south.

"I don't understand," murmured Ananias. He turned to our father. "Is there a different current out there? Something that'll help them close on us?"

Father shook his head. He ran a hand across his mouth, twisting the leathery skin. "No," he said.

"Then why . . ." Ananias didn't complete the question. There was no point, no explanation, except the most obvious of all. "He's turning around. Dare's giving up."

Father continued to stare at the ship. "He must've known he'd never catch us."

"But he could've followed us to Roanoke," I said.

"He doesn't know that's where we're heading," Ananias pointed out.

"Where else would we be heading?" I was as confused as

Father. Nothing in Dare's behavior so far had prepared me for the possibility of his giving in. "Anyway, why go back to Sumter? When we left, it was overrun with rats."

"The other men's families are there," said Jerren.

"But not Dare's."

"Maybe they didn't give Dare a choice," said Alice. "Maybe they didn't want to wait for their families to die before turning back to help them."

"Or maybe Dare wasn't alive to offer an opinion," suggested Ananias, looking at me.

"He's a seer," I protested. "Who risks his life if he knows the crew is out to get him?"

"We're a long way from Roanoke," said Father. "His visions would've been foggy, at best."

The binoculars still hung from a cord around my neck, so I raised them to my eyes and focused on the ship. I took a deep breath to prepare myself for the familiar sight of Dare standing at the prow, arm raised. Even in defeat, I expected him to be defiant. But he wasn't there at all.

I struggled to process everything. All my life Dare had been a living, breathing reminder that nothing was certain or safe. His legend had cast a shadow over our colony. Now we were emerging from that shadow, and I didn't trust the light.

That's when it hit me: No one around me was cheering either. Gulls swooped low, picking scraps of food from the deck, but we were still. Waves crashing against the hull sounded louder than ever in the face of our silence. Were we too cautious to celebrate, even when victory seemed assured?

Or was it more than that? Deep down, I'd wanted a chance to confront him, to make him pay for everything he'd done to our colony. Maybe Alice was right—maybe he'd suffered on that ship, and was suffering still, but it wasn't by my hand or Alice's. Or any of the people whose lives he had ruined. Didn't we deserve the chance to exact revenge?

I checked out the ship's deck again. The Sumter men were busy adjusting course, all their energy concentrated on returning home as quickly as possible, as if they'd forgotten that the solution even existed.

We returned to the food. Birds had been picking at it, so Alice gathered up the plates.

"Need help?" I asked her.

She didn't answer. Just took off alone for the stairs. A few moments later, I followed her. I needed to see Rose.

There was a small tub of white ointment beside Rose's cabin door. Alice had probably found it and put it there. I opened the door quietly. Rose was sleeping. Or so I thought.

"You coming in?" she whispered.

I closed the door and knelt beside her. Outside, the sun was low in the sky, and a warm orange glow lit her face. Rose had always been so calm and thoughtful and . . . *untouchable*. But the past few weeks had changed all that. Her long blond hair was gone, chopped short and pressed into a matted bundle beneath her head. Her flawless skin bore scars that would last a lifetime. I tried to tell myself that she was lucky to be alive, but there was nothing lucky about what she'd been through.

"The other ship has turned around," I said. "Dare's gone."

She managed a smile. "Good."

"I guess so."

"You *guess* so? This is what we've been waiting for. We needed a sign. Well, *this* is our sign."

She waited for me to agree, even stopped breathing momentarily so that she might hear me better. But I still couldn't get things straight in my mind, so I opened the lid to the tub instead.

"Please don't take this the wrong way, Thomas, but we've got to move on. It's our *destiny* to get back to Roanoke and start over. Can't you see that?"

"No, I can't." I dipped a finger into the ointment. I wasn't sure what it was for, but figured it couldn't do any harm.

"How else do you explain everything? Changing ships today. Escaping from Fort Sumter yesterday. Even the way Nyla got the ship moving out of Charleston Harbor in the first place."

"You didn't help her?"

"No. She raised the anchors by herself, if you can believe that. When she came back, I was almost asleep. I don't think we even spoke. She just held my hand, and . . . well, that's the last thing I remember."

Destiny. Maybe she was right. It would certainly have been easier to attribute everything to fate. But fate hadn't come to our aid in the gunroom on Fort Sumter—Dare had. And if there was one person who I was sure would never believe in fate, it was Dare.

Seeing the ointment on my finger, Rose lifted the hem

of her tunic. The knife wounds were hideous—dried blood mixed with deep purple bruising. She gritted her teeth as I applied the ointment in small, slow movements. When I paused, she released a long, low groan.

"I just want you to know," she said breathily, "that if anyone else was doing this to me, I'd scream at them."

I dipped my finger in the tub again. "I figured you'd be screaming at me too."

"Actually, so did I. Guess I really don't want you to go."

She raised her left hand and ran a finger across the back of my wrist. Her touch was feather light, but it sent tremors across my body.

My pulse grew faster. I knew the effect it would have on her as my element grew stronger, so I tried to direct the flow of energy back on myself. For a while, it worked, and the dull ache of my echo was inflicted on me. But not only me— Rose's eyes narrowed as she fought to block out the pain.

I pulled away.

"Don't," Rose pleaded. "It's all right."

"No, it's not. Not yet, anyway. You need to save your strength."

"That's all I've been doing for the past fourteen years. Maybe it's time for me to toughen up."

"You sound more like Alice every day."

"Is that such a bad thing?" Rose peered at me from the corner of her eye. "Clearly it is. Has something happened between you two?"

I almost laughed at that. *Something?* So many things had

happened that I'd lost track, but Rose didn't need to hear them. "I just like you as you are, is all," I told her.

"Then hold me."

I groaned. "You'll be better soon. I'll hold you then."

"That's all? You'll just hold me?"

"Maybe . . . kiss you too."

Rose raised her eyebrows. "Oh really?"

She probably expected me to go red, but for once, I didn't. "Yes, Rose," I said, tending once more to her wounds. "Really."

Later that night, after a turn at the wheel, I selected an empty cabin and fell asleep. I was exhausted, but sleep didn't come without nightmares: of Plague, and Dare, and the pirates we'd have to face when we reached Roanoke Island.

Someone shook me awake. I batted the hand away and rolled over without opening my eyes.

"Thomas." Alice's voice. She grabbed a flap of my tunic and yanked it hard, rolling me toward her.

I snapped my eyes open. The cabin was filling with the dull gray light of a cloudy morning. "What are you doing? What's the—" I stopped the moment I saw her. Gone was the familiar defiance, the narrowed eyes, the pursed lips. Now she appeared cautious. Scared, even. She opened her mouth, and closed it again.

"What is it, Alice? What's going on?"

"Something's happened. Something bad."

An image of Griffin—bloodied, broken, and now Plague-ridden—filled my mind. I'd known it was possible that he would contract the disease, but the news still caught me off guard.

"How is he?" I asked.

"He?"

"Griffin."

She shook her head. "This isn't about Griffin. Or Nyla," she added after a pause.

"What is it, then?"

"A rat must've gotten on board the ship before it left Sumter. Maybe more than one."

"How do you know?"

It seemed an eternity before she answered. "Because Dennis and Rose shared a cabin last night, and both of them were bitten just before sunrise. They've been exposed to the Plague," she said, spelling it out for me. "I'm sorry. I'm so sorry."

CHAPTER 11

flung the blanket aside and pushed past Alice. She grabbed my arm, but quickly let go again. "Be careful, Thom. Your element has gotten stronger since yesterday."

"Are you afraid of me?" I demanded, blind with anger.

"No. I'm afraid for Rose."

I ran along the corridor, following the sound of Marin's crying. Rose and Dennis lay side by side in the same small, sweltering cabin as Griffin and Nyla. Dennis drummed his fingers against the floor impatiently, still feeling too well to understand how serious this was. Even Rose appeared more comfortable than she had the previous evening. Seeing the four of them together was heartbreaking, as if the Plague had already claimed them all.

Rose greeted me with a wan smile. "You came," she said, like I was the first person she'd seen all day. Maybe that's how it felt to her, as if her mother weren't there at all, or only there for Dennis.

Sure enough, Marin was kneeling beside her son. She

ran the backs of her fingers across his forehead comfortingly. But what Rose couldn't see was how Marin's eyes constantly drifted to her daughter too. Maybe, like me, Marin was comparing the girl before her to the Rose we'd known back on Hatteras. If so, she must have been as disturbed as I was to see Rose's swollen right leg, and the angry red bite mark.

I wanted to tell Rose that there was still hope. I wanted to hold her hand. Instead I remained disconnected, unwilling to lie and unable to touch her without causing pain. The future was as clear to me as if I were a seer: Rose growing sicker, and dying. Rose must have seen it too—her cheeks twitched from the effort of pretending that everything was all right.

"We need to find the rats. Need to destroy them," I said. But the truth was, I just needed to get out of there before I broke down.

"I'll help," said Alice.

Jerren and Ananias were waiting outside the cabin. They knew what was going on, and were as helpless as me to do anything about it.

"How many do you think there are?" I asked.

"More than one," said Ananias. He lowered his voice. "Rose and Dennis were bitten at the same time. They woke up together. Neither of them saw anything, though, so it's hard to believe there's an entire pack of rats. Plus, we would've heard something before now, right?"

I strode along the corridor and pushed open the door to the cabin where I'd seen Rose the previous evening. It was so different from the cabins on the other ship—here the walls were perfectly straight, and there were no gaps between the floorboards. Unless the rats were tiny, it was hard to imagine how they might have gotten into the cabin at all.

Jerren moved a small wooden chest to one side, revealing a rectangular hole in the wall. It was about the size of a hand, easily big enough for a rat to crawl through. "Vents," he explained. "The ship would have had a system for circulating warm and cold air."

"So these vents are in every cabin?" I asked.

"Probably, yes."

Alice pressed her ear to the hole and raised a finger to her lips, demanding silence. For several moments she listened for the telltale sounds of rats, but heard nothing.

As she pulled away, Jerren joined her. "Let's combine," he said. "If there's a sound in there, I'll draw it toward us."

They could have settled for touching arms, but held hands instead, fingers twined. It was only a moment before Alice's eyes grew wide. She'd heard rats, all right.

"They're that way," she whispered, pointing to the front of the ship.

Ananias peered around the cabin door and along the corridor. "How far? There's only one more cabin between here and the galley in the ship's bow."

Alice and Jerren exchanged glances. "If I had to guess, I'd say they're hiding out between the galley and the other cabin," she said.

"So how do we trap them?"

"We don't. Jerren and I will go to the galley and block the ductwork. You and Thom head to the cabin next door and combine. One big flame in such a small space will kill them for sure."

"What if that's not all of the rats?" I asked.

She passed by me and began walking along the corridor, eager to begin. "They move in packs, remember? I think they'll be together."

Ananias and I slipped into the neighboring cabin and located the vent in the wall. This one had a cover, but it was easy to remove. We stared at the dark space behind, and waited for Alice's signal.

Jerren joined us almost immediately. "We've jammed a piece of wood into the duct. They won't be able to escape."

As he spoke, the sound of skittering paws echoed faintly along the duct. Frightened by activity in the galley, the rats were heading our way. Ananias stood before the hole, palm raised, poised to unleash fire. I held my hand just above his.

A moment passed. Then another. "Is Alice giving us a signal?" he asked, turning to face Jerren. "Can she hear—"

With his back to the hole, Ananias didn't see the rats appear. They were side by side, frozen in the sliver of light that penetrated the darkness. There wasn't time to warn him either. I grabbed his hand and poured my element through him.

What happened next was a blur. A giant flame shot out from his fingers and incinerated the rats. The metal duct melted instantly. And from next door came an ear-splitting scream.

Jerren sprinted back to the galley as Ananias pushed me away. My brother staggered back against the wall, petrified, both hands raised as if he was fending off an attack. "What did you do to me?" he yelled.

I shook my head uselessly. I didn't know what he was talking about.

Footsteps pounded in the galley. "Help!" shouted Jerren.

Ananias kept a wide berth as he slid around me and out of the cabin. I had to follow, but hesitated as I recalled the expression on Ananias's face. It showed more than just anger. Ananias had been *frightened*.

Ananias's was the next voice I heard. "Oh no," he cried. "Get her water. Now!"

I could barely make my legs move, let alone carry me to the galley. I hadn't even made it to the door before Tarn rushed by. "What's going on?"

Step by agonizingly slow step, I made it into the galley. Alice was trying to touch her face, but Ananias was holding her hands back. "Check her eyes," he shouted.

Tarn leaned over her daughter and stared into Alice's eyes. Alice blinked several times and gave a slow nod.

"What can we do for the burns?" asked Jerren.

"Cold damp cloths," said Tarn. "Then ointment, if there's any left."

Alice's face was red and blotchy. There was a long cut across her cheekbone where an object must have hit her—probably the charred piece of wood beside her.

"I thought it would hold," said Jerren, pointing to the

wood. He looked at Alice. "How can she be burned? She's got the element of fire."

"It's lucky she does. Otherwise she might not have any face at all," said Ananias. He breathed in and out through his teeth. "What just happened, Thomas?"

Again, I had no answer. "We . . . combined?"

Alice coughed gently. "Thom did it to me too, when we were changing ships. He took out the four Sumter men. I wasn't ready to combine, but the fire came anyway."

"What's going on?" I demanded. "Just tell me what I did!"

Maybe Ananias was swayed by seeing that Alice was going to be all right, or by the fact that I had no clue what was happening. Either way, he grew calmer. "You took over my element."

"That's impossible."

He wouldn't even look at me. "Clearly not."

I scanned the room for any sign of support. Only Tarn was watching me, and as our eyes met, she looked away quickly. "Did you already know?" I asked her.

She licked her dry lips. "You should speak to your father, Thomas." It was as close to yes as I would get.

I wanted to get out of that room, and I wanted answers, so I ran to the stairs and went up on deck. Father was at the wheel again.

My entire body was shaking, but not from fear or confusion. I was furious. "They say I can take over their elements. What are they talking about?"

He kept his eyes fixed straight ahead, probably so that he wouldn't have to look at me. "This isn't the right time, Thom—"

"It's *never* the right time. You've had sixteen years, Father. So tell me, when do I get to know who I am?"

There were several sets of footsteps on the stairs. We were about to have witnesses. That suited me fine—why shouldn't everyone else discover that I'd been lied to yet again?

"Right now you're too angry," Father said. "You need to—"

I didn't let him finish. Just grabbed his arm and gave him a taste of that anger. He whipped his head around, eyes wide. We shared the same element and I could feel him pushing back against me. But he was weak. He was swimming against a riptide, and the current favored me.

There was a flash of blinding fire. I choked on the hot air and collapsed to the deck. Ananias towered over me, tears welling in his eyes. "I can't let you hurt him, Thomas."

Father was on the deck too. Wheezing, he clasped his hand to his chest. With the anger shocked out of me, I couldn't believe what I'd done to him.

Ananias crouched down between us. "Tell Thomas what's going on, Father."

"You already know as much as me," Father said.

"He took over our elements, don't you get that? He *possessed* us." Ananias was fuming again. "Why didn't you warn him about it? Why didn't you warn *us*?"

Alice emerged at the top of the stairs, a cloth pressed

against the left side of her face. She stomped over and glared at us. "Why do you think?" she snarled. "With his element, Thomas doesn't just control machines and instruments. He controls *us*." She let the words sink in. "He can take over any element he likes. And there's nothing we can do to stop him."

CHAPTER 12

F ather led me to an empty cabin and closed the door behind us. He rested his forehead against the door, his fingers around the handle. "I didn't know," he said.

"Sure you didn't."

"I'm telling the truth."

"So what? If you hadn't lied to me about my element, hadn't kept it from me all these years, I would've found out what I can do. *All* of it."

"And if we'd told you the truth, you'd have faced this moment even sooner. Do you really believe everyone would have treated you better when they didn't even need you around? Or is it possible they'd have stayed away from you completely?"

He had a point, but I didn't want to admit it. He didn't deserve a moral victory, especially one he hadn't earned.

"Can *you* do it too?" I asked. "Take over other people's elements?"

"I used to be able to, a little—if they were tired, or didn't know what was happening. But not like you. Sounds like you can take whatever element you want, and no one can stop you."

"I don't want to *take* anything. Don't you get it? I'm not trying to frighten people off. This element has controlled my life. Even before I knew about it, it kept people away from me. Now I want to get control of it. I want to practice combining, so that we can work together."

He barked an angry laugh. "Who's going to combine with you? Not me—you can repel me without breaking a sweat. You could destroy me with a touch, if you wanted."

"Stop it! You're not the victim here."

"We're *all* victims, Thomas. Some of us are just more deserving of sympathy than others." He ran a hand through his straggly hair. He had the face of an old man—wrinkled and tired and worn. It wasn't the image of my father I remembered from a few weeks ago. I wondered how I appeared to him now. "I just discovered that your mother might still be alive, remember?" he continued softly. "You're not the only person who has been lied to."

Back to the wall, he slumped down to the floor and folded his arms across his knees. "I used to imagine she was still with me, your mother. I'd talk to her every day. Ask her what I should say to you. You were so full of questions when you were young. Would've stayed that way, I think, but we wore you down with silence."

I sat across from him. "What did Mother tell you? When you talked to her, I mean."

He closed his eyes. "Nothing. I felt like she was leaving me to decide. And look how that turned out—I couldn't have been more wrong about how I handled everything."

It was a confession and apology rolled into one, but I had nothing to say. Learning the truth about myself, my element, and the history of our colony hadn't made sense of everything. I was still in the dark, just a different kind than before.

"Tell me how to control the echo, Father."

"It takes time—"

"Well, I don't *have* time! Griffin could be dead in a couple days. Nyla too, and Dennis, and . . . Rose."

He made a little sound at the back of his throat. "I'm sorry, son. I know you like her."

He was trying to be sympathetic, but *like* was a hopelessly inadequate word—offensive and thoughtless. It was as if he was undoing everything that had happened over the past few weeks. In his eyes, I was once again that boy standing alone on the beach on Hatteras Island, watching Rose from a distance, wondering if there would ever come a time that she'd know how I felt about her. And return those feelings.

Well, if there was one thing I knew for sure, it was that.

"I know how it feels to have this element," he said finally. "The things you're going through, they aren't unique. As hard as your childhood has been, mine was hard too, in ways you can't imagine."

"How so?"

"I grew up with non-elementals, remember? Before the Exodus, we all coexisted. They didn't know my secret, of course, but the only way to preserve it was for me to stay away from everyone. I had to make sure that I didn't touch anyone, and I also had to be careful that no one accidentally touched me. When things were busy, and there were lots of people around, I had to focus on keeping space between me and others, so I wouldn't shock them."

"Did you used to hurt people?"

"Accidentally, yes. Lots of times. But if it was a one-time thing, they blew it off—called it static electricity, or something. But it would make me so nervous. It got to the point that I avoided crowds. I wouldn't play in groups. People thought I was weird. Anti-social. I wasn't weird; I was petrified. And I needed to be to survive the echo."

"But you got control of it," I pressed.

"I'll get to that, I promise." He gave a deep sigh. "There was a girl I knew—quiet, like me. Kept to herself. We became friends. We were both sixteen, and even though I knew I should keep away, I liked her. *Really* liked her. We began spending all our time together. And then, one day, she tried to kiss me. I knew what she was going to do a moment before it happened, and I panicked. I lost all control of my pulse. She didn't even get in a kiss before I pushed her away. She felt the echo, the pain. I think she wanted an explanation. And then, she didn't—she just gathered up her stuff and left. Never spoke to me again. Three years later, I fell in love with your mother. And my only regret is that I didn't have the strength to stay away from that girl when I knew it was the right thing for both of us."

"So you're saying I should stay away from Rose?"

"No! Not at all. I'm saying that you're *lucky* in one respect: Rose knows who you are. She knows what you'll do to her, and she likes you anyway. She'll work with you, Thomas. You'll deal with it together."

"I don't want to *deal* with it. I want the echo to stop."

"It won't st—"

"That's a lie. You and Mother had three children, so don't pretend you never touched."

"Of course we touched. And we tried every trick we could to make it all right. At first, we'd combine elements, so that my echo passed right through her. But touching someone isn't the same when your mind is on something else." I didn't tell him that I was already well aware of that. "After a while, I'd try to focus on my pulse, keeping it slow. That's when things began to change for us. Everything got better."

"So I should focus on slowing down my pulse?"

He hesitated. "I guess it would help, yes."

"But you're not sure."

When he spoke again, he looked defeated. "Your element is so much more powerful than mine, Thomas. I've never experienced what you can do . . . the power you produce, the way you completely take over other people's elements. I've never had to suppress that power either. And I won't lie to you—I'm not sure I ever could."

He closed his eyes and turned away. I played his words over and over in my mind, searching for another meaning, a conclusion I could bear to face. But I knew precisely what he was saying: If Rose had been exposed to the Plague, which seemed almost certain, I'd spend the next few days watching her grow sicker and die, unable to hold and comfort her.

"Hey," he said, watching me. "You saved us all, Thomas. I need you to remember that. Saved us from Dare, and saved us from Sumter. For sixteen years, we broke you down, and look at you now—strongest of all of us. I'm so proud of you. None of us deserve for you to be the boy you are."

He wanted a smile from me, or at least an acknowledgment of what I'd done. But in my mind, I was still focused on Rose. My time with her was going to be over before it had even truly begun.

CHAPTER 13

I hadn't meant to hurt Alice, and I needed to apologize to her. Plus, she knew better than anyone what it was like to exist on the edges of our colony, and was more likely to let me combine with her. We'd be reaching Roanoke soon, probably by the following morning, and I still had no idea how to control the flow of my element. What use was our greatest power when it was as likely to destroy us as the pirates we'd be fighting?

Alice wasn't on deck. She wasn't poring over maps in the radio room. She wasn't in any of the cabins, as far as I could tell. So I made my way to the galley. Faint voices came from inside—one male, one female.

I tried the door, but it was locked. "Alice?"

There were sounds of movement, but no answer.

"Alice?"

More scurrying around, and this time, a response: "Hold on."

I shook the door, but it wouldn't budge. A moment later, Alice opened it. "What?" she demanded.

So much for apologizing. As if to emphasize how much she didn't appreciate the intrusion, Alice ran a finger across the burned side of her face and squinted her left eye, reminding me of what I'd done to her. Behind her, Jerren sliced fruit with mechanical regularity.

"I get it," I said, looking from one to the other. "I'll leave you two alone."

"We're preparing food for everyone."

I snorted. "Sure you are. You've always been first to volunteer for meal preparation, Alice. Everyone knows that."

She produced a thin-lipped smile. "Sarcasm. Nice. What are you going to hit me with next, Thom? You going burn me to death with my own element?"

I stepped back. Alice was expert at offending people, but she'd never turned on me. We'd had our differences, but she'd always respected me enough to be up-front about what they were. I still didn't fully understand what was happening between us, but it was clear that she didn't want me around. Why would she, now that she had Jerren? How perfect that they could lock the door and be alone. To talk. To touch.

How perfectly unfair.

I headed straight for Rose's cabin. Except it wasn't her cabin, of course. It was a place for her to have some company while she waited to die.

The first thing I noticed as I entered was that Marin was tending to Nyla. Rose and Dennis were both sleeping, but I'd figured that the Guardian would ignore everyone except her son. Instead, she was applying ointment to Nyla's neck in a gentle circular pattern.

That's when I saw the angry black lumps. The boils migrating across Nyla's bare legs. And most horrifying of all, her ash-gray fingertips.

Marin raised a finger to her lips, warning me to hold my tongue. At first, it seemed like a ridiculous thing to do—Nyla must have been aware of her condition—but in the quiet and calm of that cabin, it actually made sense. Nyla was awake, but from the way she stared blankly at the ceiling, she obviously wasn't fully conscious of everything that was happening. Wasn't aware of the fact that her short life was already entering its final chapter.

Griffin kept vigil beside her. As much as she had deteriorated in just a few short strikes, he had recovered. The night before, his body had been a mess of blood-red wounds. Now the scabbed-over cuts were itching. He ran his hands along his arms, desperate to scratch, but knowing that he shouldn't. Hard to believe he could be bothered by something as mundane as itching after everything he had been through. It was a sign of how near he was to a full recovery.

Marin leaned back and rolled her neck. She replaced the lid on the container of ointment.

"What's it for?" I asked.

She placed the container beside her. "It has a numbing agent . . . reduces the pain. Doesn't cure anything, though." She glanced at Griffin—curing the Plague was the solution's role. But how?

"You can take a break, if you want," I said. "Alice is making food."

She gave a curt nod, and stood. A moment after she left the room, Griffin rolled over and laid a hand softly on Nyla's bruised and swollen arm. She moaned as if he was hurting her.

Griffin turned his face toward me. *Help,* he signed.

How?

Combine. He studied my reaction, and clearly didn't like what he saw. *Me. Solution.*

How could I explain that everything I'd known about combining had just been turned upside down? Even if it hadn't, even if I still believed that combining was something we could safely do, Griffin was too weak to be using his element to help someone else. He couldn't even sit up to sign with me.

Unable to find words, I stared at Nyla instead.

Me. Solution, he signed again, stabbing his chest with his free hand. *How?*

I. Not. Know, I told him.

Must. Find. Out, he insisted. *Please.*

I hated denying him this after everything he had been through, but there was no way I was combining with him. Even without me, his touch made Nyla flinch. Who was to say we wouldn't kill her instead of curing her? He must have been coming around to the same idea, because he pulled away from her. Seeing her pain had weakened his resolve as well.

"Thomas?" Rose's voice pulled me around. She smiled a little as she saw me, and the smile was genuine.

"How are you doing?"

"Better than you, I think. I look at you and all I see is hurt."
She reached out and ran a finger along the fabric of my tunic.
"It makes me sad."

I watched the progress of her finger as it slid under my
tunic and onto my skin. I felt the familiar rush, the simultane-
ous hope that she'd do more and the fear of what would happen if she did. She kept her finger still for a few moments. Her
expression was neutral, but the perspiration on her forehead
told the real story: It was hurting her to touch me.

I eased my arm away. "Please," I whispered. "Don't hurt
yourself."

"All right." She touched the hem of my tunic instead.

Behind me, Griffin let out a groan. I didn't look around,
though. I wanted Rose to know that even if we weren't touching, she still had my full attention.

"What's Griffin doing?" she whispered. "I think . . . he's hurt."

As I turned to see what was happening, my heart sank.
Blood dripped from Griffin's wrist, and ran in rivulets along
his forearm. The wound was fresh — it hadn't been there just
a moment before.

I ripped material from my tunic and wrapped it around his
wrist. *What. Happen?* I asked.

He pulled away and kept his eyes fixed on Nyla. That's when
I realized that her left wrist was bleeding too. Worse, a knife lay
between them. The edge was rimmed with their blood.

It wasn't an accident. Griffin had made both cuts.

He hid his bloodied wrist. *At. Sumter,* he protested. *Blood.
Machine.*

I remembered it perfectly: The large machine in the gun-room at Sumter—the plasmapheresis unit, Chief had called it—that would extract Griffin's blood. Chief had believed that the antibodies in Griffin's blood might provide immunity to everyone else, and prevent them from getting Plague. But that was just speculation. Did Griffin honestly believe that it would work, and that he could give Nyla his blood without the machine?

You. Crazy. The signs exploded from me. *Maybe. You. Kill. Her.*

Then. Combine, he fired right back. *Combine. Combine. Combine.*

It was only then that I understood the full meaning of what he was saying. He'd already tried to help her by himself, and hadn't seen any difference in her. He was telling me that I was his last hope. Which meant that I was Nyla's last hope too.

If. You. Do. Nothing, Griffin continued, calmer now. *She. Die.*

I placed one shaking hand over Nyla's arm. My heartbeat was so fast I thought I might throw up. I imagined that I could *see* my element spreading out from each finger like a mist—opaque, insidious.

Nyla shifted position slightly and our bodies came into fleeting contact. Where she'd appeared almost unconscious before, now she gritted her teeth and yelped. It only lasted a moment, but it was a sign.

I left the cabin immediately. Not even Rose could keep me there any longer.

CHAPTER 14

I t was a long night of short tempers. Alice seemed flustered and impatient. Marin never stopped tending to Nyla, Rose, and Dennis. Jerren couldn't bring himself to leave his sister's side. Griffin was grieving too. It left us with only a skeleton crew on deck, so we kept our shift patterns brief. It was a good idea in theory, but I found it hard to go to sleep and even harder to wake.

My father and Ananias and I were in charge as the tepid light of sunrise broke through clouds to the east. Alice emerged a few moments later, carrying a breakfast of nuts and dried fruit. She didn't look as if she'd slept at all. Dark circles hung from her eyes.

"You need to rest," I told her.

"I can't. There's too much to do." She placed the tray of food beside us and slid a map from underneath. She studied the barrier island that ran parallel to us, engaging her element, telescoping the land so that she could work out our exact location. Then she ran a finger across the map.

"We'll probably reach the Oregon Inlet in one or two strikes," she said, referring to the narrow channel that joined the Pamlico Sound to the ocean. Roanoke Island sat in the middle of the sound, just a few miles north of the inlet. We were getting close.

No one responded. Father and Ananias just stared into the distance, as if they too could see what lay ahead, and feared every part of it.

"We'll have to wait for the tide to turn," Tarn announced one strike later as we approached the Oregon Inlet. But what she really meant was that Marin and Rose weren't around to use their water element to push us against the falling tide. Neither was Dennis, with his element of wind.

We sailed past the mouth of the inlet and turned the ship around in a slow circle so that we'd be in position to move as soon as the tide turned. There was a clear edge to the turbulent water. We drew in the sails, and lowered anchor just shy of it.

A half mile ahead of us, the inlet stretched forward invitingly. The whitecaps were no more than one foot high, but they were laced together, overlapping as the water fought to escape the sound. I hadn't passed through the inlet very often, but the unpredictable currents were legendary.

"Is this where John White's crew drowned all those centuries ago?" Alice asked, breaking the silence.

The question came out of nowhere. I hadn't thought about John White's expedition since we'd left Fort Sumter two days earlier. The Guardians had told us about White's Roanoke Island settlement, but they hadn't mentioned that his crew had drowned.

"What are you talking about?" demanded Ananias.

"It's just a story I heard," said Alice, eyes fixed on her mother. "About the Oregon Inlet, and seven drowned sailors. Except, I don't think it's a story at all."

Tarn took a swig from a water canister and recapped it carefully. "A story you *heard*," she repeated.

"Exactly."

A personal war of words was playing out here, only I didn't understand the meaning. And then it hit me: Alice hadn't *heard* the story at all. She must have *read* it. And the only source for new stories about John White was the missing third journal.

I wanted to ask Alice right then if *she* had taken the journal from Rose's cabin, but why bother when the answer was clear? The more important question was *why* she had done it, and why she'd hidden the truth from me.

Tarn held her daughter's gaze for a few moments. Then, instead of answering Alice's question about John White, she sloped over to the wheel and took it from Ananias.

Alice wasn't going to let her out of the conversation so easily. "Tell us what happened to White's expedition, *Guardian Tarn*."

Although they were ten yards apart, my father stepped between them as if he were trying to avert a fight. "John White," he murmured, playing for time.

"Yes, Ordyn. John White," said Alice. "Let me refresh your memory. He led an expedition that established a settlement on Roanoke Island in 1587. The colony was in trouble, so he returned to England for extra resources. He got held up there for years. While he was gone, some of the colony's children developed the ability to control the elements. The shock of it divided the colony. Most people left instead of coexisting with the children. When White finally returned, he sent a small crew to Roanoke Island to look for the colonists. But the men never made it through the Oregon Inlet." She tilted her head. "Sound familiar?"

It sounded familiar, all right, and not just to my father. But nowhere in the Guardians' account had there been any mention of drowned crewmen.

Father looked at Tarn, but she had her back to him. He cleared his throat. "White wanted to reconnect with the colony. But as he got nearer, the weather turned suddenly— strong winds and rain. He probably thought it was bad luck, but luck had nothing to do with it. It was the young elementals. They'd seen his ship approaching, and were warning him to stay away.

"He should've given up, or waited, but White was impatient. He'd waited years to get back. So he sent an exploratory crew through the Oregon Inlet. The elementals conjured ferocious currents and powerful gusts. When the crew still pressed onward, the elementals panicked. The children probably didn't mean to hurt anyone, but they didn't have complete control of their elements yet. It only took one wave to capsize the boat." Father exhaled slowly. "Either the sailors couldn't swim, or they weren't strong enough to overcome the conditions. Seven men drowned."

I stared at the inlet and pictured the scene. It wasn't hard to imagine how it would have happened. "Why didn't the children rescue them?" I asked. "Whoever had the element of water could've swum out."

"Depends how close they were. No one knows where the children were at the time. Anyway, if they'd done that, the sailors would've discovered the truth: That the children wielded impossible power."

"Who cares?"

"Everyone cares, Thomas." This from Tarn. She spoke softly, measuring each word. "Ever since the beginning, ours has been a story of incompatible groups. Elementals and non-elementals don't coexist equally. They never have, and never will."

"It's true," agreed Father. "Even White recognized it. The next day he saw smoke rising above Roanoke, and tried to get there again. This time the elementals didn't stop him. He found them, and discovered what they could do. He was so amazed that he sketched the children. Even made notes about them. Maybe he didn't realize they were responsible for the drowned crewmen, but he knew what would happen if anyone else saw the children: They'd be burned to death as witches. That's why he lied to everyone . . . told them he hadn't found a soul on Roanoke Island."

Tarn turned to Alice, one arm loosely draped across the

wheel. "So now you know. Unless . . . there's more." She made it sound like a question.

Alice smiled, but didn't answer. "We should ready the sails," she said. "Looks to me like the tide is slowing. It'll turn soon."

She was right about that, so whatever battle of wills was playing out was momentarily put on hold. All the same, I stole a glance at Alice as I joined Ananias in turning the sail winches. Nothing she'd heard seemed to have surprised her at all. She'd known the story already, and she hadn't shared it with me. I could have forgiven her for that. But the only way she could have known the story was if she had taken the journal. Which meant that she was responsible for preventing Griffin from reading it. That was too much.

The ship kicked as the sails filled. Waves crashed against the prow. Tarn gripped the wheel tightly with both hands, struggling to hold a course against the constantly shifting currents.

We passed the southern tip of Hatteras Island—nothing but sandy beaches and dunes tufted with windswept grass. It was a wild, desolate place, but I couldn't escape the feeling that I was returning home. If only we could know what we'd find there.

A bridge had once spanned the mile-wide inlet. Now all that remained of it was a series of columns that loomed large a couple hundred yards ahead of us. It wasn't until we drew closer that I recalled the words that Alice had seen painted on one of the columns as we'd left the inlet more than a week before: *Croatoan*, and *murder*. *Croatoan* was a reference to the elementals' abandoned colony. I figured that *murder* was a reference to the drowned men from John White's exploratory crew.

Seeing the columns reminded me of the other thing I'd spotted on the day that we'd left: an abandoned settlement on the south side of the inlet. I tried to spy it again now, but couldn't. So I climbed the ladder that ran against the mast.

"What are you doing, Thomas?" my father shouted.

"There's an old settlement to the south," I said. "Tarn told us about it . . . about how you used to trade with them years ago." That wasn't all that Tarn had said. She'd explained that rats had brought Plague to the settlement, and that the people had opted to stay together, even though it was a death sentence. Hard to believe that they'd surrender so easily when survival was as simple as crossing the sound and joining us in our colony on Hatteras Island.

"You shouldn't be up there," my father protested. "These currents are unpredictable."

Not as unpredictable as they were on the day that White's men drowned, I thought. Unless . . .

An image formed in my mind then: the abandoned settlement's inhabitants crossing the sound in an attempt to escape the rats. Only something was holding them back—the very same thing that had held back John White's exploratory crew centuries earlier.

"That bridge column didn't exist when John White's men passed through the sound, did it?" Alice asked no one in particular.

Neither of the Guardians seemed eager to answer her. "No," said my father finally. "The bridge was built centuries later."

"So the words were written later too."

"What *words*," my father chided. "There's only one word."

"There are two," I called down. "The word *murder* is written on the blind side of the column. I saw it when we were leaving. But then, you already know that, don't you?"

Father and Tarn exchanged glances.

"It doesn't mean anything," said Tarn.

"The people from that settlement wanted to join you, didn't they," Alice fired back. It wasn't a question, either. "They wanted to join you, but elementals and non-elementals can't coexist, right?"

"Some of them already had the Plague," snapped Tarn.

"So? Nyla has the Plague now. Rose and Dennis too."

"Enough!" Marin emerged from below deck, hands raised as if she were surrendering. "You want to know the truth? We chose to save ourselves, yes."

"You killed them!"

"We killed *no one*. The Plague killed those people. We're convenient scapegoats, that's all. Always have been. Always will be." Even from partway up the mast I could see that Marin was crying. "When my children die of this disease,

94

you won't see *me* running away. I won't let them suffer alone through the last strikes of life."

"But that's *your* decision." Alice remained insistent, but seeing Marin clearly affected her. "They'd made a decision too, and you stopped them from saving themselves. You can be as noble as you like for yourself, but you have blood on your hands, Marin. All of you do."

Marin brushed her tears away. "Spoken like an enemy, Alice. But then, that's not so surprising, I suppose. You were always going to show your true colors eventually."

In the silence that followed I wondered what exactly Marin meant by that. And why Tarn didn't say a word in Alice's defense.

CHAPTER 15

O nce we were through the inlet and on the open waters of the Pamlico Sound, the Guardians left us. Tarn went first, as Ananias took the wheel. Father followed her. It was impossible not to wonder if they were still trying to hide something from us.

From my position on the mast, Roanoke Island appeared as a hazy outline to the north. I climbed down the ladder and savored the feel of stable planks beneath me again.

"We should anchor off the southern tip," said Ananias. "It'll keep us out of sight of the pirates."

Alice shook her head. "We'll head for the eastern shore. Anchor off Shallowbag Bay."

"Are you crazy?" I snapped. "The pirates will see us from Skeleton Town. They'll know exactly where we are."

"No, they won't. They'll see the ship, but we won't be on it." She waved her hand at a point in the distance. Maybe she was engaging her element and could already see that far.

"When we pass under the bridge that connects Roanoke and Hatteras Islands, the columns will block the pirates' view of the ship for a moment—long enough for us to jump overboard. While the pirates continue to watch the ship, we swim to shore. Then we circle around Skeleton Town and approach them from the rear. We'll have the element of surprise."

"We'll be outnumbered," warned Ananias.

"Surprise isn't our only element," Alice reminded him. "Our powers are strongest on Roanoke. Anyway, we're not looking to fight the pirates. The plan is just to rescue your mother and grandmother . . . if Tessa's still alive, I mean."

First Alice had hidden the journal from me. Now she was deciding our next move as if no one's opinion mattered except hers. I wasn't in the mood to play along. "I suppose the ship will sail itself, right?"

Alice rolled her eyes. "Rose and Dennis and Nyla aren't fit to come. Marin will want to stay with them. Between her and Tarn, anchoring the ship in Shallowbag Bay won't be a problem."

"And what if the pirates row out to the ship while we're gone? Only Tarn and Marin are strong enough to put up any resistance."

"They won't need to resist at all. If Tarn sees the pirates coming, she'll weigh anchor and Marin will use her element to move the ship away. In the meantime, we'll have fewer men to deal with on the island. It's a win-win."

"What if the pirates shoot at them?"

"We'll tell everyone to stay below deck."

Ananias seemed convinced, but I wasn't. "Even if we rescue Skya and Tessa, and somehow manage to avoid getting drawn into a fight—*then* what? We can't set off on another voyage, Alice."

"We won't have to. To be honest, I don't think the pirates are going to fight us at all. Not once they get an up-close reminder of what our elements can do." Alice flared her nostrils. "Look, if you have a better plan to offer, Thom, then go ahead. I'm listening." She waited a moment and raised her hand in mock salute. "Thought so."

She turned on her heel and strode to the prow, where she could get an unobstructed view across the sound to Roanoke Island. I followed her. "How did you know that stuff about White's expedition, Alice? About those men who drowned."

The corner of her mouth twisted upward in a smirk. "I wondered when you were going to mention that."

"Well?"

"You know perfectly well how I know. I read it in the third journal."

I froze. Somehow it had never occurred to me that she'd admit it. "So where's the journal now?"

"In the ocean. Best place for it. Trust me."

I brought my fist down on the deck railing, which gave a low metallic clang. Then I flexed my fingers to make sure that nothing was broken.

She glanced at my hand from the corner of her eye. "I

guess you want to hit me. Did you think the journal was yours, Thom? Is that what you thought?"

"Well, it sure wasn't *yours*. You know how much Griffin wanted to read it. He could've pieced together the whole story of who we are."

"Not who we *are*, Thom. Who we *were*. Anyway, it's time we started looking forward, not backward."

"Who says we can't do both? Griffin deserves to know the truth."

"The *truth*." She snorted. "The truth is that the Guardians have lied to us for years, in more ways than we can probably ever know. And about more things than we can ever forgive."

"That's not good enough, Alice. Griffin wants details. After all he has been through, don't you think he deserves that much?"

She ran dirty fingers across her chapped lips. She was staring at the sound, but her mind seemed to be elsewhere. When she spoke, her voice was gentler than before. "I thought Griffin was going to die, Thom." She exhaled slowly. "I was so angry. We rescued him from Sumter, but the next morning he seemed sicker than ever. I thought we'd been wrong about him—that he wasn't the solution after all. And, I don't know if this makes sense, but . . . I didn't want him to spend his last days reading that journal. You have to believe me—it would've raised more questions than it answered. Griffin could spend the rest of his life reading this stuff and never get to the bottom of it all. But you're right: It wasn't my place to keep the journal from him. I'm sorry. I was just so angry with all the lies, you know? They never end."

An apology—another surprise. Alice had always been impetuous and mercurial, but I'd never had such a hard time reading her before. She was always the girl with a plan. So what was the endgame this time?

"I understand that you hate me right now," she said.

"I don't hate you." It was the right thing to say—almost true, as well.

"Detest me, then. Loathe me. Whatever. You have more reasons to hate me than you even know."

Another cryptic remark, almost like she was inviting me to delve deeper. But it was also an olive branch, and I had to take it. "You saved Griffin from Sumter," I said. "After losing your sister and your father . . . you still risked everything for my brother, and I'm grateful for that."

We were reverting to our usual roles: Alice, keeper of secrets; Thomas, peacemaker. Only, Alice didn't seem reassured at all.

She pointed to the Roanoke–Hatteras bridge in the distance. "Remember a couple weeks ago when we went to spy on the pirates? How we kept to the shadow of the bridge?"

"How could I forget? I was petrified."

"You did well."

"Only because you told me what to do," I said honestly. "When Dare walked right by us on the beach, I almost screamed. Then he chopped that guy's finger off, and stuck his own hands in the fire—"

"Dare scared me too. Back then, anyway."

"Not so scary now he's gone, is he?"

"No." She chuckled, but there was no humor in it. "He doesn't scare me anymore."

She rolled her neck. Hands resting against the railing, she stared into the distance, eyes narrowed, element engaged. A few moments later, she shook her head slowly as if the element wasn't working properly, or she didn't believe what she thought she'd seen.

"What is it, Alice?"

She studied the surface of the water. "There's something out there."

I squinted in a vain attempt to see what she was seeing. "What is it?"

"A raft, I think. Yes, it's definitely a raft."

She pointed. Sure enough, there was something out there, though it was hardly more than a speck.

"Tell Ananias to steer due north," she said, voice quiet and urgent.

Something about her tone made it clear that this was no ordinary raft. I ran back across the deck and showed Ananias where to point the prow.

"What's out there?" he asked.

"A raft."

Ananias spun the wheel to the right, and we lost speed as the ship turned. "Did she see anything on it?"

"Must've done. She wouldn't have told us to shift course otherwise."

Ananias pursed his lips. "I think it's time you got Father. Tarn too. We're on enemy water now."

I shouted down the stairs for Father and Tarn to rejoin us. When I returned to Alice at the prow, I saw something on top of the raft. "Are those—"

"Bodies," said Alice. "Three of them. . . . No, four." She bit the knuckle of her thumb. "They're not moving. Something's not right."

"What is it, Alice?"

She blinked twice and stared at the water again. Whatever she saw, she didn't like it. She backed away from the rail and turned to leave.

"Where are you going?"

She looked at me, then at the steps leading below deck. I couldn't tell what was playing out in her mind. "I need to tell . . ." She didn't finish the thought, because just then, Father and Tarn emerged.

Finally I saw what she had seen: Four people on board the raft, and not one of them was moving. Three were turned away from us so that we couldn't make out their faces, but one had her head tilted slightly toward us. And as her long gray hair was ruffled by the breeze, I knew exactly who it was.

Tessa. My grandmother.

I glanced back at Alice. She was watching me with a faraway expression. "There's only one reason to stick four bodies on a raft and cast them off," she said. "And we both know what it is."

Yes, we did. I just couldn't believe that Tessa might be dead so soon after I'd begun to know her.

"You realize what this means, don't you?" she continued.

"They're all dead."

"More than that. The other three look like pirates, and I'm guessing they didn't shoot each other. Which means there must be another killer on Roanoke Island." Alice lowered her eyes, as if she was frightened by her own realization. "And I have a horrible feeling it's Plague."

CHAPTER 16

Neither Tarn nor my father wanted to check on Tessa, that much was clear. But Plague or no Plague, she was family, so we drew in the sails and coasted to a stop some distance from the raft.

Marin might have been able to manipulate the currents to draw us closer, but she was below deck tending to the sick. So Alice coiled a rope around her waist and dived into the gray-green water. She surfaced several yards from the ship and swam toward the raft.

There wasn't room for her to climb aboard—the bodies had been packed on tightly and restrained with binds—so she tossed her rope across the raft and crawled around to the far side to retrieve it. She wrapped it back around her waist. Legs braced against the thick wooden side, she gave me a nod. Ananias and I began to pull in the rope, and Alice drove the raft slowly toward us.

Tessa was by herself to the left of the raft. The three pirates must have been dead when they were placed beside her; or close to death, anyway. Their limbs overlapped awkwardly. Even from several yards away I saw the telltale signs of Plague: dark lumps around their necks, and blackened fingers. It was hard to think of them as people at all—at least, until I scanned their faces and recognized one of them.

"It's the old man from the beach," I shouted.

Alice was grimacing from the strain of forcing the raft along, but she peered up at the figures.

"When we spied on the pirates at Hatteras, there was that old man," I reminded her. "Seemed like Dare's right-hand man."

She placed both hands on the side of the raft and pulled herself up to get a better look. When she saw him and Tessa side by side, her expression shifted, as though their deaths were particularly meaningful for her.

Before I could ask Alice about it, Tarn drew alongside me. "We can't bring them aboard," she announced. "All we can do is offer blessings for safe passage."

"Forget bringing them aboard," I said. "What I want to know is: How did they die of Plague on Roanoke Island? There are no rats there."

"There *weren't* any rats there," my father corrected. "But we've been gone a week."

"Convenient timing for them to arrive," said Ananias.

I huffed. "Not convenient at all. Not if we're going to rescue our mother."

Alice raised a hand for silence. She was staring at Tessa's foot. Slowly, carefully, she placed a finger and thumb on

Tessa's bare big toe and pinched hard. The foot ticked side-ways.

"She's alive," I shouted.

Alice was already untying the rope from her waist and spooling it around Tessa. "Get her up there," she yelled. "Now."

Tarn shook her head. "No way. She has Plague."

"So have Rose and Dennis and Nyla. Are you going to throw *them* overboard?"

The stench of dead bodies drifted up on the warm breeze. The pirates weren't bloated yet, but they would be soon.

Still Father hesitated. Being so close to Tessa was stirring up old memories—I could see it in his eyes. I understood it too.

When the Guardians had decided to rewrite our colony's history, Tessa had been the lone holdout, the only person who refused to hide from the ugly events of the past. But instead of fighting for what she believed, Tessa had left the colony, choosing self-imposed exile as if it were the noble thing to do. A few months later Griffin had been born, Dare had taken our mother away, and Father was left to raise his three sons without any help. How different things might have been if Tessa had swallowed her pride and stayed.

Ananias and I began to drag Tessa up to the deck railing. Finally, reluctantly, Father joined us too. The rope slid easily over the metal. When Tessa was within reach, Father held her steady while Ananias and I heaved her on board. She collapsed onto the deck without a sound, skin bruised, clothes tattered, hair draped across her face like so much seaweed.

We helped Alice up next. She crawled across the planking and knelt beside Tessa.

"What are you doing, Alice?" cried Tarn. "She's sick."

Alice glared at her mother. "Sick, but not dead. So what's she doing on that raft?"

Alice had always seemed suspicious of Tessa when we'd first encountered her back on Roanoke. Now she pressed her ear to the old woman's mouth as though our survival rested on what the old woman might tell us. Finally Tessa mouthed something to her.

"Yes," Alice encouraged her. "We know about the solution."

Tessa was clearly dehydrated, so I grabbed a water canister. Alice didn't take it, though. Maybe she suspected that these would be Tessa's last words, and we couldn't afford to miss them.

Again Tessa opened her mouth. This time, Alice's eyes grew wide. She was perfectly still for several moments. Then she sat back on her haunches.

I tipped a little water into Tessa's mouth, but it dribbled out again. "We need to get her below deck. If we can't get water and food into her, we'll lose her."

"Don't you think we're already carrying enough dead weight?" grumbled Tarn.

"I don't think anyone's *dead* yet. Although if it weren't for Tessa, *you'd* be dead now. Or have you forgotten when you were trapped in the hold on Dare's ship?"

Tarn didn't say a word. Neither did Father. Ananias watched the old woman from several steps away. He hadn't seen Tessa since he was a small boy.

"Come on," said Father. "Let's get her below."

Ananias and Father lifted Tessa from the deck as if she weighed nothing. I was going to help them when I noticed Alice. She hadn't moved. Barely seemed aware of us at all.

"What is it, Alice?" I asked. "What did Tessa say?"

Alice was still following the old woman with her eyes.

"What did she say?" I repeated, louder this time.

Alice's hands were shaking. "She said: 'Solution is . . . death.'"

Silence. Ananias and Father lowered Tessa back onto the deck.

I waited for someone to explain what it meant, or better still, to dismiss the words as the ramblings of a feverish woman. But when Father said, "She's delusional," I could tell he was worried.

"Alice," I said softly, "are you all right?"

She startled, as if I'd woken her from a trance. "We need to get moving again," she replied, like she hadn't even heard the question. "We'll be at the bridge in less than one strike. We need to eat and drink. We must get ready to disembark."

"*Disembark?*" Ananias raised his hands. "Tessa got Plague on that island."

"We don't know that," said Alice. "The only way there can be Plague is if the pirates carried rats ashore when they landed."

"And if they *did*?"

"We can outrun a few rats. We did it on Sumter, remember? Unless . . . you don't think your mother is worth that risk."

It was a cruel thing for Alice to do, calling Ananias's bravery into question. But as Ananias turned his attention to Tessa, bringing the conversation to a close, I knew that he was going to do what she asked of him.

I took Tessa's legs and we carried her downstairs. Behind us, Alice was explaining her plan to Tarn and Father. I wondered if they'd offer any resistance, or if Alice would pass it off as a joint decision with Ananias and me.

Ananias paused at the bottom of the stairs. "We can't put Tessa with the others," he said.

He was right about that. There wasn't room, and besides, the sight of her might make them panic.

I tilted my head toward the nearest cabin, and we carried her inside.

Alice must have asked for the sails to be opened again, because the ship began moving. Light from the porthole swept across the cabin as the boat rose and fell with each wave. Tessa didn't stir as we placed her on the hard wooden floor. She didn't make a sound as Ananias left the room.

The Tessa I'd found hiding on Roanoke Island had been deceptively strong, like a strip of leather, toughened with age. But Plague had cracked and weakened her. She didn't have long to live, I was certain of that.

I poured water onto a cloth and ran it over her lips. When

she didn't respond, I leaned back against the wall and shut my eyes.

I must have fallen asleep, because I woke to the sound of the cabin door opening. "It's time," said Ananias.

I rubbed my eyes. I felt achy and disoriented. Tessa was still beside me, but her eyes were open. She was gazing at the water canister.

I tipped the canister, and she drank. When I stopped, she tried to speak, but words wouldn't come. I poured again, and she drank again, and even though I knew that she should go slowly at first, I let her have as much as she wanted. The moment I stopped, she rewarded me by tilting her head to the side and vomiting bile across the floor.

I wiped her mouth with the cloth. "You need to rest."

She opened and closed her mouth, but all I could hear was wheezing.

"I'll be back," I told her. "We're going to rescue Skya."

I figured that hearing her daughter's name might please her, but her eyes grew wide and her breathing quickened. She labored to speak, firing indistinct sounds that left spittle in the corners of her mouth. She resembled a caged animal, giving everything so that her words might break free.

"Thomas!" Ananias's voice came from the top of the stairs.

I pulled to a stand. But as I stepped toward the door, Tessa grasped my right ankle. "Solution . . . Plague."

Did she want Griffin to cure her? Probably, but there wasn't time to explain that Griffin had so far only managed to cure himself. "I'll be back soon," I told her.

I pulled free of her grasp and reached the door before she spoke again. This time, her words were clearer. "Solution is death."

She didn't sound crazy or delusional anymore. She sounded like she needed me to know the truth, even if it was the last thing she ever said.

CHAPTER 17

ee anything yet?" I asked Alice.

"Nothing," she said. "Nothing at all."

We lay on our stomachs on the deck, hidden behind a crate, eyes fixed on the Roanoke Island shoreline. Ananias and my father were with us. Jerren too, which surprised me.

"Maybe the pirates haven't seen us," I said.

"If they're alive, they'll have seen us."

The bridge column was only a hundred yards away. Tarn was crouched on the deck, one hand on the wheel to keep a steady course.

Alice craned her neck to get a view of the shore again. "It's too quiet," she murmured. "Far too quiet."

I fought the urge to look for myself. If Alice couldn't see anything, neither would I.

The bridge loomed over us. Halfway across its span was a large gap, a precaution to prevent rats from spreading from one island to another. Had rats really made it to Roanoke?

Until recently, I'd have thought it was impossible. But finding Tessa had changed everything.

"Get ready," said Alice.

The ship slid alongside the column, hiding us from the shoreline. On Alice's signal we ran to portside. Standing in a line, Ananias, Alice, Jerren, Father, and I dove overboard.

The ship continued its progress, gliding from behind the column and out onto open water. From our position, it was impossible to see that anyone was sailing it.

"Come on," said Alice. "Let's head for the reeds."

We swam in a line for two hundred yards, where the waters of the sound merged with marsh, and a reed-lined channel cut deep into Roanoke Island. Alice kept us hidden behind the reeds. Insects buzzed about us, persistent and irritating, but no one complained. Even our strokes were precise and quiet. Our best chance of success was to remain invisible and silent. At the slightest sound, the pirates might locate us, and we'd witness firsthand how they dealt with unwelcome arrivals.

We were well into the creek when I recognized it as the same one Alice and I had paddled along after spying on the pirates on Hatteras. We'd discovered a remarkable kayak near Bodie Lighthouse, and had hidden it in these very same reeds. It didn't seem accidental when Alice crawled out of the water some distance from that spot. She even shot me a quick look, defying me to mention the kayak to the others. Even now, she liked to keep secrets.

We pushed through the reeds until they ended abruptly a few hundred yards south of Skeleton Town. When Alice raised her hand to stop us, we all followed her command, even Father.

"See anything?" Jerren whispered.

Alice narrowed her eyes. Something about whatever she was seeing frustrated her. Or maybe it was what she *didn't* see that was the problem. She sighed as if she no longer trusted her own element.

"Seems clear," she said finally. "Let's keep to the south of Skeleton Town, though. Head west, then make a wide loop around the town."

We resumed walking. Alice usually moved quickly and decisively, but not now. With every irregular footstep she swept the area with her eyes. Even the sound of our breathing seemed to irritate her.

Jerren stayed at the back of our group. He was preoccupied too, although with something altogether different than Alice, I figured. I wanted to ask how Nyla was doing, but I could guess the answer to that.

"I didn't think you'd come," I told him.

He stared straight ahead. "I have to. Remember how I met your mother on Sumter? Well, she told me that help was coming, and she was right. From what I hear, she also said that Griffin would be the solution to Plague. I have to believe she's right about that as well." He cleared his throat. "Trouble is, I don't know *how* he's the solution. Something tells me we need *her* to unlock the secret. Without it, there's no solution, and my sister's as good as dead."

Just ahead of us, where tall reeds gave way to wild grass, Alice signaled for us to crouch down. We were drawing closer to the ruined stone buildings of Skeleton Town. To the northeast, the water tower tilted precariously. Below it, out of sight, was the hurricane shelter. I could still remember the night, a couple weeks ago, that the Guardians had sent us there. I could even picture Guardian Lora, our chaperone, scowling at me, wasting her dying breath to blame me for my weakness.

Well, I wasn't so weak anymore.

"I don't see anything," said Ananias, growing restless.

Alice didn't respond.

"I said—"

"Shh!" Alice hissed. "There's a street about three hundred yards away. Cuts east–west. If the pirates are on the lookout, that's where they'll see us."

"And what are you going to do about it?"

"Find out if they're on the lookout, of course."

Anger flashed across my brother's face. He wasn't aware of Alice's ability to bring sights and sounds closer, and must have thought that she was being sarcastic. Before the situation escalated, I scooted forward and tugged on his tunic. "Trust me," I whispered, "it's better to let Alice lead."

I didn't imagine that Ananias would accept that, but Father was nodding in agreement too, so he backed down. Perhaps he suspected that Alice had a talent the rest of us lacked. If so, he wasn't letting on.

"Nothing," said Alice finally. "Just silence."

I swallowed hard. "You think they're all dead, don't you?"

"I don't know. But something's wrong. Humans aren't the only things that make sound on Roanoke Island."

Jerren shuffled forward and joined Alice. Hands raised, he turned in an arc, using his element to draw all sound toward her, giving her a better chance of hearing something . . . *anything*.

"Well?" he asked.

"Where are the birds?" she murmured, more to herself than to us.

She continued walking, quicker than before. She didn't pause as we reached the street, and didn't slow down as we headed northeast to approach Skeleton Town from the blind side.

We wound through trees as the backs of the buildings came gradually into view, including one I recognized from our time on Roanoke Island: the clinic. The door was slightly ajar, inviting us to enter.

"Did we leave it open when we were here?" Alice asked me.

"I don't know. Even if we did, it's possible the pirates have been in here too."

"Hmm." She stared at the sheer gray walls, as if she might use her element to see right through them. "Stay here. I'll only be a moment."

"No, Alice. Wait."

Alice ignored me. Bent double, she padded through the grass toward the clinic.

The tall mast of the Sumter ship was just visible above the buildings. Tarn must have reefed the sails, because it wasn't moving. Strange that the pirates still hadn't approached the ship, or even fired a warning shot. *Are they scared of us,* I thought. *Or are they all dead?*

When she reached the clinic, Alice shimmied around the door and peered inside. I expected her to return to us then, but she slipped into the building instead.

I wasn't the only one who was anxious. Beside me, Jerren picked at the bark of a young pine tree.

Alice emerged a moment later, thumb raised, signaling for us to follow.

Jerren ran. The rest of us followed his lead. There was a different sense of urgency than earlier. I'd thought we knew what we'd be facing on Roanoke—hostile pirates holding my mother prisoner—but none of it had come to pass. What if the pirates had deserted the island altogether? And if so, why?

We entered the clinic through the back. Light filtered in through small windows just below the ceiling and large cracked panes of glass at the front. The place felt eerily familiar from our time in Skeleton Town. I'd tried to consign those memories to another lifetime, but now they came flooding back: how I found the lantern that had revealed my element to me; how I had discovered Tessa hiding in the space above the ceiling. So many important things had happened here.

How different my world would have been if I'd never set foot in the building.

"See anything familiar?" whispered Alice. She rested her hand on a large rectangular wooden box placed upon a table. "It's the same one, right?"

"Yes," I said. "The same." I ran my fingers along the smooth edges, recalling the evening we'd evaded Dare on Roanoke Island. With a storm approaching, his men had come ashore, and brought the box with them. There was no longer any doubt in my mind that my mother had been trapped inside it. Not anymore, though—the lid was open, and the box was empty.

Here was proof that the pirates had been in Skeleton Town. But were they still here now?

Ananias tapped my arm. He pointed to our father, who wasn't even looking at the box. Instead he stood beside a tattered chair, a faraway look on his face. "Are you all right, Father?" he asked.

Father looked up. "Yes. I just . . ." He ran his hand across the back of the chair. "This is where I was sitting the first time your mother used the word *solution*—this chair right here. Skya was pregnant with Griffin, and Tessa was checking that everything was progressing well." He smiled. "She said it so casually, like a solution was no big deal. I think maybe that's why I didn't take her seriously at first. But looking back, I think she was afraid to say exactly what she thought Griffin would be. Afraid that I'd think she was crazy."

Alice and Jerren continued to search the clinic for clues, but both stayed silent. They were listening in, learning about the past, just as we were.

"What really happened back then?" I asked.

Father sat down in the chair and ran his palms along the moth-eaten arms. "Your mother mentioned the solution a few times over the next couple months. Each time she'd watch me, like she was trying to grow the seed she'd planted weeks earlier. Trying to convince me that it was real. But I still didn't believe her. Even though she was a seer, it seemed too improbable—this vague cure. But then she woke up one night and the vision wasn't vague anymore. She couldn't have been any more specific: Dare was going to return, she said. He was going to steal the solution away from her."

"But Dare *didn't* steal the solution," said Ananias. "Mother stopped him from taking Griffin."

Father gave a melancholy smile. "Yes. And no. Your mother had a plan, see? When, as she predicted, Dare arrived, she stayed well away. It must have been obvious to him that Skya knew what was going on—he knew she was a seer—so Dare spent the night planning to kidnap her. He was so blinded by that one task, it never occurred to him that she wasn't the solution—that the solution was *inside* her.

"Your mother went into labor that night. To this day, I don't know if it was a coincidence, or fate, or stress, but Griffin was tiny. No one was certain he'd survive. For that one night, we were all together—Skya, me, Griffin, and you two. It was our first and only night as a family."

119

Father pulled to a stand. He placed a hand on the chair back and let it take his weight. He looked tired. Old.

"She was gone when I woke up. Dare and his men had rowed ashore at dawn and come looking for her. She went without a fight, content to know that Griffin—the real solution—was safe. Dare was too focused on capturing Skya to realize what had happened. It seems impossible to me now. Skya had just given birth. She was exhausted. But Dare saw only what he wished to see. That's how he always was: chasing one prize after another. And this time, he had his prize.

"I went after her, of course. Dare wouldn't let his trigger-happy men kill me, but when I began to use my element, someone panicked. I was shot three times. I managed to capsize their boat before I blacked out. The last thing I remember was seeing Skya floating facedown on the ocean. There was blood all around her. *My* blood." He pinched the skin around his mouth, rekindling a little of the pain he'd felt that day. "The Guardians said Skya died that day, and I believed them. What could be more prophetic than that I'd been too weak to save her? I figured that was the reason she never warned me exactly what was going to happen: Because she knew I'd fail her. Turns out, she was right—I failed her the moment I gave up believing that she was still alive."

He looked around the room then, as if he might find our mother standing nearby, wide-open smile assuring him that everything could be the way it had once been. He moved from place to place, looking for a sign. But apart from the wooden box, everything was exactly as we'd left it a couple weeks earlier: shattered glass covering the floor beside the entrance, and a thick coating of dust on every surface.

As his anger grew, my father moved quicker. He knocked over chairs and stripped shelves from walls. Alice and Jerren fired anxious glances my way as the noise grew louder, but Father was possessed. Tears streamed down his face.

"Father," I called out.

He took no notice.

"Father!"

He yanked open the doors of a large, floor-to-ceiling metal closet. For a brief moment he was mercifully still. Then he staggered back, hand pressed against his mouth. When he tripped and fell, he never once took his eyes away from the closet.

I ran over to him. So did the others. In the closet, hanging from a short piece of thick rope, was one of the pirates.

CHAPTER 18

What the hell is going on?" demanded Jerren. His hands were fists at his sides, but his voice cracked as he spoke.

The body was purple-red and bloated. Now that the doors had been opened, an overpowering stench filled the room.

Alice padded over to the window and scanned the street outside. "We need to get back to the ship," she said. "Everything here is just . . . *wrong*."

I pulled my tunic up so that it covered my mouth, and stepped forward until I was standing beside the body. I didn't recognize the pirate, but he had the look of one of Dare's men: malnourished and wiry; leathery, sunburned skin.

"He doesn't look like he has Plague," said Ananias.

My father drew alongside me. He lifted the dead man's hands and inspected them, looking for signs of a struggle.

The man's hands appeared no different than his arms: dirty, but not especially scratched or scarred. There was no blood or skin under the fingernails. No broken knuckles, as far as I could tell. "He died without a fight," I said.

"Unless he killed himself." Alice sounded frustrated—angry, even. She punched her thigh as if the thought offended her. As if this was somehow *personal*. "We need to go. We'll talk back at the ship."

It wasn't a suggestion anymore. There was panic in her voice. She *knew* something.

"Come on," said Jerren, leading the way.

We left the clinic by the broken front door. The street was as quiet and desolate as the rest of the island. Alice looked around frantically.

"What do you see?" I asked her.

"Nothing," she said. "That's the problem . . . *nothing*."

We headed north along the main street, Ananias leading the way. I caught a glimpse of our ship through the gaps between buildings. Tarn and Marin had lowered the anchors and moored now, but neither of them was on deck. There was no other vessel on the water. Unless the pirates had already boarded the ship, which seemed impossible, everyone on board would be fine.

Without warning, Alice veered off and approached the battered building to our right. In the space where the window used to be, three more dead pirates swung from ropes attached to a wooden beam. But unlike the other body we'd found, these showed early signs of Plague.

"They didn't want to die of Plague," said Alice. "So they took their own lives."

"But how did they get Plague in the first place?" I asked. "One or two rats couldn't do this."

"Maybe the pirates crossed to the mainland," suggested Ananias.

"No way. They're not stupid. Anyway, why are the bodies hanging here? Someone should've buried them. Or released them to the water like the ones on the raft."

"Maybe there's no one else left," said Jerren.

My father approached the dead pirates. "Or maybe they just haven't had the chance to dispose of the bodies yet. I don't think these men have been dead for long."

"What would've stopped someone from disposing of bodies?"

"Maybe us," said Ananias. "Maybe we've been seen."

Alice pointed to the northwest. "We're not the only new arrivals. There's the tip of a mast just above those trees over there."

"I don't see anything," said Ananias.

"Just trust me, all right? There's a mast. Judging by its height, I'd say the ship is a big one. At least as big as Dare's."

"You're saying you can see something the rest of us can't?" Ananias had held his tongue earlier, but now he demanded answers. "Alice?"

In response, she raised her hand. I figured she was playing for time, still determined to keep her element a secret from everyone else. But as she sank to her knees and put her ear to the ground, it was clear that she was engaging her element again. Brows furrowed, she nodded slightly as she picked up a sound that resonated along the street.

She snapped her head up. Her eyes grew wide as she stared

into the distance. I couldn't see anything but a shadow crossing the cracked surface of the street.

How could there be a shadow when the sky was cloudless?

"Run!" Alice screamed. "To the ship. Now!"

I felt frozen. So did everyone else, all of us transfixed by the shadow moving toward us, its color shifting from mottled gray to black.

There were rats on Roanoke Island after all. Thousands of them. And they were coming straight for us.

We ran back along the street, occasionally stumbling on the uneven ground. We were heading away from the ship, but we couldn't do anything about that. All that mattered was getting away and staying together.

We'd only gone a hundred yards when the familiar Skeleton Town intersection came into view. The water tower loomed ahead of us. The hurricane shelter would be just to our right. Turning left would take us toward the water. It was our only hope.

My heart was pounding against my chest. I gasped shallow breaths. With every stride I told myself there must be an explanation, and that we'd find it as soon as we returned to the ship.

I was wrong.

Alice skidded to a halt first, arms in front of her in case she fell. The rest of us stopped too, because sliding around the corner of the intersection like a vast black mist were thousands of rats. They moved quickly, never breaking formation. Moments earlier, they'd been silent. Now their relentless squeaking filled the air.

This wasn't improbable anymore. It was impossible.

I spun around. The first group of rats had made up ground on us. "What's happening?" I yelled.

"Combine," my father shouted. "It'll frighten them away."

At first, the word meant nothing to me. Even when I realized that he was talking about combining elements, I hesitated. My element was invasive, and with only Alice within arm's reach, I couldn't bring myself to make the connection. I'd stolen her element once, and injured her another time. She was better off without me.

"Combine, Thom!" she yelled, lunging for my hand.

It was a moment before I let my energy flow through her. The flame was weak, and hardly deterred the rats at all. So I increased the power until the fire shooting from Alice's right hand burned the ground before us in a two-yard arc. The size of the flame caught us both by surprise. The heat was so intense that I had to pull away. But it still didn't stop the rats. They surged forward again, crawling over cremated carcasses as if they were no obstacle at all.

Behind us, Ananias and my father were combining too, another fire that scorched the ground. They had more control over their elements than us, but somehow the flame was smaller. Rats circled around it, finding cool spots through which to launch an attack.

Jerren raised his hands in an attempt to redirect the hideous squeaking sound, but it was coming from everywhere at once. His concentration was shot, energy diffused, and he accidentally redirected the noise straight at us. It hit us with the force of a hurricane. Alice and I clapped our hands over our ears as the rats pressed their advantage.

Face twisted in agony, Alice ripped her hands away from her ears. "Again," she screamed. "Combine."

The sound moved beyond us as she grabbed my hand. But I was petrified now, and disoriented. Energy surged from me in uncontrollable bursts. When we cut down one swathe of rats, another took its place. It was like watching waves breaking on the shore, one after another, each larger and more threatening than the last.

"*More*," cried Alice.

I threw all the power I could muster. This time the flame engulfed everything in a twenty-yard radius. If the other elementals had been in front of us instead of behind, they'd have been burned to death. The buildings to the right and left were bathed in flame.

Ananias and my father were close—no more than fifteen yards away—but rats were filling the gaps between us, forcing us farther apart. Jerren was drifting away too. We were three islands now, isolated and out of touch.

That's when the rats attacked.

It happened in a single moment, a surge so organized, it was as if they'd been waiting for an instruction to pounce. Now they clawed at us, scratching, biting. Alice and I combined again, but she was afraid of bringing the flames too close to me, and the fire did nothing to stop the rats behind us. I used my free hand to bat them away. When I caught a glimpse of my fingers, they were covered in blood. *My* blood.

I let out a cry. It wasn't about the pain—all I felt was a warm, wet heat spreading across my back and legs—but because I knew that we would die here. Maybe we'd be clawed to death, or die of Plague, but one thing was certain: There was no hope of escape.

I was still screaming when the rats fell away. Again, it happened in an instant. And not just to me, but to the others as well. The rats took up positions around us, our own private guards.

The rats fell silent. Once again, Skeleton Town was thrown into eerie quiet.

"Where are you?" Alice shouted. "Show yourself."

"Who are you talking to?" I asked.

She didn't answer. She was staring at the burning buildings. Smoke had engulfed the street, and I couldn't see through it. But I could see something *in* it.

Two figures emerged: one tall, one short. A man and a boy. The boy was young, not much older than Dennis. He had an almost feral appearance, and cowed as the man bullied him along.

As they drew closer, something about the man seemed familiar. I'd seen him before, on the beach at Hatteras Island. Then it came to me: He was the young man who had attempted to murder Dare. But Dare had gotten the better of the upstart, and had cut off the young pirate's finger.

"Jossi," I said.

Alice didn't reply. Maybe she'd already worked it out for herself. Or maybe, I realized, she was transfixed by the way the rats scurried alongside them—not attacking, or rounding up, or threatening in any way. It was like Jossi and the boy were immune to the rats . . . or worse, as if they were controlling them.

The boy was speaking to Jossi in whispers I couldn't hear. I read his body language just fine, though — he didn't want to be here. This was being done against his will.

"What's he saying?" I asked Alice.

"He's saying . . . *please don't make me hurt them.*" She let the words sink in. "We have to get to the ship, Thomas."

Yes, we did. This wasn't a rescue mission for my mother anymore. We'd all been exposed to the Plague. We needed to warn the others what was going on.

As if they were responding to what Alice was thinking, the rats edged closer. But they weren't behaving like rats at all. They were clearly being controlled by the boy. He watched us from thirty yards away, read our body language, and predicted our next move. With thousands of rats at hand, he wielded a weapon more lethal than any I could comprehend — far more powerful than an element.

Alice raised a hand to cover her mouth. "There's a passage between the two buildings on the right," she whispered. "On my command, run to the shore."

What about Ananias and my father? I wanted to ask. *What about Jerren?* But there was no way we could all escape. The important thing was to get word to the others on the ship that our mission had gone disastrously wrong.

As the rats crawled over her feet, Alice lowered her hand. I braced myself, even though I was sure we stood no chance of getting away.

"Now!" she shouted.

I sprinted to the right, crunching rats underfoot. Others surrounded me, but I just kept running. They bit and clawed, but I'd already been exposed to the Plague. The pain of the attack was nothing compared to what would await me as the disease took hold.

I slipped between the buildings and stumbled on the loose ground, but I didn't fall and I didn't slow down. The rats stayed with me at first, but with every step I left more of them behind. I glanced over my shoulder to check that Alice was still with me.

She was lying beside the entrance to the passageway. Rats covered her so completely that I could only recognize her by the occasional flashes of skin as she fought them off. Tears sprang to my eyes. I wanted to help her, but in my mind I heard her yelling at me to keep running, to warn the others about the new enemy we were facing.

The rats had caught up to me again, so I ran faster than ever. Beyond the buildings the route to the shoreline opened up, a landscape of wild grass and rubble. It presented more of an obstacle to the rats than to me. I could put some distance between myself and the rats out here.

The sound of someone shouting distracted me. It was coming from behind me, but above me too. As I looked back, I tripped and fell.

Just as well too, as a bullet struck the ground just ahead of me. Dare's men were still in Skeleton Town, all right. As our eyes met, the pirate lowered his rifle once more and took aim.

CHAPTER 19

leaped up and ran. There was a low wall ahead, so I darted to the left. A moment later, a bullet grazed the brick—another lucky escape.

Surrendering wasn't an option. I could as easily die later as now, so I pushed onward.

I don't know why I changed direction again—maybe it was Alice's voice in my head—but something told me I had to, that until I was out of range, running in a straight line was just making the pirate's job easier. After that, I zigzagged through the battered remains of Skeleton Town, always keeping the ship in my sights. Sounds of gunfire shattered the quiet, but it wasn't long before the shots grew fewer. Then they stopped.

I was out of range.

The shoreline was only a half mile away. A mixture of sweat and blood dripped down my face and along my arms as I willed myself to keep sprinting. My legs felt bludgeoned. My lungs screamed. The wound in my chest had reopened yet again. I welcomed the feeling of panic—it was all that kept me from breaking down.

A quarter mile to go and I was slowing. I forced out one step after another, but the footing grew softer as I approached the shoreline. It wasn't like running on sand, but it was close.

Shouts from nearby jolted me. I looked over my shoulder and saw four pirates running after me, rifles slung across their backs. They were fresh. Their pace was faster. Even if they didn't catch me, they'd be within range again soon.

I thought of Alice lying on the ground, covered in rats. Brave Alice. She'd given the order to run, but had let me go first. It should've been *her* running to the ship as the rats picked *me* to pieces. She'd sacrificed herself for me. I couldn't let her down.

Two hundred yards to go. A shot rang out. It missed, but I imagined the bullet slicing through the air beside me. More shouting. And something dark in my peripheral vision.

I glanced left and right. Somehow rats were converging on me again. But they couldn't have made it from the street already, which meant that these were different rats. I'd thought there were thousands of rats, but I was wrong. There were tens of thousands. Maybe a hundred thousand. Enough to wipe out every human being. And Jossi and the boy controlled them.

Solution is death, Tessa had said. Finally I realized what she had meant by that. She hadn't been talking about Griffin at all. No wonder she'd been so desperate for me to stay on the ship.

I pounded out one stride after another, keeping an equal distance from both packs of rats. The ground was marshy here, but that would be harder for the rats than for me. The pirates, on the other hand—

The sound of the gunshot hit me at the same moment as the bullet itself. There was a flash of white-hot pain as it grazed my arm, followed by a dull heat. Exhausted, delirious, I told myself that he'd missed. I took it as a sign that I was winning.

I wasn't aware of the moment that land gave way to water. I just kept going until I couldn't bring my legs above the surface. Then I began swimming. My right arm wouldn't rise as high as my left, but I dragged it up and around anyway. My legs, still burning, flapped against the water.

Another bullet zipped through the water next to me. The pirates would be closing in again. How far would I be from the shore when they got there? Fifty yards? Less? Close enough that they could hit me with ease, that much was certain. My strokes were useless now.

Another shot, and another, so close that I felt the bullets shift the water beside me. I wasn't going to get away after all. I knew that now.

With a last look at the ship in the distance, I took a deep breath and dove underwater. I counted eight strokes and resurfaced. Another breath. Under again. I only managed five strokes this time. I had no idea if I was still heading for the ship.

Something slapped at my arms—a bullet, I thought. I broke

the surface and dove under again. The slapping resumed, and it wasn't bullets, or a fish. I flailed my arms, trying to fight off whatever it was, but it pressed against me, holding me tightly.

That's when I realized it was a person. Someone with the element of water.

I couldn't see anything, but I figured it must be Rose. I was too disoriented to wonder how she had recovered from her injuries enough to help me. I just relaxed into her arms and let her speed me along. The pressure of the water against my head was proof of how quickly we were moving. In moments I would be out of range of the gunmen. There was no way they'd be able to catch up to me now.

As my breath was about to give out, we surfaced momentarily. In that instant, I discovered that it wasn't Rose at all. It was Marin.

We went under again. Her legs fluttered behind us, as quick as a butterfly's wings and as powerful as a pelican's. The next time we emerged, I couldn't see the shore at all because we were hidden behind the ship.

Things happened around me in a blur of motion. A rope landed beside me, but I couldn't think of what to do with it.

"Climb, Thomas," came a voice from above us. "You must climb."

Still I stared at the rope. Beside me, Marin floated on her back, face frozen in an agonized mask. I couldn't piece it all together.

"She'll be all right," Tarn implored me. "She just needs time to recover."

It was my echo again. During the few days we'd spent on Sumter, I'd been able to stop obsessing about every fleeting touch. Now that we were on Roanoke, the memories of everyone I'd ever hurt came flooding back.

Add Marin to that list. She'd known what rescuing me would entail, and she'd come anyway. But *why*? She hated me.

I grasped the rope and eased it around her torso and under her armpits, careful not to touch her. I tied it off with a double hitch knot. I didn't want her to drift away from the ship—even someone with the element of water could, presumably, drown.

Tarn had tied her end of the rope to the ship's railing. Hand over hand, feet coiled around the rope, I began to climb. I thought of Rose in the ship, and Alice in Skeleton Town, and almost gave up. Then I glimpsed Marin below me, and Tarn above, leaning over the rail, straining to help me back on board. Just two more pulls and I'd be there.

I lost my grip as I reached for the rail, but Tarn had a tight hold on my tunic. She heaved me over the rail and onto the deck.

"You've got to help me get Marin up here," she said. "That woman just saved your life. Now it's time for you to save hers."

She pulled me to a stand and we took the rope. Gradually we pulled Marin from the water. When she was almost at rail level I anchored my feet against the edge of the ship and leaned back, a counterbalance to her weight. Tarn dragged her aboard.

We were sprawled across the deck. To the east, wisps of smoke skidded above Skeleton Town. How were the others doing? Was I a coward for leaving them?

Tarn followed my eyes. "What happened over there, Thomas?" she asked.

What *had* happened? And how could I begin to explain. "It was . . . an ambush."

"We heard shots. Is anyone hurt?"

"I don't think anyone was shot. But the others have been captured. And there are rats. Lots of them."

Tarn looked over my body—took in the blood streaks and the bite marks. "How many rats?"

"Thousands."

I wanted to see Griffin, but now I was pleased that he wasn't with us. How could I explain that after all these years, he wasn't the only solution? How could I put everything that had happened into signs when I couldn't find the words?

"The pirates control the rats," I said. "They used them to round us up. To trap us."

"That's impossible. They just made you *think* they can do that."

"I saw—"

"What they wanted you to see." Tarn huffed. "An element like that couldn't have arisen until *after* the Exodus and the Plague. That's the way elements evolve—in response to external change. Since every one of the pirates was born *before* the Plague, they couldn't possess such an ability."

"But the *boy* wasn't born before the Plague."

136

"What boy?" Tarn's expression shifted—no longer dismissive, but concerned. "What are you talking about?"

"A boy who came from the clan ship that's moored to the northwest of Roanoke." I pointed, but the mast was obscured by trees.

"If there's a clan ship, then where are the clan folk? You can't believe a boy sailed that ship through the Oregon Inlet by himself."

I shrugged. These were reasonable questions, but I had no answers. Nothing made sense anymore. "Tessa said the solution is death," I reminded her. "What if Griffin isn't the real solution? What if that boy on Roanoke is instead?"

Tarn looked at Marin. She wanted another Guardian to help her make sense of everything. But Marin hadn't moved. Only the gentle rise and fall of her chest convinced me that she was still alive.

"I need to go back," I said. "I have to help them."

"No. You need to rest."

"Your daughter is over there."

"Yes, she is. But making another hasty decision won't turn back time. What we need now is a plan."

I thought about this. "Actually, what we need is answers. And I know who has them."

I dragged myself off the deck and lumbered toward the stairs. I never made it to Tessa's cabin, though. Because halfway down the stairwell, listening in, was a perfectly healthy girl.

It wasn't until Nyla spoke that I was sure I wasn't seeing a ghost.

CHAPTER 20

Nyla bit her lip, as if she were waiting for me to appraise her and was nervous about what I'd say. But what *could* I say? The lumps on her neck had disappeared. The skin was still dark from bruising, but there were no blemishes, or fever. No more pain.

"You're cured," I murmured. It was a pointless, self-evident thing to say, but I had to say it to make it real. "How?"

She shrugged. "Griffin."

"Where is he now?"

Nyla lowered her eyes. "In the cabin. Sleeping."

Why would Griffin be sleeping in the middle of the day? When we'd left a few strikes earlier, he'd been feeling better.

I didn't bother to ask which cabin he was in. I knew where I'd find him.

Griffin was lying on the floor, sweating, teeth chattering. He looked even worse than Rose. Yet, through it all, he smiled. *Save. Nyla*, he signed. *Me. Solution.*

He had no idea about the boy on Roanoke, or the rats.

As far as Griffin was concerned, he was the solution, and his version of the solution didn't equal death at all.

I knelt beside him. I wanted to hold him, but I couldn't—it would hurt him even more. And so with nothing else to do, I broke down in tears. Tears for those I'd left behind on Roanoke, and for Rose and Dennis, and for Griffin, who'd hurt himself to save another.

"Where's my brother?" Nyla stood in the doorway. "Where's Alice?"

"They're still on Roanoke," I told her. "Now you tell me: How did you do it?"

"Do what?"

"We don't have time for this!" I didn't want to be mean to her—not with Ananias captured on Roanoke—but I had to know. "How did Griffin cure you?"

"We just held hands."

"You're lying. I saw Griffin touch you earlier. There was something wrong."

Griffin signed for me to stop—he could see that Nyla was frightened. But when he beckoned her to join him, she wouldn't. She wanted to keep her distance. It was as though she was afraid of stealing even more of his strength. Or hurting him.

Almost like me, in fact.

"What's your element, Nyla?"

She hesitated. "I don't know."

"Your brother's being held at gunpoint. If we're going to help him, we cannot have secrets. You have to tell us about your element."

139

"How can I?" she snapped. "How do *you* explain what you are? . . . What you can do?"

Tarn had helped Marin below deck now. They stood behind Nyla, but hearing this, they shrank back. It was instinct, the realization that, like me, she could hurt them without even meaning to. Especially when she was agitated.

"You have *my* element," I said.

Nyla pursed her lips. "It's not *your* element, Thomas. It's *an* element, and I hate it as much as you do."

Ideas raced through my mind, then—answers to questions I'd never thought to ask. "That's how you got the ship moving when we escaped from Sumter, isn't it? You took over Rose's element."

"I'd seen Rose catching fish, so I knew she had the element of water. But I didn't know we'd be strong enough for that." There wasn't a hint of triumph in her voice. The element was as much a burden to her as it was to me.

"So Griffin cured you by combining?"

"No. We tried that. It didn't work. So I took over his element. Cured myself by draining him." She bit her lip. "That's what you want to hear, right? That I hurt Griffin to save myself. That I could be more like you than anyone else, and still be *less* than you—less thoughtful, less kind . . ."

Her eyes welled. Having admitted everything, she couldn't bring herself to look at Griffin at all. But I could, and there was no mistaking the look on his face. The discomfort was still there, but he was smiling right through it. For the first time, his suffering was meaningful. There was a purpose to his pain.

I. Save. Rose. Now, he signed, bowing his head toward the figures on the floor. *Save. Dennis.*

Marin had been leaning against Tarn for support, but Griffin's promise seemed to give her strength. "Can he do that?"

"No," I said. "He's too weak."

"And so am I! Or did you think that rescuing you was easy for me? That holding you against me as I swam through the sound didn't rob me of my strength." Her clothes dripped onto the wooden floor.

"But he doesn't even know what happened. Nyla took over his element."

"Because I *had* to," insisted Nyla. "I couldn't give him my element and take his at the same time. I had to take it all, just like he said I would."

"Wait. Griffin told you to do it?"

"Of course he did. Maybe he could cure someone else just by touching them, but not me. And not you."

Marin slipped to the floor and rested her chin on her knees. "Look at me, Thomas. I *broke* myself to save you because it was the right thing to do. And because Rose would never forgive me if I hadn't."

Hearing her name, I glanced at Rose. I'd been putting it off, I now realized, aware that she was only getting sicker. But I hadn't realized how *much* worse. She and Dennis were sweating so hard that their clothes were as saturated as mine. But somehow her Plague seemed farther along than his—maybe because she'd been so sick before she was bitten.

I. Save. Her, signed Griffin. He even seemed excited by the prospect, as if his life had no greater purpose than this.

There was silence. Then: "Can he?" whispered Rose.

The answer was clearly *no*—Griffin needed time to recover. Since he couldn't be trusted to look out for himself, he needed me to do it for him. But Rose was slipping away with every passing strike. How could I deny her the chance to be cured? How could I deny Griffin the chance to cure her?

"You'd need me to combine with him," I told Rose. "He's weak."

"I'll do it," said Nyla.

"You've only just been cured."

"And you've only just returned from Roanoke. I think I'm stronger than you are."

I moved aside so that Griffin and Nyla could kneel beside Rose. But Rose shook her head gently. "No. Dennis first."

I felt a rush of panic. "But you're weaker than him."

"Don't care. Dennis goes first, or I won't go at all."

I turned to Marin, pleading with my eyes for her to talk some sense into Rose. But when Marin broke eye contact, I knew that she wouldn't say a word.

Dennis rolled toward his sister and took her hand. "I won't do it," he said.

"Yes, you will." She pulled his hand to her lips and kissed his fingers. "You *must*. They need you. You're special."

"But—"

"I'm next. I promise."

What if there isn't a next? I wanted to shout. But Griffin and Nyla were already lining up alongside Dennis. There was nothing I could do to stop them, either. Rose had made her feelings clear. In a way, Marin had too.

With a deep breath, Griffin gave Nyla his left hand and placed his right on Dennis's chest. There was something strange about the image, but it took me a moment to realize what it was: For years, no one had willingly touched Griffin because of his ability to foresee a person's death. But there was no hesitation now. What was the use in waiting, when the pallor of almost-death already hung over Dennis's skinny body?

I didn't expect to see the cure unfolding before us. It seemed logical to me that any transformation would take time, the Plague driven out a little more with each breath, each heartbeat. But I was wrong.

Dennis's color changed right before us. His cheeks turned red and sweat beaded on his forehead. His teeth chattered. Then the swelling around his neck and under his armpits reduced, leaving only shadowy outlines. It happened so quickly that Dennis seemed surprised when Griffin let go.

It was the miracle Dare had predicted, a solution to humanity's greatest threat. Griffin was changing the world, right before our eyes.

I looked at my brother, unable to conceal a smile. I figured that Griffin would smile right back at me, proud of what he'd done. Instead his eyes were closed, and his head lolled from side to side. His breaths were rapid and uneven.

Then he passed out.

Nyla was afraid to touch him in case she made things

worse. I felt powerless too. So it was Marin who shuffled over, lifted his head, and slid a rolled-up blanket underneath. Then she wrapped her arms around Dennis.

"I feel . . . fine," he said. "It was like he was giving me life."

Rose watched her younger brother, a smile playing on her lips. But there were tears too as she took in the sight of Griffin, out cold on the floor.

Dennis pulled away from his mother. He was probably eager to move about after so much time cramped inside the cabin. He stepped to the porthole and savored the feel of the sun on his face. Resting his head against the wall, he peered outside. "What's that?" he asked.

I joined him, but all I saw was the dark sound stretching toward the shore.

"In the water there," he tried again.

Tarn stepped quickly over to us. She peered outside, eyes narrowed, seeing things that the rest of us couldn't. "Oh no," she said.

"What is it?" I asked.

"Get on deck," she yelled. "Do it *now*."

Dennis, completely recovered, was first to react. Tarn was right behind him. Nyla and I hesitated a moment, partly because we were both exhausted and maybe because we didn't want to leave Griffin. But the horror in Tarn's voice propelled us along the corridor and up the stairs. Marin was behind us, but she was in even worse shape—spent, weak, useless.

From the higher vantage point, the water no longer

appeared uniformly dark. Instead, like a cresting wave, a clear straight line separated the regular gray-green water from a swathe of advancing black.

But it was the noise that really made me sick—thousands of tiny breathy squeaks. The rats were coming for us. And they only had twenty yards to go.

CHAPTER 21

R ats can't climb a ship, right?" Dennis shouted. "The
sides are curved. Slick."

"That's right," said Tarn. She sounded unsure,
though. Like me, she was probably racing through any and all
possibilities. Unfortunately, precious moments passed before
she yelled, "They'll climb the anchor chains."

I lumbered to the bow winch and began turning. It must
have used a gear system, because the handle turned without
much effort. Nyla raised the anchor at the stern. In mirror
image, we spun our handles around as Tarn and Dennis scurried around the deck.

Before my anchor was clear of the water, a shot rang out
from the shore. There was a long moment before I recognized
the sound. I dropped to the deck.

The chain unraveled, sending the anchor crashing back
down.

Nyla had reacted the same way. "We're out of range," I
shouted, as much to remind myself as her.

146

I pulled myself up and turned the winch again. Gunshots grew more frequent, but I didn't stop turning, and neither did she. Peering through the railing, I couldn't see any gray-green water at all anymore, which meant that the rats were close.

Tarn was unfurling the mainsail, while Dennis filled it with powerful gusts of his element. As the ship began to move slightly, they both seemed to relax.

"We might be all right," said Tarn. "I think we . . ."

She pointed toward my anchor chain. At least twenty rats were clinging to the links. As they reached the level of the deck, they jumped free and landed on the ship.

Nyla screamed, assuring us that the same thing was happening on her chain. My instinct was to let the chain slide back down into the water, but then nothing would prevent the rats from climbing. I shouted to Nyla not to let go of her winch either, but it was too late—she had already released the handle in horror.

"Get it back up," I yelled.

Tarn understood immediately. She left her station at the sail to assist Nyla. Rats were spreading across the deck now, having caught a ride on my chain. At least with the anchor stowed, there was a limit to how many more of them could come.

The rats had appeared perfectly organized as they swam across the sound. Now they crisscrossed, their movements unpredictable and chaotic. Even though I couldn't explain it, I had no doubt that even out here they were being controlled by the clan boy's awesome element.

"Watch out, Thomas," said Dennis.

They surrounded me in an instant. I didn't panic, though. Oddly, I felt immune to them. I'd already been exposed to the Plague when they bit me in Skeleton Town. Now I needed to prevent the others on board from being bitten as well.

I grabbed a coiled rope and whipped it back and forth across the deck. It was thick and heavy and knocked several rats overboard with each swing. But there were always more.

A scream from the stern pulled me around. With their anchor still partially submerged, Tarn and Nyla were being deluged with rats. Dennis left the sail and sent powerful gusts of air across the deck, like a gigantic broom sweeping everything aside. Nyla and Tarn fought to hold their ground against it as the anchor broke the surface and they locked off the chain.

The ship began to move quicker. We were pulling away from the sea of rats, but hundreds had already boarded.

"Thomas," Dennis called out. "We need to combine."

He was almost at the stern now, and I was near the bow. Neither of us could afford to stop what we were doing to race across the deck.

"Combine with Nyla," I shouted back to him.

She was crouching on the deck only a couple yards from him. He barely had time to register that she was there when she lunged for his hand and the gusts of wind accelerated. And then stopped, replaced by an eerie stillness.

"Down!" she screamed.

I dropped to the deck as the atmosphere shifted. I felt like I was caught in a vacuum, as if all the air surrounding the ship had been gathered up. Then it erupted in an explosion that cleared the deck of rats and sent several wooden crates flying through the air. I rolled away as a large one landed beside me and burst through the wooden planks.

"Nyla?" I shouted. "Tarn?" I got on my knees and surveyed the desolation. Every object not tied down had gone, bursting through the ship's steel railing as if it were made of twine.

The others heaved themselves into a seated position. Tarn stared at Dennis and Nyla, mouth open, saying nothing. The two of them looked shaken, like they couldn't quite believe what they'd done.

An odd sound distracted me then. It came from below deck, but I couldn't place it. Was it an animal? Or the weakened planks shifting beneath us? I pressed my ear against the deck.

From the corner of my eye I noticed Nyla watching me. She stood and padded swiftly toward me. "What is it?" she asked.

"I don't know," I said. "I thought I heard something."

She nodded once and headed for the stairs.

"Where are you going?" I shouted.

I was about to follow her when I heard a sound like a human cry coming from below the chest. Griffin and Rose were in a cabin at the other end of the ship, so it had to be Tessa. But the sound was coming from the galley area, immediately below the prow. If Tessa could move about, she could answer my questions. And I had plenty.

I walked lightly down the stairs. Tessa's cabin was the nearest door, so I opened it. To my surprise, she was asleep on the floor, exactly where we'd left her. There was an empty plate beside her, though, so at least she'd been able to eat.

But what had made the sound?

I continued to the end of the corridor. The galley door was ajar, and I could just make out Nyla's left shoulder. As I drew closer, I heard a series of quick, rasping breaths.

I peered around the door. Nyla had a flashlight in her left hand, and shone the beam at white panels against the far wall. I'd seen the panels before, but now there was a gap.

I eased the door open. It didn't make a sound. But as I crossed the threshold, Nyla spun around.

The flashlight momentarily blinded me. When I recovered, I realized that there was something in her right hand too: a gun. She pointed it at me.

I froze. "What are you doing, Nyla?"

"You should go."

"Jerren said there were no weapons on board."

"He was wrong." Her eyes flitted from me to the gap in the panels. One of them stood apart from the others and had been moved to the side, revealing a strikingly different *metal* panel.

"I heard someone cry out."

She shook her head, a warning for me to stop asking questions. Her finger rested precariously on the trigger.

"You're not going to shoot me," I said, edging forward. "So please put down the gun."

"I have to protect myself."

"I'm not going to hurt you."

She held her ground. "It's not you I'm worried about."

The moment her eyes flickered back to the metal panel, I pounced. In two strides I had hold of the gun barrel. I poured my element along the metal shaft, just enough to shock her into letting go. But Nyla didn't cry out. Instead, she blocked the flow and fought back with a surge of her own.

Energy built up in the space between us. I felt it like some great malevolent elemental force. When our power was evenly balanced, the energy converged on a single point. Smoke rose from the gun barrel. The metal began to bend.

Would either of us be left standing when this ended?

I took a deep breath and let her power ebb toward me. Then, as she became distracted by her own progress, I threw everything into a single massive shock.

Nyla stumbled backward and crashed against the wall. She crumpled to the floor and grabbed her head. She was bleeding.

"What's going on, Nyla?"

"They promised me everything would be all right," she said, tearing up.

I tossed the gun away. "Who did?"

"Jerren and Alice." She glanced at the metal panel again. "They said this was the only way."

Now that I had time to look, I noticed that the metal panel was a door—it had hinges on the left, and two sturdy bolts were attached to the top and bottom. When I pulled them back, the door swung easily and noiselessly toward me.

It was mostly dark inside, except for a sliver of light from a tiny crack in the ceiling. It must have happened when the chest fell against the deck. The air was stale, rancid. I figured the space couldn't be very large, as it was crammed into the shape of the ship's prow.

Something skittered across the floor toward me. It moved lightly, quickly. I stepped back as the rat reached the edge and clawed its way down the paneling and across the galley floor.

Once I'd caught my breath, I retrieved the flashlight from the floor. My heart must have been beating fast, because the light shone brightly.

"Don't," she whispered.

I shone the beam through the gap in the paneling. The space was larger than I imagined, with metal walls and ceiling—a place to store precious cargo, most likely. There was a bundle of black cloth stuffed into one corner. As my pulse slowed down, my element waned and the light became dimmer, but I could still make out colored images through holes in the cloth.

The images moved slightly. There was the sound of someone breathing. Then the cloth fell away, revealing a blood-streaked face and long lank hair.

CHAPTER 22

staggered back from the tiny space as Dare edged toward me. Behind me, Nyla closed the galley door and locked it. "Let us explain," she said—not *me*, but *us*.

I wasn't interested in an explanation. I was overcome by blinding anger, so I lunged for Dare and poured my element into him. Unlike Nyla, he didn't resist. Or couldn't. He just accepted the punishment, and when I was done, he slid through the gap and collapsed in a heap on the floor.

Blood flowed from a wound on his head. Barely conscious, Dare stared at me with a blank expression. This was my chance to kill him, to apply my element until his eyes rolled back in his head and his heart stopped beating. No one deserved to suffer as much as he did.

But then, why had he let me attack in the first place?

"Go ahead," he wheezed. "Do it."

He was a seer. He'd foreseen everything so far. He'd probably even foreseen getting captured and locked up. So what was his endgame?

Nyla passed by me and handed Dare a water canister. He tried to take it, but couldn't grip. It fell to the floor and rolled out of reach, dripping water onto the wooden planks. He closed his eyes.

I couldn't bear to look at Nyla. We'd given her a chance to survive, and she'd betrayed us. "How could you do this?" I hated how breathy and nervous I sounded.

She picked up the canister and gave it to him again, careful to make sure he had it this time. "Dare helped Alice and Jerren escape from Sumter. You and Griffin too. You'd all be dead if he hadn't turned on Chief."

"He's the one who risked our lives in the first place!"

Dare drank a little. "Where . . . Alice?" he rasped.

"She's been captured," I told him. "Her and Jerren, both."

He clicked his tongue. "I told them to take me."

"You're a seer. Don't pretend you don't know what's happened to them. What about my mother? Is she still alive?"

"*Was* alive, last time I saw her. But that was days ago."

"We found the wooden box in Skeleton Town—the one you carried her ashore in."

Dare winced as he stole short breaths. "I didn't want to do that to her, but she was distracting."

"What does that mean?"

"She seemed scared. She'd asked to come to Roanoke with me. Said she wanted to see you, and your father and brothers. But when we got here, she changed her mind—said something terrible was going to happen."

"What was it?"

"I don't know. She said she couldn't see it clearly." He looked at me at last. "I thought she was stalling, to give you time to escape from me. But a hurricane was coming and my men were worried. That's why I hid her in the wooden box. There was no distraction after that, for us *or* for you." His face relaxed, as if he was satisfied by his answer.

"Well, now she might be dead. Along with everyone else."

"My men won't hurt anyone. We'll negotiate your mother's release. Alice's and Jerren's too."

"And the clan folk? Will you negotiate for them too?"

"Of course. I was the one who radioed for them to come. I *invited* them here, Thomas. Non-elemental pirates and non-elemental clan folk—a new colony for a new future."

Despite his injuries, he seemed to be gaining energy with every word. I hated myself for having this conversation, but we were getting to the heart of something here, and I still couldn't see clearly what it was. "What about the elemental on that clan ship? The boy who controls rats."

Dare's lips twitched. "What are you talking about?"

"You *know* what I'm talking about. You're a seer."

He was concentrating now, working on the argument that would prove I was mistaken. "You saw this boy?"

"Yes. And now my father and brother are captured. Alice and Jerren too. And you want me to believe you had no idea it would happen?"

He looked away. "I told them not to go without me."

"You sent them into a trap."

I kept waiting for the Dare I thought I knew to emerge, to

fight back with words if his body wasn't up to it. But he just looked tired and wounded. "The last time I spoke to Alice we were still a long way from Roanoke. My visions were close to useless."

"Liar. My mother held Jerren's hands on Sumter and foresaw his future."

"Clearly not all of it. Anyway, you can't compare me to Skya."

"Why not? You're brother and sister. You're both seers—"

"And seeing the future is my *secondary* element." He paused to let the words sink in. "I'm not like your mother. Or Tessa. My strengths lie elsewhere."

The longer I'd been standing over Dare, the more I'd allowed myself to feel in control. The injury to his head was real. The dehydration too, I was sure of it. All too late, it occurred to me that I had no idea what other surprises he had in store.

With a deep breath, Dare raised a shaking hand upward. A moment later, a tiny flame emerged.

I flung myself at him. Grabbed his hands and jolted him. This time, his eyes rolled back. He passed out just as Nyla pulled me away.

"What are you doing?" she snapped.

"What are *you* doing? He was going to burn us. You know what he's capable of."

Nyla pressed a finger against his neck to check for a pulse. "Here," she said. "Help me get him back inside the secret room. We need to lock him up."

"No. The others need to see this. See how you've betrayed us."

Nyla punched the floor. "Don't be stupid. You really think this is all just chance? That when you and Alice were changing ships, Dare stayed here alone, just waiting for Alice to capture him?" She gritted her teeth. "Wake up, Thomas. He *wanted* to be captured."

"Why?"

"Because he knew that Alice wouldn't hurt him. Not after she read the journal that he left for her."

I wanted to tell Nyla to stop. I wanted to believe these were lies. But deep down, I knew they weren't. I felt like I was staring at a distant object through binoculars. It was getting closer and closer but I couldn't bring it into focus.

"The reason you escaped from the other ship is because Dare unloaded the men's rifles," she continued. "He meant for this to happen."

"What was in the journal?" I whispered.

Nyla looked at Dare's unconscious body. "That's what he was trying to show you. His primary element is fire. *Fire*, Thomas . . . same as Alice." She paused. "Elements are inherited, but neither of her parents had that element. So ask yourself: Who do you think she got it from?" She bowed her head. "Who do you think Alice's real father is?"

CHAPTER 23

I couldn't speak. Couldn't even breathe. I wanted to tell Nyla that she was wrong, that something so unfair couldn't be true. But the Guardians had always treated Alice differently.

Now I understood why.

Moments from the past played out in a punishing cycle: Alice being scolded, berated, bullied, demeaned, and her own father, Joven, leading the assault. I'd always thought that he was ill-equipped to handle a rebellious daughter. Turns out, he just wasn't equipped to handle a daughter who wasn't his.

Recent memories came flooding back too: Joven viciously attacking Alice on our voyage to Sumter; Alice's sister, Eleanor, who was never the same after a single brief conversation with Dare; all the arguments between Alice and Tarn on Sumter. With every recollection, I knew that what Nyla was telling me was true. I just couldn't get my head around what it meant.

"When did Alice find out?"

Nyla leaned against the wall. "She suspected something after the escape from the gunroom on Sumter. She and Jerren were outnumbered. They never would've gotten out of there if Dare hadn't helped them. There's no way *anyone* would've gotten out alive."

"And then she found the journal in Rose's cabin, I guess."

"It was kind of an accident. She was in there checking on you and Rose. When she saw the journal, she took it for Griffin. But he was in a bad way too, so she started reading it for herself. I don't know what was in it, but it was all the proof she needed." Nyla recapped her water canister and placed it carefully on a counter. "Are you going to tell Tarn?"

Tarn. I hadn't even considered her. Whatever her situation now, she must have loved Dare once. But what about Marin? Dare's men had shot and killed her husband. How could we possibly band together as long as Dare was with us?

"Come on," I said, grabbing his tunic. "Let's put him back where he belongs."

Working together we dragged him into the space. His arms and legs were twisted, but that wasn't our concern. Even though we'd spared his life, I hoped that he was uncomfortable—the more pain, the better.

We left the room together, and joined the others on deck. Dennis had stilled the wind, and Tarn was lowering the anchors. We were at least a mile to the northeast of Roanoke Island, close enough to see the tree line, and the leaning water tower and crumbling buildings in Skeleton Town. And far enough to be out of range of the pirates' rifles.

Tarn stood against the railing, staring at the island. I was sure she was engaging her element, working to bring everything closer, make everything clearer.

"See anything?" I asked her.

She peered at me from the corner of her eye. "It's so quiet. So still."

"I think the pirates are toying with us. Trying to get us to make a move."

"Well, maybe we should."

"Not yet. They could've easily shot us down. We didn't even see the gunmen on the roofs." As I placed my hands on the railing, I noticed that they were smeared with Dare's blood. I put them down before Tarn noticed. "I think the pirates want us to get Plague, not to die."

"That may end up being the same thing."

"Not if we have the solution. And they must believe we do. So they're luring us over. If they can capture Griffin, they'll control the rats *and* the solution. They'll be able to go anywhere they like. The mainland will be theirs."

She bowed her head. "So what do you suggest?"

"Let's wait until dark to go over. Give ourselves the best chance of staying hidden."

"We won't be able to see."

"As long as you're leading the way, we'll be fine."

Tarn bristled. "I don't know what you're talking about."

"Come on, Tarn," I said, keeping my voice low. "I know about your element."

She was usually so poised, but now she looked furious. "You know *nothing*."

"We have to be honest with each other from now on. Can't you see that?"

"What's there to be honest about?"

"How about Alice's father!"

Silence. I hadn't meant to say that. Whatever had happened between Tarn and Dare wasn't relevant anymore. If anyone had a right to demand answers, it was Alice, not me. But my words were out there now, and Marin and Dennis were watching us, waiting for whatever came next. Nyla hung back, unsure of her place in the unfolding drama.

"Seems you know a lot," said Tarn.

I shrugged. "I found the third journal," I lied.

"I see. And now you want to know how it could happen—how I could have a child with the man responsible for destroying our colony." She gripped the rail tighter, her knuckles turning white, and watched us.

Dennis looked horrified; Marin, sympathetic. I don't know how I appeared to her, but after a few moments Tarn's shoulders relaxed, like she was shedding a burden she'd carried for her entire life. "My husband, Joven, left the Roanoke Island colony after our daughter, Eleanor, was born," she explained. "He went to work in the Gulf of Mexico. He always talked about coming back, but things weren't good between us, so I didn't believe him. And then the Exodus happened. After that, I was sure I'd never see him again.

"I'd grown up with Dare on Roanoke Island. He'd always been my friend, the one person I could count on to listen. He wasn't like everyone else our age. Didn't seem to care what other people thought. I wanted to be more like him, I guess. After the Exodus, we became close again. Sometimes he'd look after Eleanor so that I could help out in the colony. I don't think either of us meant to fall in love. It just happened. We were strong together.

"It didn't last, though. All the elementals had made a pact not to use our powers—history showed that people with unexplained abilities don't get treated well by others—so we tried to blend in with the refugees. But when things got tough, we started using our elements in secret. After that, the colony became divided—native Roanoke Islanders versus refugees, elementals versus non-elementals. The *schism*, we called it. They knew we had more than them—more food, more water, more power. They just didn't understand *how*. And then Ordyn was involved in an accident where a boy died. After that, the non-elementals became suspicious. There was no going back.

"Dare was an elemental, like us, but he'd saved the refugees too. He believed that the future depended on all of humanity, not just elementals. So when it came time to choose a side, he chose the refugees. He wanted me to come with him too, but I couldn't. Roanoke was home for me. And Eleanor was an elemental. What would've happened to her when a non-elemental realized what she could do?"

Tarn tilted her head to the side, and closed her eyes as the sun warmed her face. "I didn't know I was pregnant when Dare left us. I never got the chance to tell him, either. A few months later, long after I'd given up hope of ever seeing him again, Joven found his way back to us on a clan ship. When Alice was born, he promised to treat her as his own daughter. He said she'd never have to know the truth of who she was. But he didn't treat her the same as Eleanor. He was a bully . . . and I let him be that way because I was scared that he'd tell Alice the truth.

"Your mother despised me for my cowardice, Thomas. Tessa did as well—it's part of the reason she left the colony, because she wouldn't agree to keep our horrible secrets anymore." Tarn blinked away tears. "I thought I was doing the right thing, but I was just weak. If I'd come clean, we could've started to heal. And I wouldn't have had to find ways to keep you and Alice apart once I realized how much she liked you. I mean, you're blood relatives," she said helplessly. "I *had* to keep you apart, you understand?"

My mouth was dry. I had questions, lots of them, but my impulse was to reassure Tarn because now wasn't the time for fighting. "Alice has Jerren now," I said, trying to be helpful.

Tarn gave an angry snort. "Now, yes. But I'm not talking about a few days, Thomas. You're the only real friend Alice has ever had. She's risked everything to stand up for you. And no matter what she's done, and what she's said to me, I've had to keep you apart."

I didn't ask what Alice had said to Tarn about me, because I didn't want to hear the answer. But I understood now why

Alice had been unwilling to harm Dare, the father she had never known. Of everyone from our tiny, close-knit colony, he was the only person who had an excuse for letting her down. The rest of us, each in our own small way, had driven her into a life of isolation and distrust.

I wanted to blame Joven. Tarn. The Guardians. But surely I was as much to blame as anyone. I'd played my role in the colony to perfection too—downtrodden victim, an easy target who spent every waking moment pining for Rose, desperate to prove that I was worthy of her attention. When had I ever bothered to ask Alice how *she* felt? . . . what was on *her* mind? If I had, she might have shared that third journal with me instead of Jerren, and I might have been able to convince her to slow down and think things through. Maybe we'd have brought Dare with us when we went ashore. Maybe we'd have known what we'd be facing in Skeleton Town. Maybe we'd all still be together. Safe.

I turned on my heel and left the others. No one was going to follow me, and that suited me fine. I had a rescue attempt to plan. And only one person on board knew exactly what we were up against.

CHAPTER 24

Tessa was awake, but she hadn't moved. I wasn't surprised. Her gray fingers and toes looked brittle, as if they might break off altogether.

I lifted the water canister to her lips and she drank. Her skin folded and cracked like sun-baked paper. "Griffin can save you," I told her.

"Many will need saving," she replied. "But not me."

"Are you giving up?"

"No. I'm making my peace. I got to see you again. Your brothers too . . . and Skya." She whispered her daughter's name as if she were making a wish. "I only wish I'd gotten to see Dare. Strange, but I can almost feel him here. So close, but . . ."

I'd had my issues with Tessa, but they seemed unimportant now. Bending down, I slid my arms under her knees and shoulders and lifted her. She was a tall woman, but so frail. She probably weighed less than Nyla.

"Why do the others hate you?" I asked.

She tried to retain eye contact, but her head lolled about. "*I* was the one who foresaw the Exodus, and the Plague . . . who told them to stay on Roanoke. I'm the reason they're alive today. They owe me their lives, and no one likes a debt that can't be repaid. Imagine how free they'll feel when I'm gone forever."

I carried her to the galley. There I placed her gently on the floor, with one blanket for a pillow and another spread over her.

I slid the wooden panel aside and drew back the metal bolts. Dare was inside, exactly where I'd left him. His breathing was labored. Grabbing the loose cloth under his armpits, I heaved him across the slick surface of the hiding space and onto the galley floor.

He collapsed in a heap. "Back so soon," he mumbled.

When I didn't respond he opened one eye. As he saw his mother lying on the floor his expression changed. He appeared younger again, and conflicted. Was it because of her disease, or shame at having abandoned her many years ago?

He crossed the room and rearranged his mother's blankets. His eyes were fixed on her, but when he spoke, it was to me: "I assume you're here because you need my help."

"Actually, you need mine. Your daughter has been captured. And the pirates answer to a new captain now."

He tried to mask his surprise. "And who might that be?"

"Jossi."

"Jossi is a fool."

"A fool who controls every rat on Roanoke," I reminded him.

Dare raked his fingers down his face. Seer or not, he hadn't foreseen this development.

Tessa cleared her throat. "You should have told your men that the clan ship was coming, Dare," she scolded. "When it arrived, the pirates panicked. Skya and I, we . . . tried to reason with them. But they were outnumbered and confused, so they let their guns do the talking. And when one accidentally discharged, everything changed."

"Changed, how?" I asked.

"A clan woman died. The other clan folk turned on the pirates, who threatened to kill everyone. But they never got the chance. Rats converged on the streets. I always thought there were no rats on Roanoke Island, but I was wrong. Some came from sewers, others from buildings. Maybe they came from the clan ship itself. But they moved as one. My cat went after them, but instead of skittering away, the rats pressed onward. Whatever survival instincts they were supposed to have were gone. They turned on my cat, and killed her. Ripped her to pieces. No matter what stood in their way, they fought to converge. That's when I realized where they were going: straight for the pirate who'd accidentally fired his rifle." Tessa dry coughed. "The rats savaged him too. He tried to fight them off, but couldn't. The way they were biting and scratching, I honestly thought they were going to kill him right there and then."

Whatever Dare imagined had happened on Roanoke, it clearly hadn't included this. "What happened then?" he asked.

"Jossi realized that a clan person must be controlling the rats. He noticed a child acting strangely—a boy named Kieran. The boy's parents were attempting to shield him.

They tried to make him stop the attack, but Kieran was completely locked in to what he was doing. So Jossi pulled the boy free and placed a gun to his head. When the parents protested, he took them hostage too. Then he convinced the rest of the pirates that other clan folk might have elements too, so they rounded everyone up and imprisoned them in the hurricane shelter. Once Jossi had control of Kieran's parents and the other clan folk, the boy obeyed his every command. Kieran is Jossi's puppet now, and also his greatest weapon."

"I saw thousands of rats, though," I said. "Where did they all come from?"

Tessa paused as Dare gave her more water. "When Jossi realized what Kieran can do, he lowered the plank across the gap in the mainland bridge and demanded that Kieran summon rats." Tessa let the image sink in, of a young man and a small boy opening a previously safe island to a scourge that might kill them all. It seemed insane, but then, who could say what was sane anymore? "Rats have been coming over from the mainland ever since. So we'd all better hope that nothing happens to Kieran's parents. If they're harmed, by Jossi or anyone else, Kieran won't distinguish between pirates and clan folk and elementals anymore. He'll make the rats attack and kill indiscriminately. And nothing we can do will stop him. He's a frightened boy playing with a weapon he cannot possibly understand."

Dare was still for a moment. When he moved, it was to dribble water into his mother's mouth. She grimaced from the pain of swallowing.

"What about Skya?" he asked.

"She's alive. A prisoner, like all the others." Tessa sighed. "The pirates believe that you're dead, Dare. But not Jossi. He's superstitious—thinks you can't be killed. So he's keeping hold of the thing that gives him power over you . . . the one thing you can't risk losing. Your sister."

Whatever meager reserves of energy she'd had were gone now. Tessa stared straight ahead, not blinking, stealing irregular, shallow breaths.

Dare leaned back against the wall. His head tilted from side to side as if he didn't have complete control of it. "For so many years, I didn't realize that Griffin is the solution," he said. "In my visions, it was Skya. I tried to argue for her to come with me, but she wouldn't. If I hadn't been so blinded by what the solution meant, I would've realized that the solution had been *inside* her—it was her baby. If only I'd realized that she'd already given birth to him the night I kidnapped her, then . . ."

"Then *what*?" I snapped. "You could've kidnapped a baby instead? Or kidnapped both of them?"

"The survival of the human race outweighs any one person, Thomas."

"Don't pretend to be noble. You're a murderer, that's all. Or are you forgetting that you shot Guardian Kyte?"

"Kyte was shot by a rogue gunman, probably in revenge for my apparent death."

"And what about Guardian Walt? You sliced his neck and set him adrift in a canoe. We found his body."

"Walt was already dead."

"Liar!" I looked around suddenly, afraid that I'd raised my voice. This wasn't a time for unwanted visitors. "I saw him myself."

"You saw, but you didn't *look*. There was no blood coming from his neck wound, was there, Thomas? It had already congealed, see? The knife wound was made postmortem."

It was true. The wound had been nothing but a thin streak across his neck, like a tidy cut through soft wood. "So why slice his neck at all?"

"To make you believe it could happen to anyone," Dare explained. "Your father. Your brother. Anyone can die at any time. And plenty *have* died while we've waited for the solution to save us."

"Plenty more of your men died trying to capture Griffin—"

"Because your Guardians left us with no other choice. Anyway, my men knew the risks. There comes a time everyone has to decide what's worth dying for." Dare gave a tired smile. "Whether or not you believe it, Thomas, I've dedicated my life to preserving the human race. When I heard about the Plague, I spent almost two years searching for survivors—people who'd been left behind; children with no parents. Every time I left the Roanoke colony I knew that I might never return. And what was my reward? Your Guardians turned the refugees away. They made life intolerable for them."

"Maybe the Guardians weren't sure that everyone could survive on Roanoke Island."

"That island once supported a population of thousands.

170

Providing for everyone wasn't a problem." He sat up straighter. Talking about the Guardians and refugees seemed to energize him, but his body had a crooked awkwardness to it. The colorful arms that had looked so powerful and intimidating through my binoculars appeared sinewy and leathery up close. "But the moment I left the colony, your father started turning refugees away."

I hesitated. "Father wouldn't do that."

"Of course he would. And he *did*. Who else do you think made that hole in the mainland bridge? He combined with the other Guardians and they used their elements to blow it apart."

"They were trying to stop the rats."

"The rats were still hundreds of miles to the west. It was refugees they were trying to stop. The Guardians wanted anyone who reached the edge of the mainland to turn around. While I was sailing up and down the coastline, risking everything to save lives, your father sentenced countless people to death."

"I don't believe you."

"It's true," murmured Tessa. "It's all true."

Dare spoke faster now, emboldened by his mother's support and my dwindling opposition. "We had competing visions of the future. I believed that elementals and non-elementals could coexist; the Guardians did not. But there's no denying who the victims were. Your so-called *Guardians* are just the latest in a centuries-long line of tyrants." He turned his piercing blue eyes on me. "History tells us that Roanoke Island was the site of the first European colony, but I say it was the site of the original civil war. John White's group was ripped apart when those four boys discovered their elements. The elders of that ancient colony tried to reason with them, teach them to use their elements responsibly. But they were *children*. And every elemental since has behaved the same way, wielding power like a petulant child who's tired of playing nicely."

"You don't know that," I spat. "We're talking about centuries here. Thousands of elementals. You can't prove any of it."

"I don't need to prove it. It's all written down in the colony's journals—every horrific event, documented so that future generations might claim to be wiser."

"The journals that have been conveniently lost, you mean?"

"Not lost, Thomas. You know as well as I do, Alice destroyed them. And if you'd read what she did, maybe you'd have destroyed them too." He leaned closer. "She knows the truth about who we are and what we've done. And she loves you enough to spare you that burden."

He was right: Alice did love me—enough to spare me from the truth, and to sacrifice herself in Skeleton Town so that I might escape. Having learned all that she was, and all that we were, she held her own life more cheaply than she held mine. It was heartbreaking.

Alice had always been an outcast. So had I. It was what had bound us together. Sharing the burden had lightened it for both of us. I needed to share her burden now.

"Tell me what she read," I told Dare. "All of it."

CHAPTER 25

You want to hear the whole history." Dare gave an admiring smile. "A noble gesture, Thomas, but no—I don't think there's any point in that. Not unless you like hearing the same tragic story told a hundred times with only minor variations."

"Then what's the tragic story?"

Dare looked around the cabin. It was like he wanted to take it all in, connect the immense past with this specific place and time. "John White believed that he had found paradise on Roanoke Island. When he left to secure more supplies from England, he couldn't have imagined what would happen. But those four boys and their elements changed everything. And then the first child *born* on Roanoke Island revealed an element too. Virginia Dare was her name—sent fire from each fingertip like it was the most natural thing in the world. Some of the colonists said it was witchcraft, and demanded that the elementals be drowned. The parents refused to give them up, though. Battle lines were drawn, but the fight never happened. Even with their massive advantage of numbers and weapons, the non-elementals realized that those children could exterminate them on a whim. So they left instead.

"They set off in the dead of night. They probably wanted to establish a colony close to the ocean, but they were afraid the elementals would find them, and destroy them. So they settled on the northern shore of Albemarle Sound, about fifty miles west of here. Theirs was an equal, self-governing, *sustainable* colony—exactly what White would have wanted. They never really felt safe, though. About two decades later, new explorers from Europe who were drafting maps of the region stumbled upon the colony. The explorers marked the colony's location on their new map, but the non-elementals begged them to hide the location out of fear that the elementals would track them down. The mapmakers figured the colonists were just superstitious, but agreed to obscure the settlement's location behind a tiny flap of paper. It worked—the site of the colony remained a mystery for centuries."

Dare closed his eyes. "The Plague was a disaster, but it was also an opportunity, Thomas. I tried to make the Guardians understand that we finally had a chance to mend the divisions once and for all. There was no room for separate colonies anymore. No time for schisms. But your Guardians refused to coexist—even refused to give non-elementals the same chance to survive. And so I did the only thing I could—I tried to make our world bigger again. I tried to take the solution, so that we could reclaim the mainland . . . so that non-elementals would have a chance to survive."

He waited a moment and looked at me. He'd stated his case and now it was my turn to respond. Perhaps he thought that I'd been swayed, but he was missing the point. "You kidnapped my mother." I tried to keep my voice steady. "We haven't seen her since the day Griffin was born. We've lost years. I don't even know who she is."

"I thought she was the solution."

"So what? You think everything would have been all right if you'd taken Griffin instead? What you did was evil. You abandoned your own mother."

I expected Tessa to agree with me, and put her son in his place. But she wasn't moving.

I edged closer. The perspiration on her forehead had evaporated. Her features were oddly relaxed. Her chest no longer rose and fell.

"She's gone," said Dare. He sidled up to his mother, and finger-combed the hair from out of her eyes.

"You don't even seem upset."

He flinched at that. It didn't seem put on, either. "I said good-bye to her many years ago. Believe me, she must have done the same."

He picked up a cloth from the floor and poured water onto it. Slowly, tenderly, he cleaned his mother's face. "Will you release her body to the water?"

I nodded, but he couldn't see. "Yes."

"Thank you." He finished by wiping her chin. Then he kissed her forehead and covered her face with the blanket. "I need you to let me escape, Thomas."

"Why?"

"Because I have to talk to Jossi."

"He'll kill you."

"Maybe. But I have to distract him long enough for you to get to Kieran's parents. If he can't control the rats, Jossi is finished."

"But the pirates still outnumber us. They have guns."

He groaned. "Weren't you listening to what I told you just now? The first elementals were outnumbered too, but they still held an advantage. Earth, water, wind, and fire. By combining, *anything* is possible."

"I have none of those elements."

"Wrong! You have *all* of them. Alice told me what you did to her—how you took over her element. Don't you see? You can harness all the elements in the world. You can make anything, *take* anything . . . destroy anything. And no one can stop you."

"They'd hate me for it."

"Being hated is better than hating yourself."

"Is that how you justify everything you've done?"

"I don't justify, or make excuses. I made peace with being hated a long time ago. I can live with it. The only thing I can't accept is regret. I stand by my actions." He conjured a flame, and snuffed it out suddenly. "If you want to end this fight, you'll use that power, Thomas. And you won't second-guess the damage it'll do."

The water canister was still beside Tessa. Dare saw me looking at it, and handed it to me. "I need to go to Roanoke," he said. "If the pirates think I'm dead, they'll either figure I'm a ghost, or they'll have to concede that I foresaw everything that would happen from the start. In any case, it'll cause a little confusion in their ranks."

His words hung between us.

"And *did* you know what would happen from the start?" I asked. "Is that why you wanted us to go to Sumter?"

He shrugged. "Seeing the future is unreliable. But it didn't matter to me whether you stayed on Roanoke or left for Sumter. The one thing I knew for certain was that Griffin would never die of the Plague. The only question was how he could save the rest of us."

"If seeing the future is unreliable, why do the pirates believe everything you say?"

"Because I notice the things they don't. Being a seer is what has made it possible for me to control my crew, but the truth is, seeing the future is less important than observing the present and remembering the past. I watch people, Thomas. Learn who they are; their strength and weaknesses. Some are cowards, some bullies. But some surprise me, risking everything for a better tomorrow. The more I know about them, the more I can predict their future. Predicting isn't *seeing*, but in a world as unpredictable as ours, it can feel like the same thing."

All filthy, corded limbs, Dare resembled a lizard as he pulled to a stand.

"I still don't understand something," I said. "Why would Jossi pick a fight with elementals? He saw what happened to the other pirates when they attacked us."

Dare opened the cabinets across the galley and removed the containers of food. He helped himself to small bites from each of them. "I rescued Jossi when he was just a young boy. He was strange, even then. Most everyone else had given up on life as we knew it, but he was an optimist. An idealist. He believed there was an order to the world, and if we could just survive, we'd find a solution to everything. He even used that word: *solution*."

"So what changed?"

"He witnessed an accident. Something that couldn't be explained, that didn't fit in the natural order of things."

"What did he see?" I asked, already dreading the answer.

"Jossi saw a boy sliced to death by a mechanical saw. Saw it all: the blood, and mangled limbs; the panic. But when he tried to talk about it, people told him he hadn't seen what he knew he'd seen." Dare stuffed his mouth with food and chewed slowly. "He's been a victim his entire life, and now, finally, he controls perhaps the greatest power of all. I might be able to reason with the other pirates, but Jossi . . . well, Jossi holds life cheaper. Because the elementals made him that way."

Not *all* the elementals. It was my father's element that had caused the saw to start moving. He'd told us about the incident while we were at Sumter—how he'd seen a boy playing with the massive blade. He'd tried to pull the boy away, but because he was focused on the blade, his energy went into that instead. The boy died instantly.

I waited for Dare to continue, to place the blame at my father's feet. But he didn't say another word. Unaware that I already knew the truth, he tried to spare me from knowing that my father was to blame. Or maybe not my father, but his element—the same element the Guardians had hidden from *me* my entire life.

Might I have accidentally killed someone too if the Guardians hadn't taken so many precautions? I wanted to ask Dare if he could read my future, let me know if injury or death lay ahead for someone I touched, just like the boy who'd died by the mechanical saw.

I looked through the porthole at the sun setting over Roanoke Island and realized that I would be asking for the wrong thing. The question wasn't whether people would die. That seemed inevitable now. What really mattered was who would be left standing when the sun rose again.

CHAPTER 26

didn't bolt the door as Dare retreated to his hiding space. He said he'd know when to sneak out, and I believed him. He said that no one would know he'd been on board. Since he'd been a stowaway on our voyages to and from Sumter, I believed that too.

Nyla was waiting outside the galley. "I've been keeping guard," she said. "Figured you didn't want any interruptions."

"Thanks. Did you hear everything?"

She peered around me to where Tessa's body was stretched across the floor. "I heard enough."

Together we lifted Tessa, and carried her along the corridor. Nyla couldn't bear to look at the old woman's Plague-ravaged body. It was a reminder of what might have happened to her if Griffin hadn't cured her, and an image of what could still happen to her brother, Jerren, if we didn't rescue him.

It felt disrespectful to blunder up the stairs, Tessa's body colliding with the walls, but we were doing our best. When we reached the deck, we placed her gently on the warm wooden planks.

Marin and Tarn stared at Tessa. They'd grown apart from the seer, but Tessa had been an important part of their lives for years. Decades, even. What part of their shared history were they seeing as they looked at her now?

Marin approached us. "We should release her body," she said.

I'd heard those words more in the past several days than I had in my entire life leading up to Dare's attack on Hatteras. How many other people would be *released* to the ocean before everything was over?

With Tarn and Marin helping, we carried Tessa to the side of the ship. Dennis joined us there. We balanced the body precariously on the railing, and paused.

"Does anyone have something they'd like to say?" asked Tarn.

It was our custom to offer thanks. But while I respected Tessa's fortitude and determination, I still didn't understand what made her do the things she'd done.

"Tessa was a woman of conviction," said Marin finally. She seemed satisfied with the sentiment, and continued, "She stood by what she believed."

"No, she didn't," I said. "Tessa chose self-imposed exile over fighting for what she knew was right."

More silence. Tarn cleared her throat. "Then let us give thanks that she was brave enough to return to us and make amends. I honestly believe that with her final words she was trying to help us."

Tarn was right about that, even though she hadn't actually heard Tessa's *final* words.

"Are you ready, Thomas?" Nyla asked.

I studied Tessa's face. Tried to see past the disease that had destroyed her. My life would have been so different if she'd never left our colony. I wished she could be a part of it now.

"Thomas?"

I nodded. "I'm ready."

We eased Tessa over the side. She landed with a splash and returned to the surface. Seeing her floating beside the ship, I felt a rush of sympathy—it was as if she wasn't quite ready to leave us.

We stood in a line and stared at the water. Watched her drift steadily away.

"When do we go ashore?" asked Dennis softly.

I expected Marin to tell him that he wouldn't be going ashore at all. Instead, she caught my eye. "He should go with you," she told me. "He'll help."

"But you need to stay on the ship," I reminded her. "Rose needs you here."

"I know." She placed a hand on Dennis's head. "With or without me, his element is special. Air is a powerful force in the right hands. I trust him to know how to use it."

"I'll go too," said Nyla.

"No. I need you to stay here," I said.

She pointed to the island. "But my brother's over there."

"If Griffin's going to cure Rose, he'll need help."

"Then *you* stay!"

"Please, Nyla. You don't know Skeleton Town like we do. You've never been there."

She took off for the stairs without another word. I needed to hear her say she'd remain on board, so I followed her below deck and along to Griffin and Rose's cabin.

My brother was propped up against the far wall, eyes closed. Perspiration covered his face. Nyla ran a cloth across his forehead, down his cheeks, and around his jawline. She was careful not to touch him directly, but as she brushed his lips her fingers slipped, and they were skin to skin. Her pulse must have been fast, because his eyes flashed open. He smiled to find Nyla before him, but there was no mistaking that her element had startled him.

"How do you do it?" she asked me. "How do you touch someone when your element is strong?"

"It's only this strong at Roanoke Island."

"Well, we're next to Roanoke *now*. And live or die, there's a chance we'll never leave. I can't go through life never touching anyone. So how do you stop the hurt?"

She stared at me, waiting. When I returned her stare, the truth dawned on her at last: That I *hadn't* made it work. That I'd spent a childhood in physical isolation. That there was no easy answer to her question, or any answer at all, as far as I knew. Combining was a poor substitute for direct touch.

She bowed her head. "I see. Well then, maybe this is my punishment. I always figured there'd be a price to pay for what I did."

I felt the room go suddenly still. "What did you do, Nyla?"

She raised her hands, and in faltering signs tried to help Griffin understand what she needed to tell me in words: "I've always had the element, just like you. On Fort Dauphin it was weak. No one felt my power unless I was angry. But I fought all the time. I was stupid. Every person on that island was superstitious. They'd heard stories of the so-called elementals . . . how they stole land and food, and killed people for fun. Every colony needs a bogeyman, and for us, it was elementals. Lucky for me, the other children were too scared to tell anyone what it felt like when I hurt them.

"Jerren had an element too. He was practicing, learning to control it. One day I got into a bad fight, so he twisted sound, made noises to distract everyone. He was trying to help me, but it wasn't even his fight, and I got so mad at him for ending it. So I . . . I grabbed his hand. At first, I only meant to shock him. But then I thought about the sound he was twisting. Suddenly it was moving wherever I wanted."

Nyla closed her eyes. Her signs became smaller. "I only turned the noise on the kids for a moment. Just so they'd think twice before messing with me again. But they covered their ears and screamed. Turns out, there was an adult watching too . . . *one* adult. But it changed everything.

"Our parents didn't wait to see what happened next. Didn't even stop to pack up our belongings. We ran to the shore and took the colony's fastest sailboat. The last thing I remember about Fort Dauphin was watching every last person line up against the breaking waves. They didn't chase us, and they didn't shout. They held hands and bowed their heads and prayed. They were praying for us never to come back. They thought every single one of us had been sent by the devil."

I didn't know what to say. The story that Jerren had told us about their escape from Fort Dauphin had been a lie. Why hadn't Nyla realized that if anyone could be sympathetic to her plight, it would be me?

As she watched me, her hands folded into fists in her lap. "You wonder why we lied to you. But you lied to us too, when you hid your elements from us. The difference is that you don't have to wake up every morning knowing it's your fault that your parents had to leave everything behind. That it's your fault they're dead."

She wrapped her arms around her knees, hugging herself. Her signs for Griffin hadn't communicated even half of what she'd told me, but he read her body language clearly enough. He reached out as if he wanted to touch her, but she leaned away. I understood why too—she didn't want Griffin to suffer, just so he could prove how much he cared for her.

As Nyla left the cabin, I followed. In the corridor, I touched her arm—gently, but I still figured she'd pull away. Instead, she leaned into me, let me wrap my arms around her and pull her close. Energy flowed easily between us as she cried against my neck. Her breaths were quick and warm. When would either of us be able to hold someone else that way again? Without trepidation, and pain.

"What if death is all we're good for?" she whispered.

"I can't accept that," I said. "And neither can you."

I returned to the cabin alone. Griffin was lying down now,

eyes closed. But Rose had stirred. In the sliver of light that came through the porthole her neck appeared grisly. Now, in addition to the knife wounds she'd suffered at Sumter, her neck showed the telltale symptoms of Plague—swelling, and dark lumps.

There was a water canister beside the door, so I offered it to her.

"Save it," she croaked.

"Why? You can find more fresh water for us when we run out."

She returned a wan smile, but I saw right through it. She was preparing me for a time when she might not be able to test the purity of our drinking water. A time when she might not be around at all.

"We're almost back to where we started," she said. "Feels like a lifetime ago that the Guardians sent us to the shelter in Skeleton Town."

"I think it *was* a lifetime ago. I wish I could go back and change everything."

"Me too." Rose furrowed her brows. "I wish I could go back three years and tell myself that the boy I like really likes me too." Tears gathered in the corners of her eyes. She blinked them away. "I made it so easy for the Guardians to control me. Why didn't I fight them?"

I was blinking back tears as well. These were the regrets of a dying girl, and I wasn't willing to accept that. "What about Sumter?" I fired back, sounding angry even though I didn't mean to. "You were the one who risked everything to find out the truth. Without you we'd all be dead."

She gave me a hard stare. "I want you to hold me."

How could she know that a similar scene had just played out between Nyla and Griffin? "You know I can't do that. It'll hurt."

"Then get the canister, and channel through me. Just don't let go of me. Promise you won't let go."

I lay down beside her and held her hand. At first, I tried to control my pulse, but it clearly wasn't working. So I concentrated on the canister instead. With my energy passing right through her, I drew the water out in a narrow stream. On Sumter I'd pulled off a similar trick, but this time I had complete control. I was able to savor the feel of her against me, even as I separated the water into molecules. I brought them down as a gentle mist that settled on her hair and face, glistening in the low light of approaching sunset.

"Thomas," Rose whispered.

"Yes."

"I—"

The door opened, cutting her off. Rose gasped as I lost my concentration. It was only a moment, but with nowhere to go, the full force of my element was turned on her.

I rolled away, but the damage was done. Rose breathed in and out slowly, managing the pain.

"I'm sorry," said Marin. "I didn't realize . . ." She retreated along the corridor, leaving us alone.

"I shouldn't have done that," I said.

Rose faced me. "Don't be sad."

"I hate my element."

"Shh." She ran a finger along the fabric of my tunic. "The echo only hurts because your pulse is fast."

"It's always fast when I'm with you—"

"Which is how I know that I matter to you. Don't you see? Your heartbeat tells the truth of how you feel."

It was a beautiful idea, but I wasn't in the mood for moral victories. I didn't have time for them anymore. Not with Jossi waiting for us in Skeleton Town, and Rose growing weaker every moment.

Outside the porthole, smoke was rising over Roanoke. It was a slender band, probably from a small fire. Perhaps the pirates were cooking food . . . or cremating the remains of yet more Plague victims.

I sensed that I was losing Rose to sleep. I wanted to say good-bye, but the thought that I didn't know when I'd see her again made my chest tighten. In my mind I begged for her to be alive when I returned.

CHAPTER 27

brought food to Griffin. Told him about our plan to return to Roanoke Island. He promised me that by the time I returned, he would've cured Rose. I believed him too.

I took food up on deck, and we ate our fill. Drank all the water we needed. We wouldn't be carrying any supplies with us—Alice had taught me that.

We waited until nightfall to return to Shallowbag Bay; specifically, a point just to the north of the bay, where we'd be partially hidden from the pirates. Our ship had drifted almost a mile across the sound, but I figured that might work in our favor. If the pirates on shore thought that we'd lost control of the vessel, maybe they would let their guard down.

Now that he had recovered, Dennis was eager to unfurl the sails and use his element. That wasn't an option, though. Even though it was night, the sky was clear and the bright white sails were likely to be seen in the moonlight. No, we'd need a different element to help us this time.

Marin stood at the prow, eyes fixed on the water before

us. Beneath the ship the sound stirred like a creature awakened from sleep. The surface frothed as she turned the water against the tidal flow, but the ship barely moved.

Nyla joined her. Marin was hesitant to combine, but when they linked hands the water around us came alive with eddies and rapidly shifting currents. The ship turned in an impossibly steep arc. We were moving toward our target, fast enough that a breeze played against my face.

Dennis lay on his back and stared at the stars, breathing deeply, relaxing while he still had the chance. I was tempted to join him, to seek comfort in the night-sky canopy and remind myself that we were small and the universe was infinite and somehow nothing was as horrifying as it seemed. Not even death. But Tarn was staring at the island, and I wanted to know what she saw.

"Nothing," she said, before I'd even had a chance to ask. "No movement on the shore. I can't get a clear view of Skeleton Town, but I figure they'll be waiting for us."

"If we get that far before the rats find us, we'll be doing well."

"I suppose that's true. Another glorious chapter in elemental history." Her voice was quiet, but not so much that the others couldn't hear her. "Tell me, Thomas—now that you've seen them, have you wondered why we kept those journals?"

"You wanted a history of the elementals, I guess."

"Not exactly. The earliest entries were by John White himself. He found the elementals, drew their portraits, and kept their secrets. But he was so blinded by the miracle of the elements, it was like he forgot to mention the conflict between elementals and non-elementals. After that, each generation added to the journals, keeping a record of every argument and skirmish, hoping against hope that the *next* generation would be the one to learn from these lessons, and avoid conflict altogether. But it has never happened, and I wonder if it ever can. History is intellect; the present is all emotion. I did what I did to survive, Thomas. I could apologize—I know, I *should*—but if I had to do it all over again, I'd probably do everything just the same."

There was a point to all this, I could tell. But Tarn wouldn't be rushed.

"When the dust settles, everyone has an opinion about the things we've done," she continued. "Especially those who weren't there. But I was going on instinct, and that instinct is what has kept me alive. It'll keep you alive too, so please don't second-guess it. Tonight, I honestly believe we're fighting for our lives."

Marin raised a hand, and the ship slowed. The night was eerily quiet.

"I still don't see anything," said Tarn. "If we're going ashore, now is as good a time as any."

Nyla gave me a brief, pain-free hug. "Please bring my brother back."

"I will," I said.

Dennis crawled over the rail and stepped onto the ladder. Tarn followed him. With barely a splash, they slipped into the water.

As I straddled the railing, Marin tugged my tunic. "I'll be here," she said. "Waiting for you. All of you." She couldn't look me in the eye. "And Thomas, I . . . I'm sorry."

I figured that she was talking about interrupting Rose and me in the cabin. "You couldn't have known—"

"No. I mean . . . I'm sorry for *everything*." She squeezed her eyes shut. "I always thought Rose and I were alike, that she was comfortable with her role in the colony. When she began arguing with me on Sumter, it was as if she was rejecting me. Rejecting everything we'd done together. I thought that if we placed ourselves in Chief's hands, he'd look after us the way Kyte had. I thought that you and Rose were jeopardizing our future." Her face creased up, and tears fell. "I've let her down, Thomas. I let you both down."

It was strange to see Marin like this. She'd always been an imperious woman, distant and often mean-spirited. I knew how difficult it must be for her to apologize, but she was apologizing to the wrong person.

"You need to tell Rose that," I said. "And when Griffin's ready—"

"I know. He and Nyla will save Rose. I truly believe it."

The others were waiting for me in the water. They sculled their arms back and forth, holding position. I climbed down the ladder and joined them. Without a word, we began swimming, with Tarn in the front.

The water was calm. The breezes that had propelled the ship from Sumter were gone, so that the only noise was the gentle splash of our arms breaking the surface. Tarn set a slow, steady pace, more interested in conserving energy than in getting there quickly. Ahead of us, Skeleton Town was a black outline against the sky.

It felt strange to be approaching Roanoke in secret, as trespassers. We slowed as we got to within thirty yards, and stopped as soon as we touched the ground. Tarn held up her hand, demanding silence. She turned her head back and forth, looking and listening.

It seemed like forever before she gave us the all clear to wade ashore. We left the water and scanned the island for signs of the rats that we were convinced must be lying in wait nearby.

"We'll head straight for Skeleton Town," Tarn whispered. "If I raise my hand, it's because I've seen pirates. Find a hiding place immediately."

"What about rats?" asked Dennis.

Tarn hesitated. I couldn't see her face clearly in the darkness, but I guessed what she was thinking: That sooner or later we certainly *would* see rats, and there'd be little we could do about it. "If you see rats, I suggest you run," she said.

The night was dry but cool, and my wet clothes felt chilly against me. Beside me, Dennis shivered. "Keep moving," I told him. "We'll warm up soon."

We kept tight formation as we picked our way through the crumbled foundations of buildings. Wild grass and rubble covered the ground, making it difficult to see where we were stepping, but we weren't in a rush. As the evening grew late, our chances of catching the pirates by surprise improved. At least, that's what I told myself. But we'd already encountered a seemingly desolate town once earlier that day, and look how that had turned out.

Tarn raised a hand, and I almost stumbled in my haste to stop. She pointed to a dark silhouette at least a mile away. "Light," she said.

I narrowed my eyes and tried to make out what she was seeing. It took a while, but then I saw it: a dull glow above one of the buildings.

"It's firelight," she continued. "A torch. Whoever's holding it is moving, but only a little." Still she peered into the darkness, searching for answers, or at least clues about what lay ahead. Finally she lowered her hand. "Let's keep moving."

I was so focused on the uneven footing that I was surprised when, a short while later, I looked up and discovered we were nearing the center of Skeleton Town. We approached the main street from between two buildings. The walls were battered and the windows broken, but they hid us from view. At the end of the passageway, Tarn raised her hand again. I pulled alongside her and peered around the corner at the desolate street.

The torch, or whatever it was that Tarn had seen, was gone. The street seemed empty. But Tarn remained on edge.

"What do you see?" I asked.

She shook her head. "Nothing. But there are voices."

"Whose?"

"I don't know."

We both stepped back as a pirate emerged from a building

about fifty yards to the south. He had a candle in his right hand, and in its flickering flame I made out a rifle in his left hand. He crossed the street and sat cross-legged before a doorway.

"Strange," murmured Tarn. "That building is dark, but he isn't entering. It doesn't look like he's resting, either. So what's he doing there?"

"Maybe he's guarding something," I said. "Something that mustn't escape."

"The clan folk," offered Dennis hopefully. "They could be inside."

"No. Tessa said the clan folk are in the hurricane shelter."

"Shh." Tarn was peering into the darkness again, straining to make sense of what she was hearing, even though it was inaudible to me.

As we waited, another pirate left the building and handed something to the new arrival. What if Kieran's parents were inside?

A cry went up at the end of the street. It was loud and sudden and deep—a man's cry. Even the pirate guard left his post beside the door to look at the spectacle unfolding no more than a couple hundred yards away.

There were noises from down the street now—voices, and pounding footsteps—but I still couldn't see anything until Jossi emerged from behind a building, carrying a torch. In the yellow glow the scene became horribly clear.

Four figures were organized in a line across the street: Father, Ananias, Alice, and Jerren. They were perched on crates, teetering, about to fall at any moment. From the rigid way they stood, arms behind their backs and feet close together, I was sure that they were bound. I had no idea how long they'd been standing there, but they looked exhausted. How had they remained upright at all after everything they'd been through?

Then I got my answer. A few yards above them, a metal beam ran across the street, attached to the roofs of two buildings. And dangling from the beam were four identical ropes, which were wrapped around each of their necks.

CHAPTER 28

Tarn stepped forward. I had the feeling she would have run into the street if I hadn't grabbed her sleeve.

"Alice needs me," she hissed.

"They all need us," I said. "But if you step out there, you'll be captured too."

Tarn breathed in and out, struggling to stay calm. I kept hold of her sleeve as she craned her neck around the building.

"That voice," she murmured. "I know it."

I looked too. The scene had shifted. The pirates were no longer interested in whoever had cried out, but in something else I couldn't see. There must have been half a dozen pirates, and every one raised his rifle in warning. From so far away their voices merged together.

Dare emerged from the shadows, colorful arms swinging loosely at his sides.

The pirates didn't look as if they were in a welcoming mood. Neither did my father, or Ananias. Only Alice and Jerren seemed unsurprised by Dare's arrival.

Dennis wormed under my arm to check out the scene. Then he froze. "That's Dare," he said. "It's Dare, I know it is."

I pushed him back. In his panic, he wasn't aware of how loudly he was speaking.

Dennis struggled against me. "Alice told us she watched Dare board the other ship." He grasped fistfuls of hair. "She lied to us . . . about *Dare*."

He clearly expected me to share his outrage. When I didn't speak, he narrowed his eyes. "You knew, didn't you?"

Tarn was shocked too, but seemed more concerned with the noise that Dennis was making than with Dare. She placed her hands on the boy's shoulders. "Alice lied to us . . . *all* of us," she told him. "But if the pirates are pointing their guns at Dare, that means he's no longer their captain."

"So?"

"So maybe he's here to help us. Alice is his daughter. Ananias is his nephew. Right now, he doesn't look like a man who plans to watch them die."

"But . . . he's *Dare*."

"And for this night, on this island, you are more powerful than a hundred Dares."

We grew quiet as Dare stepped closer to the men who'd once answered to him. They kept their rifles raised. I couldn't hear what was being said, but it hardly mattered. The pirates were distracted. This was our chance.

"We need to get in there," I said, pointing at the building across the street, where the pirate had returned to his place at the doorway. "That's the only building with an armed guard."

Tarn mulled over my suggestion. "What if the pirates see us crossing the street?"

"Dare's distracting them. It's dark. As long as we keep low and stay quiet, I say it's our best shot."

"But Dare's a seer," said Dennis. "What if *he* knows what we're doing? What if he tells them?"

"He won't," Tarn answered confidently. "As long as they're pointing rifles at him, he won't give us away."

Satisfied, Dennis followed me across the street, while Tarn brought up the rear. I kept my footsteps light and quick, and my eyes fixed on the pirate guard. When we reached the opposite side, we stayed tight to the buildings and headed south.

We were only twenty yards away when the pirate moved suddenly. We shuffled into the space between two buildings and remained completely still.

Several moments later, Tarn leaned forward to get a view of the street. She exhaled deeply. "He's not looking this way," she whispered, "but he's agitated. Dare coming back wasn't part of the pirates' plan."

"Then let's hope he can keep them occupied a while longer," I said.

There was no way we could tackle the guard, and approaching the building from the front would only attract his attention. So we walked along the side to the rear, where overgrown bushes engulfed the stone. We took it in turns to crawl under the gnarled branches.

"It's the next building down," said Dennis.

The battered back door was slightly ajar. It might have

made a noise if we'd tried to open it more, so Tarn slid through the gap instead. I wanted to go in too, but hers was the only element that counted now. We had to know exactly who or what we were up against.

She was only gone for a moment. "There are two guards inside, plus the one outside," she said. "You'll hear them talking."

"Who are they guarding?" I asked.

"I couldn't see. But I don't think Kieran's parents warrant a three-man guard. I'm guessing that it's Kieran himself."

"Are the guards armed?"

"They must be, right?"

We were silent after that. Nothing that Tarn had told us was a surprise, but the danger felt especially real as we closed in on our target.

Dennis peered up at me. "Can you take them down, Thomas? With your element, I mean."

"One of them, sure. But I'll be lucky to get close enough to do that."

"What if I distract them?"

"How?"

"A little breeze." His voice shook, but he didn't sound scared. If anything, he appeared alert and determined. "Just enough to make them look away. To make sure they don't hear any noise we make."

"We'll need to stay close," said Tarn. "You won't be able to see as well as me, so follow my lead."

"What if we can't see *you?*" Dennis asked.

"Just hold on to my tunic. We'll go slow and steady. Surprise is key."

We followed Tarn through the gap in the door. The building reeked of damp and mold, and the floor was coated in a layer of dust so thick that our footsteps made almost no sound at all as we edged closer to the guards. Unable to see anything, I closed my eyes and allowed Tarn to steer me.

The guards' voices were quiet, but their words grew more urgent with every tentative step. "Dare" was repeated over and over between them, like a new word they were trying out but didn't fully understand. They were on guard in more ways than one now.

When I opened my eyes I saw them in silhouette against the broken windows. They held their rifles close, while their nervous hands kept the barrels moving in tiny circles above them. It wasn't going to take much for them to use those rifles, I was sure of it. Or to shout for help.

As we drew to within fifteen yards of the pirates, I saw Kieran at last. It was difficult to believe that this was the same child who had commanded an army of rats. He was lying on the floor, fast asleep. In the darkness he resembled Dennis, only with lighter, longer hair. He was small, maybe ten years old, a child caught in the crossfire of a battle in which he should never have had a stake. I even felt sorry for him. Then I realized that we hadn't seen a single rat since we stepped ashore, which meant that Kieran must have maintained some measure of control over his element even in sleep. If we rescued him, could we really be so sure he wouldn't turn that power on us?

We were only ten yards away from the guards now. My heartbeat was so strong that I was certain they would hear it. I wanted Tarn to stop moving, and for Dennis to distract the men, but she kept going. I had no choice but to follow as the distance separating us from the pirates slipped away.

Then one of the guards stood.

"What are you doing?" asked the other.

"Going to see him for myself. Dare was dead. We watched him drown. And I ain't never seen a ghost before."

"Then I'm coming too. Here," he said, nudging Kieran with his foot, "we can't leave the kid behind."

Kieran stirred, but didn't get up. As he rolled over, I got a look at his face, twisted with pain. Maybe he was sick. Or maybe this was his echo, the lingering discomfort from a day spent exercising his element.

The guard gave him another nudge, harder this time. "Wake up. Time to move."

As Kieran opened his eyes, he caught sight of us. He probably couldn't see us any more clearly than we could see him, but he knew we weren't supposed to be there. When he opened his mouth, I was sure he was going to alert the guards.

He didn't get the chance. Dennis created a breeze that spilled through the cracked window and fluttered the guards' clothes. It was just enough to make them turn away from us, momentarily distracted.

I didn't hesitate. Three quick steps and I lunged at the pirates. We tumbled to the ground together. I didn't want to kill them, but I couldn't afford for them to make a sound either, so I made the flow of energy brief but intense. They didn't make a sound as their bodies went limp beneath me.

Kieran sat up, dazed, and watched me from the corner of his eye. "Who are you?"

"Friends," Tarn whispered. "We're here to free—"

She was interrupted by a sound coming from the entrance. I'd forgotten about the outside guard. Now he stood in the doorway, rifle at the ready. "What the—"

I tried to spring up, but using my element had left me slower. Weaker. By the time I grasped the rifle barrel, he was already shouting for help.

CHAPTER 29

The guard stopped shouting as soon as I touched the rifle. I focused on driving my element along the barrel and into the pirate. He fought back, teeth gritted and gums bared, but didn't fall.

Tarn took one of the rifles from the unconscious pirates and swung it at the man's head. He toppled as suddenly as a tree limb struck by lightning.

"Who are you?" cried Kieran. "You shouldn't be here."

"Keep your voice down. We're here to rescue you," said Tarn.

"If Jossi sees you here, he'll hurt my parents. He took them away from me."

"We know. They're probably with the other clan folk in the hurricane shelter. We're going to free them too."

Kieran didn't look convinced. "He swore he'd kill them if he had to."

"We won't let that happen—" She stopped speaking as two more pairs of footsteps pounded along the street toward us. "We have to go!"

"I can't."

Dennis touched Kieran lightly on the arm. "We're elementals, like you. We can help, but we need to get to your parents right now. Before Jossi knows what's happening."

The footsteps were growing louder. The men were probably within fifty yards. "You have to go," I said. "Wait for me before moving in on the shelter. I'll stay here and deal with these men."

"Not alone, you won't," said Dennis.

There wasn't time to argue with him. Besides, I was feeling even more sluggish than before. "Let's get these bodies out the way, then. One look at this and they'll raise the alarm for sure."

Tarn dragged one man behind an upturned table. Then she and Dennis took another, while I pulled the last away from the center of the floor and added him to the heap. We covered them in blankets.

The footsteps outside drew closer, but the men were slowing down. They'd probably noticed that the outside guard was missing, and wanted to be cautious.

"Go!" I said.

Reluctantly, Kieran turned on his heel and followed Tarn through the building.

I picked up two of the rifles. Dennis took the third. "Do you know how to use one of these?" he whispered.

"No. We can't afford to, either. One shot, and Jossi will panic."

"Maybe he'll send all his men here. We could head around the back to the shelter."

"Or maybe he'll send them to the shelter instead, and Tarn won't get near the place. Right now, those pirates out on the street are focused on Dare. Let's keep it that way."

We padded deep into the store and hid behind large cabinets pressed against the wall. I figured that as long as we had a view of the doorway, we'd be able to see the pirates more easily than they could see us.

I was wrong. If I'd thought to look outside, I'd have noticed the amber glow from a pair of torches. As two more pirates crept through the doorway, they had a perfect view of the scene before them.

"Everyone's gone," said one. "Why'd they leave?"

"Don't be so sure they *did* leave," replied the other. "Something ain't right here."

Crouched in the shadow of the cabinet, I watched the glow of their torch flames reflected on every exposed patch of wall. It made it easy for me to track their progress across the room, which is how I knew they were about to stumble upon the bodies of the other men.

I grabbed a tiny glass bottle from the shelf beside me and hurled it toward the back of the building. It crashed against a wall and shattered across the floor.

The torches stopped moving. There was the ominous sound of two rifles being cocked.

"This ain't a good time for playing games, little boy," came a voice. "We need you to be good, now, you understand? Your momma and papa need you to be good too. They're counting on you."

The glow of firelight danced on the floor as they edged closer. The area in shadow became smaller. Dennis inhaled slowly and held his breath. I did too.

"Don't make us look for you, boy," snarled the second pirate. "We got no patience for your kind anymore, you hear me?"

Dennis peered over me to get a look at the pirates. From the angle of his eyes I knew they were right behind me. I braced myself for another attack.

A rush of air came from the front of the building. It converged on the space immediately behind the pirates. They heard the noise before they felt the wind, and turned to face it.

With a flick of one wrist, Dennis extinguished the torches. With a turn of the other, he spun the wind into a twister. As irresistible as a whirlpool, it sucked both pirates in and lifted them half a yard off the ground. Oddly, they didn't cry out as their bodies reeled in space; or maybe they couldn't. When Dennis sent them crashing to the ground with a simple flick of his wrist, I was fairly sure they'd never make a sound again.

I didn't check for a pulse because I didn't want Dennis to know if he had killed them. If we survived, there would be time to weigh the consequences of all that we had done. But that time was not now.

"Come on," I said, tugging his sleeve.

But Dennis didn't move. He stared at his hands as if he didn't recognize them. No wonder—through a simple series of gestures he'd reduced two men to sacks of flesh and bones.

"We have to go, Dennis. The others are out there with ropes around their necks." I kicked the pirates. "And these men helped to put them there. We're just defending ourselves. We didn't start this fight, remember?"

Even as I said the words I didn't completely believe them. If Tessa and Dare were telling the truth, this fight went back years. Centuries, even. We'd been born into it, but that didn't mean we weren't responsible. Our kind, elementals, bore as much guilt as anyone.

Tarn's words came back to me then—about how important it was that we not second-guess ourselves. "I couldn't have fought them alone," I continued. "You saved us, Dennis."

Still he didn't respond. Didn't even nod.

I slung the two rifles over my shoulders and headed for the main entrance. The view along the street hadn't changed much, although we were a little closer here than we had been earlier. My father, Ananias, Jerren, and Alice remained standing on the crates, looking haggard and forlorn in the soft glow of three torches.

But there was one crucial difference: "What's Dare doing?" I whispered.

Dennis came alongside me. "Kneeling, I think."

It worried me, that, but I decided that he was probably just playing with Jossi. Tricking him. Dare was a master manipulator. He knew his men better than anyone, their strengths and weaknesses. He'd know how to win them around.

My theory didn't hold up for long. In a flash, Jossi silenced Dare with his rifle butt. There was a faint crunch of wood against bone, and Dare sank to all fours. He had his back to us, so I couldn't see his face, but I was sure he must be bleeding.

Jossi towered over his former captain. Flanked by nine other pirates, he reveled in his power. "You shouldn't have come back, Dare. There's worse ways to die than drowning." He was shouting, an exaggerated performance that was as unnecessary as striking a man on his knees.

Dare wiped his sleeve across his face. "You don't know what you're doing, Jossi."

"Says the washed-up man bleeding on the ground." Jossi turned around to share a laugh with the other pirates. "Says the man who *deserted* us."

"I didn't—"

Jossi swung his rifle around and caught Dare on the cheek. Dare went down again, and this time he didn't pull himself back up.

"I've been seeing through your lies for years now, Dare. But the other men . . . you got 'em all scared, don't you? Too scared to say anything. Even after all them visions, no one wanted to call you an elemental to your face." He wasn't shouting now, but his words were just as clear as before. And for the first time, Jossi didn't seem like a desperate bully, but someone who would kill without a second thought. "I knew about you *all along*, you hear me? I knew it the day I watched my brother die—cut to death by a blade what had no business moving. My *brother*, Dare. My only family. And I came to you and I told you what happened, and what did you do? What did you *do*?" He spat at Dare. "You covered for the man who murdered him. This one right *here!*"

Jossi turned around and kicked the nearest crate. Rope tight around his neck, my father braced for the fall.

CHAPTER 30

nanias cried out as Father's crate rocked backward. I watched helpless as Father flicked his head and body forward, fighting to regain his balance. The rope bit into his neck.

It seemed like an eternity passed before the rocking stopped and Father was upright again. His chest heaved as he struggled to catch his breath.

Beside him, Jossi slow-clapped admiringly. "That was close, Ordyn. I thought you was a goner that time. You're like a cat with nine lives, ain't you? Or maybe you're just lucky. Lucky to have a friend like Dare."

The other pirates had been enjoying the spectacle too, but with those last words they grew restless. Whether or not they were answering to Dare, they clearly hadn't painted him in the role of enemy yet. But that's precisely what Jossi was doing.

"That's right," Jossi told them. "Remember how all this started? How we burned down the colony on Hatteras, and took them Guardians prisoner? Sure you do. But maybe you're forgetting how Dare only picked a fight with one man: Orydn. Beat him up something good, I'll grant you, but only 'cause he knew I had other plans for old Ordyn." He crouched down beside Dare. "It's true, ain't it? You knew I was going to kill him. I had a *right* to kill him too. An eye for an eye. So you got to him first. Even stuck him in a cage on the ship. Gave him his own special guard, so you could keep an eye on him." Jossi bore his teeth like an animal, snarling and braced for a fight. "You *spared* him, Dare. You know full well he killed my brother, and you spared him anyway."

Dare raised his head, but didn't even attempt to get up. "I told you before: Life is too precious to waste."

"Says who? If life's so damned precious, why in the hell is almost everyone dead?" Jossi slapped Dare's cheek, a pointless action to remind everyone that he was in charge. "We don't need you no more, Dare. We have our own solution, see? And before the night is out, we'll probably have *your* solution too, wherever he is. As for life, it'll carry on just fine—without you, and without my brother's killer. Or his son."

Jossi strode over to Ananias. He raised his rifle and pre- pared to strike my brother when Dare cried out, "Don't do it! . . . Please."

Jossi spun the rifle around and rested it across his shoul- ders. "I've got to tell you, Dare, I never knew you were so sentimental. Makes me want to keep you alive after all. Makes me think you ought to be around to see what kills these elementals first. I mean, they ain't going to stand on them crates forever, right? Plague's coming to all four of them, I can guarantee you that. As for Ordyn, I can't decide if he'll choose to fall first so he don't have to see his own son die, or if he'll try to hang on, hoping for one more miracle."

Dennis pulled me back. I hadn't even realized I was edging forward. "We have to help them," I said. "There isn't time to rescue Kieran's parents first."

"If we release his parents, all the clan folk get out too," he said. "That's a lot of extra people to shake things up."

"The clan folk will be guarded."

"And so are *they*," Dennis protested, pointing down the street.

Having silenced Dare, Jossi walked along the row of crates. He kicked each one, and watched Ananias and Jerren struggle to keep their balance. Then he came to Alice.

"Who dies first?" he asked her.

Alice didn't answer.

"Ordyn, maybe? He's old. A murderer too. Or what about his son? Or this one?" Jossi nodded at Jerren. "He ain't one of your clan, even I can see that. You ain't going to tell me you'd feel sorry for a boy who has no right being here in the first place, are you?"

He stood back and waited for a response. Perhaps he thought that Alice was the weak link. It was clear that he expected her to answer.

Still Alice said nothing.

"Time's a-wasting, girl."

Alice lowered her eyes and stared at him. It was a look of defiance. A look of challenge.

Jossi flicked his rifle around so that the barrel faced her. "Have it your way."

Before Jossi could fire, or kick her crate out from under her, Dare staggered up and ran headlong into him. The older pirate even got in a punch that sent Jossi reeling. But as he raised his fist again, a shot rang out.

Dare tumbled to the ground. This time, he didn't get up.

Beside me, Dennis gasped. "We have to get help."

With Dare lying on the ground, possibly dead, I knew that he was right. It wasn't going to be enough to steal Jossi's secret weapon—we needed to rescue Kieran's parents so that he'd turn the rats against the pirates.

We hurried back through the building. It was pitch-black, and with each step we seemed to crush something on the ground. But there was no one inside to hear us, or to threaten us. No one to avoid.

At the back of the building, we fought through bushes and weeds in pursuit of Tarn and Kieran. As we slipped past the openings between buildings, the pirates' voices grew closer and louder. Several people were speaking at once. Jossi had established control, but whoever shot Dare seemed to have upset the new balance of power. The confusion worked to our advantage, but I hoped that Dare hadn't paid for it with his life. Alice had kept him alive for a reason. Having lost so much else, she deserved a chance to know her father.

Finally it seemed as though the commotion was coming from behind us, which meant that we were getting near to the hurricane shelter. Sure enough, two shadowy figures stood in the cover of a small tree just ahead of us. Tarn shifted branches to get a clearer look at the open street beyond, especially the low stone shelter on the opposite side. Kieran was looking to the west, toward the mainland bridge, as if he were watching something that no one else could see.

Dennis and I crouched down beside them. "Are you all right, Kieran?" I asked.

He didn't answer. I wasn't sure he'd even heard me. I didn't press him, though—there must have been so much going on inside of him.

Tarn pointed across the street. "There's only one guard."

"Where are the others?" I asked.

"They left when they heard the gun go off. What happened back there?"

How to answer? Tarn had loved Dare once. How would she react if she believed that he was dead? "I-I don't know," I said. "I couldn't really tell."

Tarn saw right through my hesitation. Her face fell. Too late it occurred to me that she was contemplating the even more horrific possibility that Alice had been the victim.

She shook her head once, shutting out all doubts and concerns. "Let's move. One guard at the door is better than three, and the others won't be gone long."

"Then take this." I handed her a rifle. "There must be more guards inside the shelter."

Tarn held the rifle at arm's length. "I don't know how it works."

"You swing it," said Dennis. "It hurts."

Tarn didn't say anything to that. She seemed preoccupied by Kieran. He was staring at the street, but his head was moving very slightly, as if he were tracking an animal . . . or a rodent.

Tarn froze, but it was a few moments before I heard the faint clicking and shuffling as rats surged toward us. At first there were only a dozen, then hundreds, thousands, and finally a mass of rats so wide that they blanketed the street. Kieran wasn't following the rats with his eyes, either. He was *directing* them.

"What are you doing?" I snapped.

Once again, he didn't reply. Maybe he was trying to help, or attempting to stop us before we could jeopardize his deal with Jossi. I touched him lightly on the shoulder to get his attention.

Kieran flinched. On the street, the rats responded with a series of squeaks.

Dennis shrank back. He'd already been sick from Plague once and knew better than any of us how it felt. Instinct told me to keep my distance too, even though I'd already been exposed. Any battle in which we were so badly outnumbered was a battle we should avoid.

The pirate who was standing guard outside the hurricane shelter looked at the swathe of black approaching from the west. He held his post for a moment longer, and then ran, shouting, toward the intersection.

There was no time to lose.

I jumped out from behind the tree and sprinted across the street a couple yards ahead of the advancing rats. The door

216

to the hurricane shelter was open and heavy footsteps were pounding up the stone staircase inside. I slid the rifle off my shoulder, stepped inside, and swung. I caught the pirate in the ribs. He tumbled backward down the stairs.

In the torchlight from below, I saw other pirates watching me. They raised their rifles, but not before Dennis pulled alongside me.

I just had time to grab the stair rail as a gust of wind whipped through the doorway. It pulled my feet from under me and funneled down the staircase, blasting the men below. They were scattered across the floor, their rifles strewn about like driftwood after a storm.

As I ran down the stairs, I expected to see the clan folk joining our attack. Instead, they watched me with the same wary expressions they gave the pirates. Precious moments passed before they claimed the weapons for themselves.

Having decided that I was the lesser threat, some of the clan folk pinned the pirates to the floor. Others fled from the shelter, dragging screaming children away before pirate reinforcements could arrive. Kieran appeared beside me and together we pressed against the tide of evacuees.

"We'll find your parents," I assured him.

No answer again. Whatever his motives in bringing the rats, we'd forced his hand. At least now he would be reunited with his parents. Jossi's greatest weapon would be ours. Whether or not we could save the other elementals, we could end this conflict.

"Kieran!" A woman was shouting from the back of the shelter. She waved her arm back and forth to get his attention.

As Kieran hurried to meet her, the other clan folk parted to let him through. It wasn't a mark of respect, either—they were scared of him. Maybe they'd never known what he could do. Maybe he'd kept it hidden, or had been too far from Roanoke to use the element effectively. But now they'd seen the rats firsthand, and they wanted no part of him.

It didn't matter. His mother was calling to him. All would be well.

It wasn't until they came together that I noticed how old the woman looked—too old to be his mother.

"Where are they?" cried Kieran. "Where are my parents?"

She looked away. Her lip quivered. "They're gone, child. The pirates took them away."

CHAPTER 31

Kieran's face grew red. Was he panicking for his parents, or furious at the pirates for taking them away? From the street above us came the sound of screaming. The timing wasn't an accident, I was sure of it.

"Where are his parents now?" I asked the old woman.

"I don't know."

"When did the pirates take them away?"

"This afternoon."

I turned to Kieran and stood directly in his line of sight. Even then, I wasn't sure he was seeing me. "We'll find them," I shouted. "You have to trust me."

But he didn't trust me. Why would he? His parents had been gone several strikes. They could be anywhere on the island. Maybe even on the mainland.

I grabbed a flap of his tunic and dragged him toward the stairs. There was no time to waste. The pirates would've heard the clan folk by now and known they'd escaped. They'd also know that Kieran was gone too. And Jossi's only hope of regaining control would be to bring Kieran back in line.

Wherever Jossi went next, that's where Kieran's parents would be.

We were halfway up the stairs when I heard someone calling my name. It was a woman's voice, but before I could scan the faces around me, the rising tide of clan folk forced me up to the street. I figured it must have been Tarn, but she was already outside, waiting.

What if it was my mother? I was about to turn around and fight my way back down when Dennis yelled, "You've got to stop this." He was appealing to Kieran, not me, but the clan boy still didn't respond.

Rats surged along the street into town, a black mass so large that it threatened to overwhelm everyone and everything. Incredibly, none of the rats were biting or scratching, but the destructive potential was all too real. With a single thought, Kieran could kill us all.

Tarn was the next to plead with Kieran. She placed her hands on his shoulders. "We need you to control this," she said, flicking her head at the flood of rats. "We have to focus on your parents now."

Her words had the opposite effect. Reminded once again that his parents were in trouble, Kieran seemed to grow frantic. The rats responded to his chaotic thoughts, scurrying around aimlessly, crushing each other in their blind determination to move somewhere . . . *anywhere.*

"Let's head to the main street," I said. "Wherever they are, the pirates'll have to give them up now."

Tarn wrapped her arm around Kieran and hurried him toward the intersection of the two streets. Dennis and I ran after them. We watched our feet, careful not to trip, but it was hopeless. As we stepped on the rodents, they reacted with sharp claws and quick teeth. I'd only gone about twenty yards when I felt warmth spreading from a bloody wound. If I'd been attacked, it seemed certain that everyone else had been too. No one would escape the Plague this night.

We were only a few yards from the intersection when Tarn stopped suddenly. "Get back," she cried.

I shoved Dennis into a doorway and joined him there. With our backs against the wall, we listened to a fresh round of gunfire.

Tarn and Kieran were hiding in the gap between two buildings. She pointed to the intersection, where the rats were coming from all directions. Kieran had refocused now, so that they moved with purpose again. But as they came together, there was nowhere left for the rats to go. So they trampled each other, forming one new layer after another. The rats on the bottom would be crushed to death.

Why was Kieran summoning them? Who did he think was the enemy? There was no use in imploring him to stop—he was locked into this single task. As long as he lived, the rats would keep coming. But we couldn't let him die. He didn't deserve to pay for our war with Jossi.

The pirates had been taking aim at the clan folk, but now they used their weapons to frighten the rats away instead. It didn't work. The rats clawed at loose clothing and used it to climb. The pirates who didn't run were smothered. When one of them fell down, he was covered so quickly that I couldn't tell where he'd fallen. It was as if he'd disappeared entirely, drowned in a sea of black.

The clan folk were scattering too. They ran behind buildings, anything to steer clear of the rats. All around us was chaos.

I ran toward the intersection, staying close to the buildings where the layer of rats was thinner. Tarn ran out to join me, and she dragged Kieran with her. As we turned the corner, a scream split the air.

"No!" cried Tarn, but I couldn't take in the scene as quickly as her. Several beats passed before I realized that only three elementals remained on crates.

My father was swinging from a rope, legs thrust out, kicking. Beside him, Ananias strained against his rope, trying to get closer.

I broke into a sprint. The mass of rats tripped me, but I refused to fall. Falling would take time that Father didn't have. The large group of pirates had shrunk to just a few. Two of them took aim at me, but it was dark and they were distracted. I didn't even change course as their shots passed harmlessly by.

"Thomas, wait!" Tarn shouted. But I couldn't wait. Of anyone, she should have been able to see that.

As I drew closer the pirates took aim again. This time they didn't even get to fire. A funnel of wind whipped past me, so concentrated, it seemed to bend and twist the atmosphere.

The force of it knocked the pirates onto their backs. I'd thank Dennis for that later.

The other pirates disbanded immediately. Three of them ran, but Jossi wasn't among them. The two who had been knocked down threw off the opportunistic rats and pulled to a stand, ready to fight again.

I was only ten yards away when my father stopped struggling. I panicked that he was dead, but then I noticed his hands, still bound, and the small flames rising from his fingers. He was focusing his remaining energy on burning through the binds. Ananias must have realized too, because he followed Father's lead and conjured a flame so powerful it incinerated the rope that was binding his own wrists. He thrust his free hands up, ready to remove the rope.

He didn't get the chance. The pirates ran by, kicking the crates away. One after another the elementals fell several inches, until the rope jarred them to a halt. It was enough to strangle them, but not to snap their necks. They dangled together, fighting an impossible race against their disappearing breath.

As I reached them, Ananias was gripping the top of the rope with both hands. He pulled himself up a little, releasing the tension on the rope. Able to gasp another full breath, he produced more flame.

I went straight to my father and pulled the burned, frayed binds from his hands. I expected him to do as Ananais had done and take the stress off his neck, but he didn't move. I crouched underneath him and raised him up on my shoulders.

Beside me, Ananias fought to sear the rope. The flame was shrinking as his arm grew tired and his energy waned, but finally the rope snapped and he collapsed to the ground. From there, he fired another flame at Father's rope. It singed my face, but I didn't care. When the rope snapped, Father fell off the back of my shoulders. I couldn't catch him. His head collided with the ground.

"Leave him," Ananias rasped. He yanked me around. "We have to get the others down. They'll die."

I followed him past Alice. She was burning through the rope, just as he had done. But the impressive flame she wielded wasn't just her doing: Dare was beside her. He'd linked one hand with her, while he pressed the other hard against his bleeding chest. He was grimacing and wheezing, desperate for breath and yet anxious not to breathe because of the pain. One thing was clear, though: He wouldn't let his daughter die.

I lumbered under Jerren, placed his legs on my shoulders, and lifted him up, just as I'd done for Father. This time, it felt different. Jerren groaned as my element worked its way through him. I tried to limit the effect, but I was suffering too. As I grew breathless and my pulse quickened, energy burned away like steam from boiling water.

I wanted to slide out and let Ananias take my place under Jerren, but my brother was focused on burning through the rope. White-hot flames spun from his fingertips. I closed my eyes and willed Ananias to be quick.

Tarn caught up to us at the moment that the rope snapped and Jerren collapsed on top of me. By the time Tarn dragged him off me, I couldn't move. The sickening odor of burning flesh surrounded us, but Jerren didn't complain. He didn't make a sound at all.

Alice crawled over to him. She ran her hands across his cheeks and scraped dust from his lips. "Come on, Jerren," she muttered. "Come on!"

Finally Jerren opened his eyes. It was a tiny gesture, but it gave us hope. Alice ran her hands across his face and kissed him lightly on the cheek.

"Where's Dare?" I shouted. "He was right here."

"He's gone," said Dennis. "Took a rifle with him. Kieran's gone as well."

"What?"

"He fell. We called to you to wait, but you didn't hear."

I scanned the street. Kieran was capable of killing us all. Without Tarn's comforting hands and voice, that seemed more likely than ever. "Where is he now?"

"I don't know."

Everywhere I looked I saw rats, thousands and thousands of them, scurrying along, fighting, driven by an irresistible force toward the intersection. But there was nothing haphazard about their movement. Wherever he was, Kieran had reestablished complete control over them.

That's when I noticed the torches arranged in a row at the top of the water tower. The flames weren't large, just enough to illuminate a pirate and the two clan folk he held at gunpoint . . . and the shadowy outlines of the two figures climbing the ladder just below.

"Please, no," I whispered. But somehow I already knew who the figures were. Sure enough, a sliver of light cut across the ladder and revealed Kieran and Jossi.

Whoever controlled the rats, controlled the island. With Kieran as his prisoner once more, Jossi had that power. Looking around me, I couldn't imagine a scenario in which a single one of us might survive.

"We need to get to him," I said.

No one responded.

"Come on." I faced the others. "We need to—"

I froze as I saw Ananias. He was leaning over our father, hands limp at his sides. As he turned to face me, my brother didn't say a word. But then, with tears streaming down his face, he didn't need to.

Jossi had claimed another victim.

I crawled over to my father's dead body.

CHAPTER 32

'm sorry," said Tarn.

I didn't respond. There weren't words to express what I was feeling.

"What should we do?" she asked, though what she really meant was: *Do we keep fighting?*

It was a sympathetic question. No one would blame Ananias and me for giving up the fight. But looking at my father — scarred, broken, and finally beaten into eternal submission — I knew what I had to do.

"Grab the rifles," I said, pointing to the ground.

"We don't know how to fire them," said Dennis.

"I'll find a way."

Tarn sighed. "They'll be out of bullets. That's why the pirates left them here. It's why they kicked over these crates instead of shooting everyone." She tilted her head toward my father, coaxing me to join Ananias. To kneel beside my father and say good-bye. To offer a blessing for safe passage long after I'd stopped believing in any such thing.

Unable to do anything more for my father, Tarn turned her attention to Jerren. Up the street, to the north, the clan folk were climbing onto roofs to escape the pirates and rats. Maybe they'd stay there for days, huddled together, ignoring the destruction all around them, and pretending the threat was temporary. Less than a month ago, I'd have done the same thing. Now I had only one thought and one objective: to end this, once and for all.

The others called after me as I began the slow march toward the intersection, but I didn't look back. I had no time for condolences, or vague promises of a better future. The future was now, and it was bleak and evil and lonely.

I was halfway to the intersection when I heard footsteps behind me. I had no right to expect company, but Dennis took his place beside me, head high, chin jutting out. Ananias joined us a moment later. Then Alice.

With the others alongside me, I chanced a look back. Tarn was tending to Jerren, but her eyes were fixed on me. She gave a single nod, a gesture of support and respect. I nodded back, realizing at last that this was the moment the Guardians had most feared, the one they'd spent years trying to avoid: when their children realized the extent of their power and took ownership of it, whatever the result may be.

We pressed onward. By matching our strides to the speed of the rats, we were able to walk more easily. They scratched at my ankles, but it felt accidental, not aggressive, as if I was simply in their way.

Everything changed at the intersection. Here, the rats

were buried three deep. Those that were still alive bit me as I stepped on them. There was no way around them, though. The mound grew deeper with every yard of hard-earned progress; the noise, louder. They weren't congregating at the intersection at all, but at the base of the water tower.

The tower was close, less than twenty yards away, but we were barely moving. The fresh wave of rats came above my knees. When my foot slipped through the crushed pile of bones and blood, the rats came almost to my waist.

The others weren't beside me anymore. We'd been separated, driven apart in our quest to find the easiest path. But there were no easy paths. I wanted Ananias to scare off the rats with flames, but it was Dennis who caught my eye. Shorter than the rest of us, he was almost submerged in black. The rats weren't just biting his legs, but also his chest, which bled through his tunic. When he lost his balance, he slid down a few inches.

A moment later, he was gone.

"Dennis." I kept my eyes on the spot where he'd disappeared, certain that if I looked away I'd never find him again. "Dennis!"

The others had seen him go under too. His name rang out from all directions, but none of us was close to him.

I forced my way over, flinging rats from my path. When I was a few yards away, the sea of rats throbbed like an enormous heartbeat. The spot where Dennis had disappeared swelled slightly. I just had time to cover my face before hundreds of rats shot into the sky, and Dennis emerged, gasping for air.

Ananias was nearest. He grabbed a flap of Dennis's tunic to keep him above the rats. I expected Dennis to scream, but he didn't. His face was a mask. Looking into his eyes was like seeing a reflection of Kieran . . . or myself. Dennis seemed capable of anything in that moment. He just needed an outlet for his fear and anger.

Ahead of us, the pirates who had chosen not to escape were surrounded. They waved their blazing torches haphazardly, but still the rats came. At the foot of the steps the rodent mound grew faster and faster. Pirates who had been above the pile only moments ago found themselves being dragged under with the deathly efficiency of a coastal riptide. As I clambered up the mound of rats, a pirate's hand shot out of the blackness to pull me down. I kicked at it. I had no room for empathy anymore.

"You've got to stay on the surface," Ananias shouted. "Don't slip under."

I crawled the last few yards to the water tower and reached for the ladder. A pirate was fighting his way over too, recognizing it as his last hope of escape, but the rats overwhelmed him. More than that, they attacked him, biting and clawing until he writhed in pain, thrashing his limbs about in an attempt to free himself from them.

Having subdued another victim, the rats turned on me. I threw myself at the iron rungs, and climbed the ladder. Ananias was close behind me. He had hold of Dennis, and wouldn't let the boy go. But Alice was still several yards away, and slowly disappearing beneath the blackness.

Dennis didn't hesitate. As Alice covered her eyes, he took Ananias's hand and they combined, sending a band of fire that momentarily cleared the area. Free again, Alice grabbed the nearest rung.

Hand over hand, foot over foot, I pressed on. From ten yards above the ground, I had a clear view of Skeleton Town's ongoing destruction. The surviving pirates worked their way from roof to roof, setting fire to everything they saw. Maybe they thought it was the only way to combat the rats. Or perhaps they thought that this night would mark the end of everything, and they wanted to be the cause of it.

The remaining clan folk had gathered on a far distant roof, insulated from the mayhem. On the street, my father's body was almost too small to see, even as the fires in the buildings spread, bathing the scene in a red-orange glow. Tarn tended to him, and she wasn't alone. There was someone else beside her: a woman, I thought, though I couldn't be sure. They were fighting a losing battle against the never-ending tide of rats.

The other woman turned around then, as though she wanted me to see her—a face I recalled from a picture I'd found in Bodie Lighthouse weeks earlier. I took in the first view of my mother in thirteen long years.

Watching my father die had stripped me of anything but the need for revenge. But seeing my mother reminded me there were others to save, and others to live for. Griffin deserved the chance to meet the mother he'd never known.

I climbed again, faster than before. When I was halfway up the steps, Jossi appeared high above me. He held a lantern close to his face, presumably so that I could see his expression: crazed, unhinged. "Don't come any closer," he yelled.

"Let them go," I shouted back. "Before everyone dies."

"Why? Brings on the rats, I say. Let them come. Look around you. This is how we'll *all* go, the only way elementals will suffer the way that *we* have suffered. This'll be remembered as the day the earth was purged."

Below me, Dennis, Ananias, and Alice had continued climbing, and the ancient ladder was rocking back and forth under the strain. Several of the supporting clamps had rusted away.

"I told y'all to *stop!*" Jossi screamed. He leaned over the railing. "One more step and I shoot."

I had no choice. I stopped, and the others did too. The ladder continued to sway. Would Jossi even let us go back down, or was he planning to hold us there until the ladder buckled? Never mind that *he* wouldn't be able to get down either. He'd clearly seen how devastating this night would be, and had made peace with it.

I surveyed the town again: the burning buildings; Tarn and my mother dragging Father's body away from the stream of rats; and on the roof of the hurricane shelter beside us, a man who lay on his back, rifle pointed toward the sky.

A shot rang out. Above me, Jossi collapsed against the railing with a jarring clang. Down on the shelter roof, the man took aim again, but couldn't seem to hold the rifle steady. When he dropped the gun, he didn't even attempt to retrieve it.

It was *Dare*.

"Go!" Alice screamed.

I climbed. The ladder shook, but I didn't care. My fingers barely grazed the iron rungs as I heaved myself toward the tower platform, where several heavy footsteps pounded against the metal grate, and bodies collided with the massive water drum. Kieran's parents were fighting back.

The tussle ended as suddenly as it began. Only this time, no one hit the railing. Instead, a body was thrown clear over it. It passed by me with a rush of air, and landed on the mountain of rats below. I had no idea who had just died.

It didn't take long to find out.

Kieran's father teetered on the edge of the platform above me. Jossi was on top of him, landing punches to his face. As I neared the gap where the stairs connected to the platform, I got a clear view of Kieran's mother holding her son back, protecting him at any cost.

The victim must have been the other pirate. Which meant that Jossi was fighting alone.

I slapped my fingers onto the edge and pulled myself up the final step. Seeing me from the corner of his eye, Jossi pushed away from Kieran's father and staggered toward Kieran. As I swung a leg onto the platform, the boy's mother intercepted the pirate and they crashed against the railing. The suddenness of it, the sheer force, ruptured the rusted metal bars. They had no chance to stop their progress. There wouldn't have been anything to hold on to, anyway.

Jossi fell first. His hands were wrapped around Kieran's mother's arm, and she fell too. Together they hurtled past the broken railing and over the edge, plummeting toward earth. Arms outstretched, they almost brushed against Dennis, Ananias, and Alice, who were still climbing. A half yard to the side and Jossi would have taken all the elementals down with him.

"Mother!" Kieran's voice was high-pitched and frantic.

His father lay dead or unconscious on the platform. Kieran stood beside the gap, toes overhanging the edge, face frozen in horror. The tower was leaning, groaning under the strain. I crawled toward him. When I was only a yard away, he turned to me. I expected to see horror in his face, or desolation, or anger. Instead I saw only defeat. Kieran had endured so much, and done unimaginable things in the hope of being reunited with his parents. Now his mother was gone.

Kieran bowed his head and climbed over the railing.

CHAPTER 33

I leaped at Kieran and got a good hold on his ankle. Yanked the foot back before his momentum carried him over. He slid forward, but only his torso went over the railing.

Alice appeared beside me and tended to Kieran's father. I hoped it would placate Kieran to see that his father wasn't dead, but he wasn't even looking. Instead, he kicked at me with his free leg, hell-bent on breaking away.

I curled my other hand around the ankle as his foot connected with my cheekbone. White-hot pain flared across the left side of my face, and my pulse kicked. My element was misfiring, powered up and with only one place to go. Kieran unleashed a sound that was part scream, part gargle.

Having thrown everything into saving him, now I was killing him instead.

The others had staggered onto the platform, which began to sway under our weight. Ananias and Dennis grabbed Kieran too, and tried to heave him back up, but he was thrashing about so hard, they couldn't. I was sure he'd fall if I let go.

I stopped fighting my element and combined with Kieran instead—imagined my element flowing straight through him, a direct line between me and the rats. I did it to save his life, but it was a relief for me as well. Draining, yes, but we were working together now. He didn't kick me anymore. He didn't cry out. He just closed his eyes and allowed the combination to take full effect.

I heard voices. Kieran's father was groaning. Dennis was asking who had tumbled from the platform. Then everyone fell silent. They were all looking down.

I tilted my head to look through the grate. Directly below, the black mass of rats roiled like an ocean in a hurricane.

"The rats are climbing the steps," said Ananias.

"Not the steps," Alice said. "Each other. They're using themselves to get to us."

If I hadn't seen it with my own eyes, I wouldn't have believed it. The top of the pile resembled the skinny, pointed sand-drip towers we used to make on the beach. And just like those towers, no matter how many times the rat-tower toppled, it always grew back even higher than before as the base grew wider, just by force of numbers. The rats were already a quarter of the way up the steps. And they weren't coming for us.

They were coming *to* Kieran.

"Make them stop, Thom," shouted Alice. "You have to take over his element—turn the rats away."

As I regained control of my breathing, I reduced the amount of energy pouring through him. I didn't want to take over his element entirely—Jossi had already used Kieran to serve his own ends—I just wanted to slow things down, and give us a chance to think. But Kieran responded with a keening wail that resonated through every part of me. It was a cry of agony and hopelessness. A cry for the end of the world. And still the rats came. And still the town burned. And the rats ignored their instincts and scurried into the flames, until the heat that rose to greet us was tinged with the rancid odor of burning flesh.

Alice was right: I had to do something to stop the rats and the searing heat.

But Dennis had other ideas. He linked hands with Ananias and Alice and pulled them to the railing. "Combine!" he yelled.

The result was immediate and awe-inspiring: Wind took the flames leaping from Ananias's and Alice's hands and turned them into a firestorm. It cascaded down from the tower like a waterfall, incinerating the rats as they converged below.

Beside me, Kieran screamed for his mother. He must have known the fall had killed her, but the fire raining down left no shadow of doubt. I kept waiting for him to give in, to relinquish control of the rats now that neither Jossi nor anyone else had any power over him, but he seemed more determined than ever. He drew them to himself, rank after rank, and watched them die by the thousand in the inferno.

That's when I understood. Kieran wasn't trying to punish Jossi, or the pirates, or us. He wanted to kill as many rats as possible. Burning . . . crushing . . . it didn't matter *how* they died, just as long as they were destroyed.

With a loud metallic groan, the tower shifted slightly

beneath us. I couldn't even see the base of the stilts any-more—they were hidden behind flames and under the smol-dering remains of countless rats. We all knew what that sound meant, and there was nothing we could do about it. No time to climb down, and no way to survive the hell below, even if we did. The inferno would kill us as quickly as the fall.

I thought of Rose and Griffin then. Mother too. If Kieran and I could kill the rats before the tower collapsed, wouldn't our lives have meant something? Surely the survivors—clan folk and elementals—could coexist peacefully on an island without rats. In time, Griffin and Nyla could cure those who had contracted Plague. There would be a future here. Even without us, there would be that.

Kieran wasn't trying to pull away anymore. There was no need. Why jump, when falling was inevitable? Instead, he grew quiet, all his energy focused on the rats. I did the same. Together, the two of us brought even the stragglers toward the tower, until a clear perimeter emerged a few hundred yards away. The heat from the burning carcasses was overwhelm-ing. I gagged on the rancid air.

This time there was no warning sound, just a violent shift as the tower leaned ever more precariously to one side. The other elementals were jolted against the railing, but it didn't break. They didn't miss a beat, either, but rejoined hands and continued their combined assault.

I looked at each of them in turn: Dennis, who like me had lived in fear of displeasing the Guardians; Alice, the outsider, always fighting for what was right while enduring everyone's criticism; Ananias, who had only ever wanted the Guardians to respect him. I wanted them to live. I wanted all of us to live. But I said good-bye to each of them anyway, silently, so they wouldn't have to hear.

Another hideous groan as the aching stilts warped and fractured under us. The railing couldn't hold us back much longer. I didn't even have to look through the platform to see the firestorm below anymore. Limbs dangling through gaps in the railing, I could see everything perfectly because I was already facing down.

The rats plowed on to certain death, lured by Kieran's siren call. With every passing moment we were purging the island. But as the others began to tire, I knew it wouldn't be enough. Their trail of fire retreated like the ocean after high tide. With the tower straining, we were measuring life in heartbeats—ten if we were lucky, one if we weren't. Neither was long enough to rid the island of rats. They were so close too, concentrated within a radius of a hundred yards at most.

Ananias, Alice, and Dennis closed their eyes and gritted their teeth, trying to eke out something more. They must have known they were going to die here, and were determined to give everything. It wasn't enough, though. It could never be enough . . .

Unless I took over their elements. I might kill them in the process, but they were already as good as dead. Hadn't Tarn and Dare told me this moment would come?

I broke contact with Kieran. He didn't fall. He just stared at the rats and tried to hold them in his thrall.

Dennis screamed as I wrapped my arms around him. Alice and Ananias tried to resist as I placed my hands on their arms, but I wouldn't let go. They weren't elementals anymore; they were conduits, and I controlled the flow of all energy. *I* was fire and wind. Raw power flooded from me like water through a broken dam.

Fire no longer cascaded down from us. Instead, like a hurricane squeezed into a canister and unleashed in a moment, the inferno exploded. Flames radiated in an unstoppable ring, incinerating everything in their path. No rat could escape. No human either. Even high above, I was sure my skin was melting.

Ananias passed out first, unable to give any more of himself, and unable to stop me from taking from him anyway. Alice followed him into unconsciousness. I barely noticed. I didn't need their minds, just their elements. Such a betrayal to treat them like objects, but who would be alive to know what I had done?

I'd waited a lifetime to matter. To be *someone*. Now, as the world beneath me burned, I was so much more than that. I was a star—incandescent and all-powerful. And so bone-crushingly tired that I craved the moment when I'd be extinguished, and the echo would finally stop.

It was almost a relief when the first stilt gave out. The tower buckled backward, twisted sideways, and fell. I closed my eyes and let myself go.

CHAPTER 34

ombine!" Someone was holding my hand. I didn't know
who it was—Dennis, maybe. "Combine!"

Plummeting through the air, I thought of the wind
and unleashed a single pulse of my element.

There was a jolt of air from under me, so powerful it was as
if the earth itself had risen up and stopped my fall. My insides
lurched as I flew upward, caught on the drafts of an enormous
funnel. Below, the tower collapsed into the flames. The stilts
were mangled, as twig-like as the bones of a dead bird.

The chute of air weakened. Hand in hand, Dennis and
I began to turn. He must have wanted me to give him more
power, but I couldn't do it. I just focused on the ground, and
the need to stay conscious as the world twisted around me.

I wasn't sure which way was up. I thought I caught a
glimpse of the others beside me. The raging fires blurred with
the darkness until the entire island appeared bathed in furious orange.

I stopped rising, and began to free-fall. The heat grew more intense. Thick smoke filled the air. By the time I was able to get a look at the island, I saw something too bizarre to be real: A tidal wave crashed through Skeleton Town, large and unstoppable. And near the crest of the wave, a ship.

I willed myself not to look away. If I was dreaming, it was a dream I welcomed.

Another rapid turn through the air, but the ship was still there. Marin and Rose stood on the prow, with Nyla between them.

I braced to hit earth, but landed with a splash instead. Just as I'd been tossed about in the air, now I was twisted around in the water. It shocked me. Revived me. But I couldn't breathe.

My back scraped along what I figured was the ground, so I planted my right foot against it and pushed upward, surfacing almost immediately. About fifty yards away, the ship collided with the top corner of one of the buildings, ripping the hull to pieces.

I looked for Rose and Marin and Nyla, but I couldn't see them. I could hear Dennis's voice, though. He was close by and floundering in the shifting currents. The water level was dropping, but as it sank it created eddies that sucked objects under before tossing them out again. By the look of it, Dennis had been caught in one. I swam the couple yards over to him and grabbed his tunic. Once he saw me beside him, Dennis went limp. He was completely spent.

Kieran was nearby too. I heard him screaming, but as the last of the fires was extinguished by the advancing tide, I couldn't see him. Keeping one hand on Dennis, I swam toward the voice. Kieran let out a single, short cry. Then nothing.

"Kieran," I shouted.

Not a sound.

"Kieran!"

Something erupted from the water beside me. A figure cleared the surface entirely before splashing down beside me. Rose.

I couldn't make sense of how well she appeared, and how strong. There wasn't time to ask, either. "Kieran," I said, pointing in the direction of his last cry, and even though Rose had never seen the boy, she took off to find a child in the murky gray water.

While she was gone the water receded enough that I could touch the ground again. I couldn't anchor myself, though, as the currents continued to swirl, so I allowed myself to float about. Dennis bobbed up and down on his back next to me. Apart from the ebb and flow of water, the scene was oddly quiet, so I tried to hone in on voices. I didn't hear anyone.

Rose surfaced a short distance away. Kieran seemed lifeless in her arms. "Take him," she said, swimming to me.

Before I could ask where the others were, she was gone again. I figured it meant that someone was still underwater. I grabbed Kieran's tunic just as I'd taken Dennis's. The water level was below my armpits now, and I was able to stand. Occasionally I'd touch the two boys, and even though I was so weak I could barely keep moving, they would moan in response. I couldn't let go of them, though. In the darkness, with unpredictable currents, there was no guarantee I'd ever find them again.

A voice cut through the night: "Kieran?" It was the boy's father, calling from the direction of the wrecked ship.

"He's here," I called back.

Slowly, painfully, we made our way toward each other. He was helping Alice. She was conscious, but weak.

Rose swam toward us. Nyla had her arms clamped around Rose's neck, which meant that almost everyone was accounted for.

"Does Marin have Ananias?" I asked.

"I don't know," said Rose. "Marin was mostly worried about Griffin."

So that was why Rose looked well—because Griffin had cured her. But at what cost to himself? And if Marin didn't have Ananias with her, where was he? He was a strong swimmer, but if he was in the same state as Alice or Dennis, that might not be enough.

"Ananias," I called. No response. "We need light, Alice. I can't see."

She raised her hand, and lowered it again. "Please," she begged. "Just give me a moment."

I reached out. One simple touch and I could conjure a flame, whether Alice wanted me to or not. I'd used that power already, and seen what I could accomplish with it. But Alice had seen the power too, and there was no mistaking the look on her face. She was afraid of me. Afraid of what I might do to her.

If I stole her element from her now, how would she ever trust me again?

I bowed my head and stayed back. I needed Alice to see that I wasn't like Jossi or Dare.

A moment later, she produced a flame and the hideous scene became clearer. The tidal wave had carried the dead rats away, but now the carcasses floated back toward us, mingled with the cremated remains of the pirates who had chosen to stay and fight. I told myself that we hadn't started this battle. We'd been defending ourselves. I'd been trying to save lives. But seeing so many charred bodies, it was impossible to ignore that *I* had taken over everyone's element. I'd taken a precise wall of flame and turned it into an uncontrollable fireball. Who apart from Jossi would have allowed so much destruction to occur?

And what about the other people who had been on the street a short time before? Tarn and my mother had been kneeling on the ground, tending to Jerren. Then they'd moved to the side to escape the wave of rats. But what had happened after that?

My chest tightened. For at least a hundred yards down the street the buildings were blackened shells. Even beyond that they bore the scars of the devastation I'd rained down on Skeleton Town. The clan folk had taken refuge on roofs beyond that, but how had they fared in the heat? Were they choking to death on the smoke?

No one spoke. There was nothing to say.

I waded through the water as the level dropped to my

ankles. When Kieran's tunic slipped out from between my fingers, I didn't help him up. He wouldn't drown anymore, and besides, only one thought consumed me—the bleakest reality of all.

I'd killed my mother. And Tarn. And Jerren. And Ananias was gone too.

I staggered along the street, blinded by darkness, stumbling over dead rats and sharp debris. "Ananias," I called out.

Nobody answered.

"Tarn!" Strange that hers should be the name I chose next, but I couldn't seem to make my mouth produce the word *mother*. Better not to say the word at all if she was dead so soon after reentering our lives.

"Jerren!" Still no answer. The water was almost at street level now, and I moved faster, quick enough that I fell hard as I tripped over a large dark object lying in front of me.

I struck the ground with the force and grace of a toppled tree. I wasn't able to brace myself, so my nose and forehead made contact with the inch-deep puddle and the cracked street. I tilted my head to the side to breathe, but I didn't move. It was time to stop. Time to rest.

Something shifted under my foot. I figured it was a rat, or a piece of driftwood brought in on Rose's massive wave. Then it moved again. And moaned.

CHAPTER 35

rolled over. Crawled on all fours to the body that lay crumpled at my feet. I couldn't make out anything—skin or clothes—so I patted the person to the left and then to the right until I felt the head. Beneath my fingertips the skin felt like dried clay, but with a sticky coating that I was certain was blood.

"Over here." I tried to shout, but it came out as a wheeze.

Alice was first to reach me. She crouched down and produced a flickering flame. In the weak light I saw a man's face, but I couldn't identify him. His clothes were burned. The explosion had blasted part of his face away. Swathes of skin had been scorched.

It wasn't until he smiled that I knew it was Dare. There was a time that smile had chilled me, but I wasn't frightened anymore. I couldn't even bring myself to hate the man. Whatever he'd done was in the past, unchangeable. He'd helped to save Ananias and Alice and Jerren. He was going to pay for it with his life too.

Maybe there was another reason I forgave him so quickly. I'd been afraid that the body was Ananias's. But Ananias couldn't have been so badly burned when he was on the tower with us.

Alice leaned closer. Trembling, she placed her palm gently on what was left of Dare's cheek, and regarded her father silently. He must have been in agony, but showed no sign of it.

"My whole life . . ." Alice blinked. Tears traced lines down her dirty cheeks, and she didn't wipe them away. "I always knew. *Always* . . . that there was something else . . . something missing."

Dare didn't move a muscle, but his smile seemed frozen now, something he needed to maintain no matter what was churning inside of him.

"You could've shown me the world," she said.

Finally he flinched. Was it pain? Or the realization that he'd have no more part in her future than he'd had in her past?

"Ananias is over here!" Rose's voice cut through the silence. "But he's . . ." Her voice fell at the end, a tiny shift with an enormous effect. Something was wrong. Terribly wrong.

As I pushed to a stand, Dare inhaled sharply. "Griffin," he mumbled. "Must . . . draw me."

I didn't know what he was talking about, and I didn't care. If Ananias was in trouble, there was no time to waste.

He grasped my ankle. "Griffin must *draw* me." His voice had the same quiet desperation as Tessa's when she'd warned us, *solution is death.* "Draw me!"

248

I didn't want to disrespect Dare or Alice, but these were the ramblings of a dying man. As I pulled my foot free, he cried "No," but I didn't stop, and I didn't turn around. Ananias was nearby, and he needed my help.

"Thomas?" Rose called out to me.

I ran the last few yards and took my place beside her. Nearby, Marin was helping Griffin to join us too. I wanted to hug Griffin, to tell him how happy I was that he was alive, and to thank him for saving Rose. But one look at Ananias and I forgot everything else.

"I can't feel his heartbeat," said Rose. She pressed a finger against his neck. "He was breathing just a moment ago. When I called to you, he was still breathing. I swear!"

Marin sank to her knees and pressed Ananias's chest, trying to restart his heart. Rose breathed for him. I just stared at my older brother, unable to make sense of what was happening.

Griffin clapped his hands to get my attention. *Who. Dead?* he asked, pointing at where Alice was crouching.

Dare. I signed in a daze. *Not. Dead. Yet.* My hands moved slowly, as if they were unusually heavy. *He. Want. You. Draw. Him.*

Griffin looked away sharply. Countless conflicting emotions played across his face. Then he stared at Ananias again, and finally at me.

That's when everything came together.

Griffin had the worn, wizened expression of someone who knew this day would come—when I'd look beyond coincidence and see what was there all along. How on the day that he'd foreseen our father's death, Griffin had drawn a portrait of Guardian Lora, and watched her die instead. How he'd foreseen Nyla's death on Sumter, only for Chief to die instead, another of Griffin's portraits tucked in his pocket.

Now Dare was begging for release. Would the exchange be made too late?

Please, I signed. *You. Can. Save. Ananias.*

Griffin shook his head. *Too. Late.*

You. Must. Try.

He began to cry. *I. Kill. Other,* he replied, reminding me that the exchange wasn't without a cost.

Griffin didn't know that Father was dead. Or that our mother hadn't reappeared. I pitied him, I really did, but I couldn't let Ananias go without a fight.

I reached across, grabbed Griffin's arm, and pulled him up. Dragged him, hobbling, to Dare.

The pirate stared at Griffin with glassy eyes. He couldn't speak anymore, and Griffin wouldn't have heard him anyway. But Dare looked peaceful. He looked *ready.*

Griffin scanned the ground. There was nothing but dirt and puddles. *How. Draw?* he asked.

I stripped off my shredded tunic and handed it to him. While he straightened it out on his lap I found a piece of broken glass on the street. It didn't even hurt as I sliced it along my forearm.

I held my arm out to Griffin as blood trickled from the wound. He didn't ask me what I was doing. He'd seen Dare too now, and from his expression I was sure he realized he wasn't stealing a life. He was stealing a man's final moments. Perhaps these were just mind games, telling ourselves whatever we needed to hear to assuage the pain and guilt. Didn't matter. Griffin dipped his finger in my blood and smeared it across my tunic.

He kept his eyes fixed on Dare the whole time. But watching Griffin, I had the feeling he wasn't looking at Dare at all. He had the distant expression of someone whose mind is wandering to something completely different. Or *someone*. I didn't need to ask if that person was Ananias.

The portrait didn't resemble Dare. It was barely recognizable as a face. But Griffin knew what he was doing, and he seemed determined to do the best job of it he could, as if it were a mark of respect for the person whose life he was ending.

"Let him see it," said Alice.

I eased the tunic from Griffin's fingers and held it up for Dare to see. He didn't react at all, but his eyes were open, taking everything in. The portrait was probably meaningless to him, though; the artist was all that mattered. With his last breath, and after years of searching, Dare had momentarily ensnared the solution.

I'd accused Dare of being a tyrant. A killer. But his final act was to save another. He'd told me that every person has to decide what's worth dying for. This was his choice.

Even though he was gone, Alice held Dare's hand, her thumb gliding back and forth, rhythmic and calming. It was a gesture of love. Forgiveness too, most likely.

"He's breathing!" Rose's voice pulled me around. She was

standing over Ananias, hand raised triumphantly. "Marin and me—we saved him."

She obviously expected us to join her. In her mind, she'd returned our brother from the dead. How could we not celebrate this miracle with her? But Alice was still hand in hand with Dare, grieving the father she'd never known, and I didn't have the heart to leave either of them.

I didn't know what to say, so I kept my mouth shut and touched her sleeve, just so that she'd know I was there for her. Eyes fixed on her father, Alice raised her pinky finger until we were skin to skin. Friends. Cousins. Survivors.

And we weren't alone. As Alice broke contact and stood to leave, three figures emerged from a building fifty yards up the street: Jerren, Tarn, and Skya, the mother I'd been certain I would never see again.

CHAPTER 36

Tarn, Jerren, and my mother looked just as injured as the rest of us. Jerren was leaning heavily on Tarn. They took small but laborious steps, heads bowed low as if they didn't have the energy to look up at us. I caught glimpses of the whites of Tarn's eyes, though, and knew that she was watching us too. From the way I was kneeling, she must have realized that someone lay dying or dead beside me, and she was about to find out that it was Dare—a man she had once loved.

My mother walked slowly behind them. She was going to be reunited with my brothers and me, but our father was gone. Thirteen years ago, she'd been taken away from him before he could say good-bye. Now she was the one left behind.

Alice and I met them halfway. She slid under Jerren's free arm and they supported each other. "I thought you were dead," she whispered.

"We would've been," he replied. "But Skya told us to move inside the building. There was a storage room. She sealed the door with pieces of cloth. After that, everything was just noise."

My mother and I stood facing each other, but a few yards apart. If she'd known to take shelter in that room, had she also foreseen that our father would die? And Tessa? Was this part of some inexplicable trade: her husband's and mother's lives in return for her children's? I knew I ought to be relieved—the battle was finally over, and we were embarking on a new future, free of rats and Plague. But would things truly be different this time? How could we coexist with the non-elementals now, when we'd failed so badly in the past? When they'd been forced to huddle on a distant rooftop and watch us decimate the town?

I looked past my mother at the bodies scattered across the ground—pirates and clan folk, wounded or dead. In the distance, other clan folk descended from the roofs where they'd been sheltering. They hurried to tend to their fallen relatives. Faced with so much carnage, children wailed, while parents mourned their loved ones in desolate silence. I didn't want to look too closely at the bodies myself. They hadn't died of the Plague, or gunshot wounds. They'd been burned to death in the moment I took over everyone's elements. Without me, they'd still be alive.

Ananias and Griffin joined me, one on each side. We stood in a line, facing our mother. She stepped forward and regarded each of our faces in turn, eyes narrowed as if she were filling in thirteen years of growth and change. Raising her hand, she brushed her fingers across Griffin's cheek. He closed his eyes and savored the kind of touch he'd never known.

Ananias stepped across and hugged her then. It was stiff and unnatural, more like something he knew he ought to do than something he wanted to do. But Mother hugged him back, and pulled Griffin in tightly too.

Finally she turned her attention to me again. She tilted her head to the side and watched me with a quizzical expression. Had she forgotten what I could do? How much it would hurt her to touch me? I felt like a child, desperate to be held and angry at being overlooked. But I also didn't want her to flinch, or pull away from me suddenly. I didn't want to hear her apologize to me, to assure me that it wasn't my fault, and that it would take time for me to harness my element, just as it had for my father before me. Father's power was nothing compared to mine, after all. That's why, as Mother reached up to touch me too, I leaned away. Better to accept our limits now than to risk hurting her and driving her away.

She continued to watch me for a moment, and lowered her hand purposefully. Then she looked behind her at the clan folk. I looked too.

At least half of them were watching us. Even though they had injured friends and relatives to attend to, they studied us instead, wondering if the devastation was over, or if this was just the eye of the storm, the lure of perfect calm before we wreaked havoc again. The fifty yards of street that separated us from them was a no-man's-land.

Griffin tapped my arm and nodded in the direction of the clan folk, as if he wanted me to cross the divide with him.

Dangerous, I signed.

He mulled over this, and signed back, *They. Need. Help.*

I was still unsure, but as Nyla joined Griffin and they began the slow, awkward march along the street, I knew I had no choice. For years, Griffin's life had been as mundane as mine. Now he was the solution, and he was determined to save.

We stopped several yards from a group of three men. They stood shoulder to shoulder, flexing their fingers, anxious not to start a fight but unwilling to back down.

I kept my voice clear and straight. "Do you have Plague?"

The men hesitated. "Why do you ask?" demanded the largest of them, a tall man with a straggly beard.

"Because we can cure it."

This announcement was greeted by muted chatter that circulated to the far reaches of the group. Meanwhile, the men confided in whispers.

"Will it hurt?" he asked.

"Not much," Nyla answered. "But Plague sure does."

Once again they talked. Reluctantly, they waved us over to an old man lying on the ground. He looked frail, but his Plague was no more advanced than Dennis's had been. Surely there were more hopeless cases than him?

Test, signed Griffin, watching me. *They. Not. Trust. Us.*

I fought back the urge to plead with the clan folk. Now wasn't the time for a test. Griffin's element was too precious and fragile for that. We were weak. We couldn't guarantee how many lives would be saved. Or if some might be lost by waiting.

But Griffin wasn't in the mood to argue. Kneeling, he placed his hands palm-down against the old man's chest. Nyla laced her fingers with Griffin's right hand, while I laid mine on his left. When I reached my free arm around his back, I was surprised to find Nyla's hand waiting for me. We linked, and the flow of energy between us and through Griffin became steady and uniform.

I looked past Griffin to the east. The sky was shifting color, a hint of blue-gray after a long night of black. The birds that had become eerily silent since our return to Roanoke announced their arrival. Surely the timing wasn't a coincidence. This was the beginning of a new era of reconciliation. Griffin was making sure of it.

I wished that he would hurry, though. Being in the center of Skeleton Town seemed to be making him more powerful than before, but the adrenaline that had kept me going all night was fading now. I needed to rest.

Nyla loosed hands. I figured she'd had enough, that the pain was too much for her, but she was listening as the old man spoke. Although he was still frail, the lumps on his neck had receded. He'd been healed as suddenly as Dennis and Rose. When he raised a hand and waved at a small group nearby, the clan folk's murmuring became louder.

Eyes closed, Griffin rocked back and forth. Sweat glistened on his forehead. He breathed in and out slowly, trying to conserve energy, unable to take any pride in what he'd just done.

A woman ran toward us then. She had what looked like a sandbag slung over her shoulder, but it was actually a child—a young girl, maybe five or six years old. The mother laid her daughter tenderly before us. "Please," she begged. "Please save her."

Just as I'd feared: There were far sicker people here than the old man we'd just helped. And this girl was one of them.

"Is she . . ." *Alive*, I was going to say, but I couldn't ask the woman that. So I put my ear to the girl's mouth and felt her shallow breaths warm me.

"Can you do it?" the woman asked. "Can you save her?"

We were so tired, and I didn't want to risk Griffin's health. Even if we helped the girl, who was to say that she'd survive? I was about to explain all this when Griffin leaned forward and placed his palms on the girl. With or without me, he was going to try.

Reluctantly, Nyla and I linked hands. Joined with Griffin again, we combined. This time progress was slower. The girl was in a bad way, and we had so little left to give. I tried to stay upright, but as my vision grew fuzzy, I lost balance, broke contact, and fell away from him.

I got back up—I couldn't let Nyla and Griffin do this alone—but quickly fell back down again. In the distance I saw Kieran's father holding him close, just as my father had once held me. It was as if the world were being turned upside down, so I closed my eyes. I just needed a moment to recover.

My eyes snapped open as someone jostled against me. The small girl was gone—cured, I guessed—and in her place were at least twenty people: men and women and children. They clamored for attention, and ignored each other's pleas. Griffin had presented them with an easy and immediate cure for Plague. No one was willing to be patient.

Beside me, Griffin was shaking his head. Curing the girl must have made him woozy, because he lost balance and fell backward. A strange sound was coming from his mouth, and I just had time to turn his head to the side as he vomited onto the street.

"Enough," I tried to say, but the word was drowned out by the clan folks' appeals. "Please," I said, but it was pointless. They surged forward.

A man grabbed Griffin's arm. He had dark, sunken eyes, and blood-red welts around his neck. "Help me," he moaned.

Griffin was crying. He wanted to cure them all, but he couldn't even keep his eyes open.

"I said, 'help me!'" the man yelled. He shook Griffin.

I lunged forward and took the man's wrist. Full of panic, I got in a single powerful shock before we fell away from each other. The man crashed into his neighbors, I fell back, and Griffin was unconscious. He'd suffered too.

I held my breath. If the clan folk were ever going to attack, now was the moment. We were too weak to defend ourselves. But none of them were looking at us. Instead, they edged back as the other elementals took up positions behind us.

Marin stepped into the no-man's-land. The woman who had once treated my brother and me like we were barely human was now our protector. And Skya was with her.

"Our elements have limits," my mother shouted. "If you

don't let these children rest, they won't be able to cure any of you. For your own sakes, give them space."

I waited for the clan folk to respond. There was muttering, but no consensus.

Before I passed out, I saw the sun peeking over the battered shells of Skeleton Town. It was a new dawn, but I'd seen that sun before. I'd seen it as I'd stood on the beach at Hatteras, dreaming of a time when I might be useful to the colony. I'd seen it on Sumter when I'd woken beside Rose, sure at last that we'd found a place that was safe. How often had that sun reeled me in with its promise of hope and change? And I'd believed it every time.

But I'd been missing the point. My future wasn't about one day, and it certainly didn't rest on something as reliable as the sunrise. Every day that I lived, my future was about me and my element. There was nothing more unpredictable in the world.

CHAPTER 37

I t was the smell that woke me: something burning. As soon as I covered my mouth with the edge of my tunic, the smoke changed course.

The sun was high—early afternoon, I figured. Close by, clan folk were using broken timbers to shuffle bloated rat carcasses into sacks. Other people collected the sacks, and traipsed away in a perfect straight line. I couldn't see where they were headed, but I was sure they would be burying the rats, preferably a long way from Skeleton Town. From the thousands that remained, they'd be doing the same job for the rest of the day.

I tried to stand, and thought better of it. I needed a moment to get my balance. Every part of me felt tightly wound, like a knot that might never come undone. As I lay there, I began to sweat, just from being awake.

I rolled onto all fours. When I was sure I wouldn't pass out, I stood and took a few tentative steps. The clan folk line snaked northwest past the buildings, toward the plume of smoke that rose diagonally even though there was no wind.

As they waited for their sacks to be filled, the clan folk watched me. I felt like I was like being observed by a dozen Guardians, suspicious and disapproving. But none of them threatened me. Whatever Mother had said to them at dawn had at least won us a reprieve, if not the clan folks' complete trust.

I joined the line too, mostly to show that I was willing to do my part in the recovery process. As I took my place, all conversation ceased. They knew who I was, and they must have known I'd played a part in what had transpired on the water tower. How much more uncomfortable would they be if they realized the extent of what I'd done?

The young man beside me pulled a water canister from the hook on his thick leather belt. "Here. Looks like you could do with some water." He held out his canister. "Go ahead. There's plenty more where this came from." I must have looked puzzled, because he continued: "Two of your kind can test the purity of water. We'll have all the drinking water we need."

Your kind. There was no mistaking those words—we may be coexisting, but ours was still a fractured colony. In their excitement over unlimited drinking water, the clan folk might be willing to overlook our other elements. But one day, those elements would resurface. Would they still appreciate us then?

"You're dehydrated." The man refused to give up. "You *have* to drink."

I surrendered, resigned to playing my role in this forgiving new world. But as our hands came together on the canister, my element passed through the metal. He inhaled sharply.

"I'm sorry," I said. The apology was a reflex—one I'd probably get to use a lot from now on.

"It was nothing," he lied.

I raised the canister to my lips and drank. The water was cool—maybe the finest water I'd ever tasted. I fought the urge to finish it.

"Listen," the man said, "I'm sorry about your father. I lost my father too this week. He was older than yours, but I loved him. I wish he was here to see this."

I held out the canister for him, but then thought better of it and placed it on the ground instead.

"I'm Brent, by the way." Smiling.

We didn't shake hands. "Thomas."

"Well, that canister is yours now, Thomas. Drink it wisely." Before I could refuse, he received a sack of rats and rejoined the line.

A few moments later, I followed him. Beyond the buildings, the clan folk had worn a clear path through the wild grass. At the end of it they emptied their sacks into a large pit. Ananias stood at the bottom of the pit, shirtless, setting the carcasses alight with both hands. Dennis stood at the rim and used his element to fan the flames. When the smoke climbed vertically upward, he redirected it away from us with the slightest flick of his fingers. Eventually, all evidence of the rats would be gone from Roanoke Island. The moment couldn't come soon enough.

When he saw me, Ananias ran up the bank. He was only a step away from me, arms outstretched, when he hesitated—he didn't want to be hurt. Then, shutting out his fear, he pulled me into a tight hug.

It was uncomfortable for me, and no doubt worse for him, but he still didn't let go. Surrounded by strangers, he clung to me.

"Where are the others?" I asked.

We broke the connection. "Marin and Rose are by the water tower," he answered. "The tank still holds a little water. Griffin and Nyla are in the shelter with Skya."

Skya, not *Mother*. How long would it be before that word felt real to us?

"We'll release the dead tonight," he continued. "Or bury them. The clan folk need a day to think things through. To mourn."

"And you?" I asked. "Do you need a day to mourn?"

He leaned back, so that we were eye to eye. Tears mingled with sweat. "When we were standing on the street yesterday, with those ropes around our necks, Jossi said stuff about how the Guardians used to treat non-elementals. I called him a liar . . . but Alice didn't. And neither did Father. I wanted Father to deny everything, but he wouldn't. He *couldn't*." He stared at the ever-growing mound of rats. "Do you remember when we were young—how Father would carry the three of us . . . one on his back, and one on each arm?"

"Yes," I said. "I remember."

"I used to think he was the strongest man in the world. Back then, I didn't know there were different kinds of strength . . . that on the inside, he was weak."

"He wasn't weak, Ananias. He carried all three of us, and he ran through the waves, and you and Griffin never even felt his element. Or mine, which means he must've been keeping me away from you. The control that must have taken—the willpower—I just hope I can find a small part of it for myself."

Ananias was growing restless. As so often before, he needed a moment alone, but duty called. "Who am I now, Thomas? I'm definitely not one of them"—he pointed to the line of clan folk—"but I'm ashamed to be an elemental. Where does that leave me?"

The clan folk were working well together, calm and methodical. They were also glancing at Ananias as they emptied their bags, each and every one of them. And I didn't see suspicion or frustration in their eyes; I saw admiration for what he was able to accomplish. Their version of Ananias was the same as mine: tough, relentless, uncomplaining.

"You're in the middle of everything now," I told him. "And that's exactly where you need to be. You're a bridge . . . the link we need to make this work."

"And you?" he asked.

"Me?" I thought about it. "I just need to stay out of the way, so I don't shock anyone."

Ananias chuckled at that. It didn't occur to him that I was serious.

"I should keep going," he said. He trudged down the bank into the smoldering pit. "If you see Alice, tell her I could do with some help. I'm tired."

Was it tiredness, or Plague? It had only been one day since we'd come into contact with the rats. It might take another day before the symptoms showed—for me, as well as for him. "Why Alice?" I shouted.

He wiped his arm across his forehead, but he was so covered in sweat and grime that it didn't help at all. Soot from the fire traced shadows across his chest that made him appear even more muscular than usual. "Now that Father's gone, she's the only one with fire."

Dennis had been watching us the whole time from the other side of the pit. I joined him there. "Ananias isn't the only one who's tired," he said. "I was in the shelter earlier. Griffin and Nyla can't keep up." I must have looked confused, because he continued: "Lots of people need healing, but there's only one solution. It's tough when no one can take your place."

Was he talking about Griffin now? Or himself? After all, he was the only one left who could control the wind. But he made it look so effortless. He sculpted the air as we talked, and never missed a beat. I reminded myself that he was still the same nine-year-old Dennis who had wailed as we left our Hatteras Island colony a few weeks earlier. But he *wasn't* that boy. Recent events had left their mark in every look and action. Age had never seemed so meaningless.

I could tell he had something more to say. "What is it, Dennis?"

"Are you going to take over my element again? Like you did on the tower." He turned his fingers, gathering the smoke into a tight spiral.

"No. I won't do it again."

He nodded, accepting the answer. But it wasn't enough, of course. As long as I could steal his greatest power, how could he ever trust me again?

"I'm sorry," I said. And I was sorry—more than he could know.

I left the pit and cut through the buildings. Picked up my pace as I reached the street. In the distance, Rose and Marin worked beside the crumpled remains of the water tower. For years they'd been an efficient team, and finally they were together again. But something had changed: Rose was in charge now. I could see it in the way her mother followed as she pointed, and the way Rose planted her hands on her hips—if it wasn't a look of defiance, it was certainly a gesture of independence. I wanted to speak to her, but I wasn't sure what to say. And as I reached the intersection, something else caught my eye.

Another line of clan folk snaked across the street in front of the shelter. But this line wasn't moving. These people weren't working. Most weren't even standing. Quietly, patiently, they waited to discover if my brother could perform yet another miracle. Or if the Plague that was so visibly consuming them would claim them first.

CHAPTER 38

There's a line," a man shouted as I headed for the shelter door. Then he saw me and a flicker of recognition passed across his face. "I'm sorry. I didn't realize you were one of them." He stepped back, hands raised defensively, and almost tripped over rat carcasses. "You're not going to hurt me, are you?"

The people behind him were silent now.

"No," I said.

The shelter door opened, and my mother stepped out. Her features bore a striking resemblance to mine. There was an older woman with her too. Between them, they supported a young woman not much older than Ananias. Her neck was bruised, but I guessed that she was in much better shape now than when she'd entered the shelter. She stopped when she saw me. "Are you his brother?"

I knew she was talking about Griffin. "Yes," I said, eyes still fixed on my mother.

She nodded. "He's the answer to my prayers. I woke

believing that this would be my final day on earth. But I was wrong." Her eyes sparkled, the only part of her untouched by disease. "I look around me and I don't even see dead rats and broken buildings anymore. I see hope. I see the start of something new."

Her eyes flitted between me and my mother. She wanted us to say that we saw it too, this world transformed, this time of breathless optimism. Mother gave her a smile, but how could I agree when my mother and I were staring at each other like the strangers we were? I didn't know her any better than the young woman she supported. If I had been anyone other than who I was, at least we would've hugged, but even that was out of the question.

"We need to talk, Thomas," Mother said finally. A tear pricked the corner of her eye. "There's so much to say."

"Yes, there is."

The young woman slid out from under Mother's arm, and the older woman shepherded her away. Meanwhile, Mother surveyed the line as if she were looking for the ripest piece of fruit on a heavily laden tree. She settled on a man who was probably the same age as Father had been.

"Thomas, can you help . . ." She trailed off as she remembered that no, I couldn't help this man—not without hurting him. "Hold the door, will you?"

I kept it open as she passed through, her arm wrapped tightly around the man. Two elderly clan folk followed him, too weak to help, but too concerned to leave his side. His parents, I guessed.

The smell from the rats was almost as bad inside the shelter as it had been outside. The tiny windows near the ceiling had withstood countless storms, but last night's explosion had destroyed them all. It was quieter, though. Calmer.

Griffin sat in the corner, back pressed against the wall. Dark shadows circled his eyes. His bony shoulders curved forward. Nyla was next to him. If anything, she looked even worse than he did.

Mother laid the man before them. He didn't move as Griffin and Nyla twined fingers and placed their hands on his chest. The process was eerily efficient, as if they'd already done this several times. The man moaned slightly, but otherwise remained still.

At first, I watched Griffin and Nyla. When their faces grew tense and tired I turned my attention to the man. At some point in the past few days he would've had to come to terms with his own mortality. Now his life could start again. Surely he would recognize it for what it was: a gift from an elemental.

A movement from the shadows pulled me around. The two elderly clan folk lingered in the space behind the stairs, waiting for their loved one to be cured. Even with me watching them, they never took their eyes off the man. Or was it Griffin who commanded their attention? It took me a while to read their expressions, simultaneously distrustful and needy; the same expressions I'd seen on the people waiting outside. The scene playing out before them wasn't a miracle; it was an unfortunate necessity. They didn't care for Griffin, only for what Griffin could provide. What would happen when everyone had been cured? Would we coexist peacefully when they no longer had any use for us? When non-elementals outnumbered us five to one?

The process didn't take long. The man was still too weak to stand, let alone walk unaided, but he knew that he'd been cured. He rolled away from Griffin and summoned a weak smile for the couple watching from across the room. They responded with relieved nods.

The man offered Griffin and Nyla a heartfelt thank-you, words rattling around his parched mouth. Then, supported by my mother, he left, his parents trailing behind as before, but with lighter footsteps now.

Nyla lay down gently on the floor, while Griffin leaned back. He wore a peaceful expression that obscured the pain and exhaustion, although both were still there.

I approached him. *You. All. Right?*

He nodded.

I sat cross-legged. Sunlight filtered through the broken window, casting a bright strip of yellow across the floor. I felt it on my shoulder. Griffin was in shadow.

You . . . I began, but I wasn't sure how to say the things I needed to say. *You. Not. Safe.*

Safe? Griffin raised an eyebrow. *Me. Fine.*

I'd chosen the wrong word. Or maybe there was no right word. It was obvious to me that he was so determined to cure others that he was harming himself. But more than that, I worried about what would come afterward, when everyone was cured.

They. You. Not. Care.

He mulled this over. *So?*

They. You. Not. Respect, I signed, the gestures larger and sharper now.

He stared at me blankly. *Me. Not. Need. Respect*. He seemed almost offended by the idea. *Me. Matter. Now.*

Now. Yes, I agreed, picking up on his word. *But. Tomorrow?*

He shook his head gently, the way the older Guardians used to do when they told us off. There was an underlying wisdom in his expression that I recognized well.

Me. Cure. Plague, he signed, as if I hadn't noticed what he could do. *No. One. Else*. He paused. *Just. Me.*

It was a circular argument, and I was tired of playing my part. I might have left then, but Griffin didn't look annoyed or angry. He wasn't interested in fighting me, or anyone else. If anything, he looked like he was at peace, like he'd finally found his time and place. His *meaning*.

"Is he ready for another?" The voice came from the stairs—Mother, returning. But there was no one with her.

"I think they need a rest," I told her.

Nyla didn't correct me. She was grateful for a break.

"That's all right," said Mother. "Griffin won't need her to cure you."

Me. I felt fine, but she was right—I'd been exposed to Plague too.

"I've been watching him," she continued. "He's becoming more efficient. It's impossible to describe, but I can *see* it. The victims with advanced Plague still take more out of him, but you're not even showing signs yet, so it'll be easy, I think."

"Is that what you're doing outside? Selecting the ones with advanced Plague?"

She coiled a strand of hair behind her ear. "I'm trying to work out which of the clan folk is likely to die next, so that Griffin can give them life."

It was a strange, stilted conversation to be having with my mother, but maybe it was what we needed—to talk about something outside of us. How could we talk about anything deeper when I wasn't used to the sound of her voice?

On Mother's signal, Griffin shuffled forward and took my hand. Energy passed between us. I focused on keeping the flow toward me—it would exhaust him faster, but wouldn't be as painful.

He broke the connection much sooner than I expected. I still felt tired as we loosed hands, but also transformed. Not because I was Plague-free—the disease hadn't even begun to show—but because, for those few precious moments, I'd seen the world through Griffin's eyes. With him, I'd faced death down and been rewarded with new life.

Griffin watched me closely as thoughts played through my mind. He was patient, content to let me understand him in my own time. And I *did* understand now. Here at last was his chance to *matter*. After years of existing on the fringes of our colony, Griffin was at the center of everything. No other elemental had ever had so much to offer. And who else would have shared such a gift as freely as he did now?

His life of confusion had come into sharp focus. And come

what may, I had to let him live the present in whatever way *he* wanted.

Nyla stirred, and Griffin ran a finger along the fabric of her tunic. Our mother sat beside him and held his free hand. After all the terrible events of the past few weeks, it was impossible not to look at my brother and feel there had been some point to everything. Our mother had returned. In Nyla, he had a true friend at last. Perhaps he'd have less time for me now, less *need*. But that was always destined to happen. If we were going to be less reliant on each other from now on, at least it had been his decision. It was how I would've wanted things to play out.

I was happy for him. Happy for Ananias too, who commanded respect, even if he didn't completely realize it yet. And for Dennis and Rose, who were using their elements to improve life for everyone. But what was *my* place in this colony—especially now that my father, the person who might have been able to guide me, was gone?

One look at Griffin, and I knew the answer.

I took a seat beside my brother. *Ready?* I asked.

Yes, he replied. *Always.*

Mother gazed at us. She couldn't have known that we'd been inseparable ever since Griffin was born, but she saw the connection now. She wiped a tear away. "I'll go get another person," she said.

I listened to the sound of Griffin breathing, and wondered whose life we'd save next.

CHAPTER 39

The sun was low in the sky—a couple strikes before sun-down, I guessed—when a bell was rung some distance away. By then Griffin, Nyla, and I had cured the most advanced cases of Plague. The rest could wait until later. I wouldn't let Griffin continue until he had rested.

We trudged out of the shelter. Clan folk filed along the street, drawn by the bell's pure, sweet sound. Like us, their footsteps were labored, heads bowed, faces solemn.

I didn't need to ask why we were being summoned. The dead needed to be released within a day of passing. But how many dead would there be? And how many of them were killed in the inferno that *I* had created?

A lone figure walked against the tide of clan folk—a child, not much bigger than Dennis. I signaled to the others to go on without me, and followed the child. I was sure that it was Kieran.

He stopped before the remains of the Sumter ship, which straddled the street like a beached whale. Some of it would be salvaged, I figured—the large pieces of wooden hull, and the metal winches—but we'd never be able to rebuild such an enormous craft.

I joined him. "Hard to believe this ship used to be bigger than a building."

Kieran didn't look at me. "Nothing's as big once it dies. Nothing that matters, anyway," he added, looking around him at the bloated rats.

He picked his way around the ship's timbers and continued walking toward the edge of Skeleton Town. I fell in step with him. I was worried, and I didn't want him to be alone. I'd seen last night's events from the same vantage point as him, so I knew the images that must be playing through his mind.

We were past the buildings when he said sharply, "You told me you'd rescue them."

I nodded, though he still wasn't watching. "I know. I . . . I'm sorry. How is your father now?"

"He's not my father," said Kieran quietly. "And she wasn't really my mother. They were my protectors. My parents were elementals, like me. We lived on a tiny island in Chesapeake Bay. It's not far from Roanoke Island, so I got to see their elements working. And when a few rats came ashore during a storm, I found out what I can do too."

"Why did you leave?"

"We were there six years. But after every storm, the island got smaller. The water level rose too. It got so we could walk around the island and see each other the whole time. There wasn't enough room to grow food. Mother got scared—said we wouldn't make it through the winter. So they built a raft and we headed south for Roanoke."

We were heading for the mainland bridge now. Hard to believe that Roanoke Island had been his parents' destination. I didn't need to ask if they had made it. We'd have seen them, if they had.

"A storm came through and pushed us off course," he continued. "We grounded on the mainland. Rats found us. I controlled them—kept them away. But it was tiring. And then we ran aground again. The rats had followed us along the shore—thousands of them. I think . . ." He hesitated. "I think it was because I was controlling them. Father tried to keep us away from the shore, but he couldn't do it. The wind and waves kept pushing us back. And every time we touched land, the rats attacked, until I couldn't stop them anymore." He took a deep breath. "Once the storm was over, my parents started paddling again. Kept going, even when they got Plague. They wanted to reach Roanoke Island. But we didn't even get out of Chesapeake Bay."

"What happened then?"

"I gave up. I knew I was going to die too. I drifted ashore again, and I didn't even paddle away. I let the rats come to me. And then I held them there for almost a whole day . . . just a few feet away from me. They couldn't move. Couldn't eat. Couldn't drink. They just stayed where they were, even when I fell asleep. I wanted to punish them. I wanted them to die.

"When I woke up, there was a clan ship nearby. A woman who was out fishing in a canoe saw me. She dragged me away

277

from the shore. She didn't know I was controlling the rats, but she risked her life for me anyway. She took me back to the clan ship. The others wouldn't let me on, in case I had Plague. So she stayed with me on the raft. For three days her husband passed us food and water. Then they let me on."

"Did they know you could control the rats?"

"No. I practiced when we got near shore, but only in secret."

We were on the bridge now, but Kieran wasn't showing any signs of slowing down.

"What happened when you got to Roanoke?" I asked.

"Jossi told us to leave. We should've just gone, but the Elders wanted to trade. Roanoke was a new place, and they wanted to explore. We never would've taken anything, but Jossi went crazy. He attacked us. Threatened to kill the Elders. That's when I made the rats attack the pirates. Everything went wrong after that. And now the woman who saved my life is dead."

"This isn't your fault, Kieran."

"So what? Nothing will stop the hurt."

My mind returned to the scene during the night. It hadn't occurred to me before, but now I understood why Kieran's protectors hadn't used their elements in self-defense—because they weren't elementals.

We continued in silence. It was a long walk to the gap in the bridge, and I was sure that's where Kieran was headed. Sure enough, he didn't slow down until we were toeing the edge. Instinctively I put a hand in front of him.

"I'm not going to jump," he said.

"Good. It's a long way down. Kind of painful. I tried it once—wouldn't recommend it."

The plank was still down, connecting the two parts of the bridge. I'd make sure that it was gone before we left.

Kieran stared at the far shore, where the sun hovered just above the horizon. "Will you combine with me? Like you did last night."

"I think your element is powerful enough without my help."

"What element? If the rats are gone, I have nothing."

I hadn't thought about that. "I still need to know what your element actually *is*. How it *feels*."

"Why? You combined with me fine last night."

"Because I could *see* what you were trying to do. I just willed the same thing to happen—for those rats to come closer and closer." I could tell that he still didn't understand. "Look, when I combine with Ananias, I imagine the flame. With Dennis, it's a gust of wind. Even Griffin—I think of energy pouring through him, as if I can force the cure to shift from person to person. I guess I need to know what it is that you want."

Kieran was undeterred. He pointed to the mainland. "There are rats out there—have to be. And I . . . I want to send them a message."

"What kind of message?"

"To stay away. If I have to, I'll tell them every day for the rest of my life."

He'd answered my question. Now it was my turn to follow through.

I closed my eyes and visualized rats on the mainland. Taking Kieran's hand in mine, I implored them to listen to him. It felt slightly ridiculous and strangely *empty*, but I kept the connection, and our elements combined.

Several moments passed before we loosed hands. It wasn't like usual, either. He didn't pull away as if the work had been completed, but remained still, staring at the horizon with a puzzled expression.

"What is it, Kieran?"

He shook his head. "Nothing. There's nothing out there."

"You mean . . . *all* the rats are gone?"

"No. There'll be more. But there aren't any around here— not for miles. Which means we can go over there, right? We can grow food. And hunt."

Sixteen years of warnings told me no, that it was impossible. But I believed him. I'd seen what Kieran could do, and there was no doubt in my mind that he was right now.

"Will the clan folk believe it?" I asked.

"I don't know. I guess not right away. I'm not like them, you know? I'm an elemental, like you." He sighed. "Doesn't matter, anyway. Right now, this is the first time some of them have been able to live on land. Who can't see the miracle in that?"

CHAPTER 40

Kieran and I were the last to arrive at dinner. Clan folk and elementals clustered in separate groups on a patch of rubble to the east of Skeleton Town. Fish, too numerous to count, crisped in the embers of a makeshift fire. Rose and Marin had probably used their elements to summon the fish to the shore. Ananias used his element to control the fire, emphasizing heat over flame. We'd eat well tonight.

The young woman who Griffin had cured earlier was handing out plates. Someone must have made a trip out to the clan ship, and brought supplies ashore. If so, it meant that the clan folk were definitely planning to stay. Given the way they stared at Kieran and me as we made our late arrival, that wasn't a particularly reassuring thought.

Kieran's father received his portion and surveyed the separate groups before him. Breaking the trend, he took a place beside Griffin. The woman who'd handed me a plate joined him there. Then Dennis stood and, with an approving smile from his mother, made his way over to the clan folk.

Perhaps it was all for show—a mask to hide how we really felt—but people were making an effort. That had to count for something.

Working quickly, Rose filled each plate from a large metal pan. When she reached me she didn't make eye contact and she didn't speak, but she gave me a little more than she should have.

I sat beside Alice because she was alone. Now that Roanoke Island was secure, she stared across the sound to Hatteras Island, as if she were looking for new adventures, or remembering old ones.

"I told Griffin about the third journal," she said. "Everything I could think of, anyway."

I looked around me to make sure that no one was listening. "Did the journal mention anything about Griffin's drawings?"

"No."

"So no one else has been able to do that? To take one person's life and save another."

"Would you admit it if you could?" She took a piece of fish from my plate. "He told me it's something he's always known about, though. Just couldn't explain *how*."

"And what about you? How long did you know about Dare being your father?"

She chewed the fish. "Not as long as I should've. I've been different since I was born. The amazing thing is that I was too blind to see it until I read the last journal."

I put the plate between us so that she could help herself.

She'd probably noticed I had more than my share as soon as I sat down. "You couldn't have known—"

"Why not? When we were sailing to Sumter, my so-called father's dying words were that I should have died instead of my sister. The same sister who was traumatized after one conversation with Dare. How obvious did I need it to be?"

"I'm sorry."

"For what? For Dare being my father? Or for losing him before I ever knew him?" Even though I heard it in her voice, I was surprised to see tears welling in her eyes. "The only thing I'm sorry about is that I lost my sister. Eleanor shouldn't have died."

"She chose that, though." I wanted to ease Alice's guilt, but maybe extending the conversation was its own form of pain.

Alice shook her head. "I was there when she died, remember? Ananias and I were at the top of the ship's mast with her. He honestly thinks she jumped, but she didn't. She let go."

"There's a difference?"

"Yes. I don't think she was choosing death. I believe she just needed a sign. Everyone and everything she'd ever trusted had turned out to be a lie, and she was tired of fighting for a cause she didn't believe in."

"But it was no different for the rest of us," I reminded her. "We kept fighting, so why didn't she?"

"Because we had a cause, Thom. That's the difference. I was fighting for answers. You were fighting for Griffin. And . . . and Rose was fighting for you." She swiped at her tears as if she were annoyed at herself, but she didn't need to worry—it was dark now. No one but me could see her. "I admit it: I always thought Rose was the weak link. I thought that if Eleanor couldn't handle the truth, what chance did Rose and Dennis have? But I was wrong. Now I think Eleanor was just waiting to be set free."

So here it was: grudging acceptance of Rose. But the way I looked at it, Rose wasn't free at all. We couldn't touch anymore. She'd lost her father, and even though they'd reconciled now, her mother had let her down. What was the point of freedom when it left you with so little?

"You don't believe me," she said. "I can see it in your eyes. But you didn't see what Rose did last night. How she and your mother took control of the situation when you passed out. How she told everyone they needed to organize, and work together. She demanded patience, and the clan folk gave it. They respect her, Thom. Do you really believe she'd turn back time, even if she could?"

No, I didn't believe that at all. And maybe that was part of the problem. Rose really was better off now. Even if that meant being apart from me.

"So what do the clan folk make of me?" I tried to hide the edge in my voice. "Do they respect me too?"

"They'll do what you say, yes."

"That's not what I was asking."

Alice was never one for lying. "They fear you, Thom. They've seen everyone else's elements at work, but you're a mystery. All they know for sure is that you're the link between our elements and an inferno powerful enough to destroy a town. I figure they're scared of what'll come next." She narrowed her eyes. "But that's up to you. You can do anything. You don't have to be the sum of their fears."

If Alice had been born with my element, I would have believed that. She'd have known how to use it. She probably would've gotten control of it early, and by now she'd be capable of anything. Me, I was capable of anything too; but just like my father, I couldn't be sure what the consequences would be—or if I could live with them.

Alice waited for a reply—something to convince her that I was ready to demand respect. Ready to assume control. But all I could think was how much had happened over the past few weeks to bring us right back to where we started. And as I looked around me I had the overwhelming feeling that while everything had changed, some things hadn't changed at all.

Skeleton Town fell silent almost as soon as dinner was over. People were tired and, apart from Ananias's fire, the island was dark.

The clan folk slept in the open, mostly huddled together. A few adults sat on the perimeter—I could see the whites of their eyes. I figured that if they were keeping guard, it was probably me they feared, so I left the area. I wasn't ready to sleep, but I didn't want to stop them from getting some rest.

I wound toward the main street. The buildings near the intersection were unrecognizable now, but I found the clinic anyway.

Someone was already there. "Are you all right, Thomas?" my mother asked.

I could have answered that in a hundred different ways. "No," I said.

"Hmm. Me neither." She peered into what remained of the building, but there wouldn't have been much to see even if it were light. "I've lived among pirates for thirteen years. They were the closest thing I had to a family. Now Dare and his men are dead. Tessa and Ordyn too."

"Why didn't you tell Dare to bring you back sooner? You knew you weren't the solution."

"Yes. But *Dare* didn't realize that." She sighed. "I held out all this time because I knew that his visions would become clearer as we closed in on Roanoke. Once he knew the truth about the solution, nothing would stop him from coming for Griffin. Then everyone would suffer. Everyone *has* suffered."

"So why come back at all?"

"Because I wanted to see you again—you and your brothers. I've never stopped thinking about you, even for a moment. I thought that I could reason with Dare once we got here, but he wouldn't listen." From the way her voice shook, I could tell she was crying. "I know you blame yourself for a lot of what has happened here, but if anyone's to blame, it's me. All I had to do was stay silent. Coming here was selfish."

I was fighting tears too. "I'm glad you came. Griffin deserves to know you."

"And what about you? How do you . . ." She turned away.

"I'm sorry. You need time to get used to this. For all you can remember, I may never have existed at all."

I flicked debris with my foot. "I saw a picture of us together outside this clinic. I found it among Tessa's things in Bodie Lighthouse."

Even in the darkness, I could see her face brighten. "This one, you mean?" She slid something from her pants pocket and handed it to me.

It was a piece of paper, crumpled and slick. I studied it in the moonlight. It was identical to Tessa's picture. "Where did you find it?"

"I've always had it. It's called a photograph. The Guardians didn't approve of old technology like this, but I'd foreseen the future—a time when we'd move to Hatteras Island and leave everything we'd ever known behind. I didn't want to go to that new world without a relic of the old. And neither did Tessa."

She moved behind me and raised her fingers in front of her face so that they formed a rectangle. "Stay right there," she said.

I turned to face her. "What are you doing?"

"I'm updating the picture."

"The clinic isn't looking so good anymore."

"True," she said. "But I'm not looking at the clinic. I only care about the boy." She smiled. "And he's more perfect than I could've imagined."

CHAPTER 41

We worked for six straight days. With all the rats cremated and the earthen pit filled in, memories of Jossi and Plague felt less vivid. The divisions between clan folk and elementals became blurred.

Every salvageable item in every building was stored and catalogued. While the buildings farthest from the water tower were cleaned out and made fit for living, the clan folk carpenters made snug-fitting shutters to replace the broken windows. By then they'd already built two fully operational water harvesters. Skeleton Town no longer belonged to the elementals, but it didn't feel much like a skeleton town either.

Mother worked hand in hand with Griffin and Nyla and me, until everyone was cured. No one who had been cured contracted Plague again, but with all the rats gone, it was impossible to know for sure if we were immune. Mother was optimistic, though. She was a seer, and she saw no reason to be afraid anymore. I just nodded and thought of the mainland, and a life without elements.

Every day, Rose watched me from the corner of her eye, settling for empty words when what we really wanted was so much more. For all the horrors we'd endured at Fort Sumter, I longed to recapture those moments when I'd woken beside her, and kissed her. Now I was caught in an endless in-between, neither elemental nor non-elemental, living with everyone but apart from them too.

On the seventh day we rested, and the clan folk spoke of a new world.

And I watched them.

I left two nights later. Griffin and Ananias were asleep. Mother was beside them. I felt guilty that we didn't get to say goodbye, but she knew me well enough now to know I'd be back. Or maybe she'd seen the future and knew it for a fact.

There was a light drizzle. Heavy cloud cover made it even darker than usual. I slung the bag of supplies over my shoulder and headed south.

The wind had changed direction and blew from the north, bringing the first hint of fall chill. Not cold, just a reminder that the seasons were changing, and that I shouldn't wait any longer to leave.

I only made it as far as the clinic when I sensed someone else on the street with me. I lightened my footsteps and honed in on the sound. Instinct told me it would be Alice, always alert, always watching, but I wouldn't have detected her until she was right next to me. No, this person wasn't a natural tracker. When I slowed down, my shadow kept up the pace.

"Who's there?" I turned around. "I know someone's out there."

The footsteps drew closer, but the person didn't speak. I couldn't see who it was until she was about ten yards away.

"Rose?" As she pulled alongside me I realized that she was carrying a bag too. "What are you doing?"

"The same as you," she replied.

"What are you talking about?"

She stood close to me. Her short, uneven hair was a mess and she carried an air of determination that hadn't existed a few weeks ago, but in every other way she was still Rose. Beautiful, caring Rose.

"I don't need to be a seer to know your mind, Thomas," she said softly. "I've been watching you pull away from everyone. I've seen you gathering supplies. I know how you feel here, and I know you think there's another place out there for you. So I told my mother and Dennis, I'm going too."

I didn't know what to say. I'd planned to go alone, but only because I hadn't dared to believe that Rose would want to come with me.

"There *is* another place," I insisted. "Alice read about it in the third journal. It's the original non-elemental colony, about fifty miles west of here. People didn't just survive there, either. They thrived. And then they moved beyond it, to other parts of the mainland. If we're immune to Plague, we have to explore. We have to reclaim the mainland."

"What about our elements?"

"What about them?" I started walking again, and she

290

stayed with me. "We'll still be close enough to Roanoke to have some control over them. Tarn says there are machines out there that can do almost any task. I'll be able to make them work."

"What if your element becomes too weak?"

I knew the answer, but it was a harder one to share. To explain why I'd surrender everything on Roanoke for a chance to find out who I was without an element. But with Rose beside me, the answer seemed simple. "Then I'll be able to touch you again," I said.

We didn't say anything after that. There would be time for talking and planning, and for holding each other too. The future was uncertain, but with Rose beside me, it was much brighter than before.

We passed the remains of the water tower and the hurricane shelter, and kept heading south. I'd figured it wasn't going to be easy to find what I was looking for, but something was glowing above the reeds ahead of us. Rose seemed less concerned by it than I was.

As we drew closer, the source of the glow became clear. Alice held her hand above her. Flames danced on her fingertips. Jerren was preparing the kayak that she and I had found during a nighttime trip to Hatteras Island a few weeks earlier.

"What are you doing?" I asked.

Alice didn't miss a beat. "Rose told me what you've been up to. You can't do this alone."

"I won't be alone."

She and Rose sighed together. "You're paddling fifty miles

with no way to measure distance," Alice reminded me. "You never even saw the location of the new colony in the third journal — I did. I checked it against the clan folks' maps, and I can tell you right now, you'll never find it without me."

I had to give it to Alice — even after everything we'd been through, no one was more effective at making me feel incompetent than she was.

Jerren took our bags and added them to several more that he'd attached to a sleek-looking raft. "We'll tow the supplies," he said. "No need to crush everything into the kayak." He took up position in the middle of the kayak, and made himself comfortable. It wouldn't be easy, with four of us fighting for space.

"What about Nyla?" I asked him. "Won't she miss you?"

"I told her I'll be back," he said. "Your mother and Griffin said they'll look out for her."

"Wait. They know about this?"

"Yes, Thom, they know," scolded Alice. "They even made me promise to bring you back alive." She suppressed the grin that was threatening to appear at any moment.

"But why do you both want to come at all?"

Alice took the place in front of Jerren. "You know the answer to that, Thom. I've spent my life waiting to escape, to see what else is out there. Now we need to know the answer to that more than ever. Elementals and non-elementals have fought for centuries. Griffin and Kieran are solutions for today, but they can't guarantee peace tomorrow. One day, something will happen that'll upset the balance. And when it does, we have to be willing to leave Roanoke once and for all. I'm ready for that. Are *you?*"

Yes, I was ready. So was Rose. Like me, Jerren had grown up with only the slightest understanding of what he could do, and seemed content to put it behind him. We were ready to move on. Together.

I took the place at the back of the kayak. It sunk lower into the water. "This is going to be impossible to paddle," I said.

Rose looked at the small space in front of me. It was the only place remaining.

"I don't think you should—" I began, but Rose was already climbing in. She managed to leave a sliver of air between us, but how long could she stay like that before she needed to stretch out?

I took the paddle and pushed us free from the reeds. The water on the creek was still, but choppier water lay ahead. It would lap over the sides unless we could keep the waves behind us. What if the tide was going out? How would we make any progress at all?

Rose shuffled back slightly. She was already uncomfortable, but I couldn't risk her touching me. Nothing would doom our expedition quicker than that.

Still she edged back. "No," I whispered. "You mustn't."

She peered at me over her shoulder. Somehow she was smiling. "Give me that," she said, taking the paddle. Then she whispered, "Now combine."

Rose leaned back against me, melting into my arms. Beneath us, the sluggish kayak rose on the water, propelled by our elements. We moved faster and faster, as the reeds blurred and the salt breeze whipped against us.

As long as we held hands, there would be no need for paddling at all. Limbs coiled, hearts working as one, I honestly believed I'd never move again. I closed my eyes and clasped my hands with hers, buried my face in her hair and felt only the promise of what lay ahead.

We left the creek and entered the sound. The wind was strong and the swell was choppy, but my pulse was quick and we didn't slow down. Roanoke Island was passing to my left, but I didn't look at it, or spare a thought for what we were leaving behind. The future lay before us now, and for the first time in my life, I welcomed every part of it.

ACKNOWLEDGMENTS

Writing a trilogy is a major undertaking, and I couldn't have done it without extraordinary support. Heartfelt thanks to . . .

My agent, Ted Malawer, who planted the seed for these books, and dispensed excellent advice as I was writing them.

The National Park Service rangers on Roanoke Island and in Charleston, who made my research trips such fun.

Audrey and Clare, who read and critiqued every book, often many times.

Tony Sahara, designer of the stunning covers; and Steve Stankiewicz, creator of the beautiful maps.

The librarians at St. Louis Public Library and St. Louis County Library, and the countless school librarians across Missouri who have encouraged teens to give these books a read.

The folks at my local indie bookstore, Left Bank Books—especially Kris Kleindienst, Jarek Steele, Sarah Holt, and Shane Mullen. I couldn't ask for more supportive neighbors.

Danielle Borsch at Vroman's Bookstore, for taking my books with her when she headed west.

The Dial team: Kate Harrison, Regina Castillo, Jasmin Rubero, Heather Alexander, Lauri Hornik, Kathy Dawson, and Scottie Bowditch.

Liz Waniewski, my extraordinarily talented, thoughtful, dedicated, and inspiring editor, for making the entire journey an unbridled joy.

ALSO FROM ANTONY JOHN:

"An absolutely fantastic start to a new series. Completely gripping and full of intrigue, revelation, mystery, and suspense. I highly recommend this book."

—James Dashner, *New York Times* bestselling author of *The Maze Runner*

"An unexpectedly emotional story of survival and self-discovery." —*VOYA*

"Plenty of mystery, adventure, and action."

—*Publishers Weekly*

"Jam-packed with action." —*Booklist*

"A page-turner with a dose of mystery and adventure, this series will interest fans of fantasy, history, and romance." —*VOYA*

Winner of the Schneider Family Award

"I loved it and laughed out loud. Hilarious and so smart. *Dumb* proves that everyone, no matter what, deserves to be heard."
—Catherine Gilbert Murdock, author of *Dairy Queen*

"Complex characterizations, authentic dialogue and realistic ups-and-downs give this title chart-topping potential."
—*Kirkus Reviews*

"A highly readable balance of humor, heart, self-discovery, and shenanigans."
—*BCCB*